MIRRORS 2:

REFLECTIONS

BY

LAZETTE GIFFORD

Copyright 2013 Lazette Gifford

An ACOA Publication

www.aconspiracyofauthors.com

ISBN: 978-1-936507-58-0

Mirrors

A Conspiracy of Authors Publication

www.aconspiracyofauthors.com

Copyright 2015, Lazette Gifford

ISBN: 978-1-936507-61-0

Cover Art Copyright 2015, Lazette Gifford

First Print Edition, July, 2016

TABLE OF CONTENTS

Hither and thither spins
The windborne, mirroring soul;
A thousand glimpses wins
And never sees the whole.
Empedocles on Etna, Act 1 (1852)
  --- Mathew Arnold

DAY ONE:

CHAPTER ONE

Something, somewhere, had gone wrong, and I felt the trouble coming my way.

I put aside my harp, packing the ancient instrument back into the case and placing it in the cupboard by my desk. This was not a day to play music. The late afternoon had already gone gray and dull. Snow brushed against the large window obscuring the view of the street from my second-story apartment. A chill took me as I watched the wall of white outside, even though the apartment felt -- and looked -- like a jungle. I like warm and green and often asked myself why I haven't left for somewhere warmer because I could go anywhere.

I should have left years ago when my mother took me to the bus station and told me never to come back home.

She gave me a thousand dollars. I should have gone to California. Or Hawaii. The idea of tropical beaches appealed to me until I thought about the news stories that covered tropical storms. I at least understood snow storms.

Yes, fear has kept me here. I've learned to hide among these humans, who never look beneath my carefully chosen clothing to see that I am not one of them. Back then, when my mother abandoned me, I had never been out of the house alone and had never left the city. Even now I haven't traveled far.

Well, as long as you didn't count a quick, and exceedingly chilly, trip to the fae lands across the Veil when a few rather annoying members of the Topaz clan tried to kill me. I'm not popular with many of the fae. Darion Sapphire Wilding likes me, but that's because he met my cousin Cherry through me, and he *really likes her*, even though she is human.

I live in an odd world. I do my detective work -- small scale jobs -- and it pays well enough finding lost dogs and stolen trinkets. The rest of the time I can hide out in my jungle of an apartment. I'm happy, except I don't like snow and watching the growing wild white of the current blizzard made me want to curl up in bed and not come out until spring. I couldn't stay hidden here, though because. . . .

There was something in the air, besides the snowflakes, that made me suspect I would be out in the weather soon. I made a mental note of where my hat and scarf were, and to make certain, I left food for the tame mice and the persistent squirrel who often came to the door. I wanted to retrieve my harp and play so I could bury the sense of trouble, but instead, I pulled up the ledger for McFaelyn Investigations and did the math. Not my favorite job, but the work took my attention and kept me focused on anything but the storm and growing dread that kept seeping in around my attempt at concentration. I had made a profit for the first time in a few months. Not just a few dollars over my bills, but enough to bank some money. That was a pleasant thought

The last case had tipped the scale. I had found a dog for someone. Not just any dog; this was a very expensive Shih Tzu worth close to two thousand dollars. Someone had stolen the pooch from the owner while they walked in the park, a slick job of getting the human's attention just long enough to grab the animal. I knew from the start that this had been a professional job. I used a little magic and not only located him, but I also lead the police to a band of people who were stealing expensive dogs and selling them overseas. The case even made the news, with my name there, for all to see. I hoped it brought in a few more solid cases. This one had come by way of Ted Weaver -- yes, the man everyone says will be the next president. He didn't know what part I'd played in helping to find his missing daughter (who was now Queen of the Fae), but he seemed to like me.

I need little work. I want enough to keep the power company happy and the mice fed.

My life keeps changing, though. A few months ago, I was nothing more than a half-breed fae, mistrusted by my father's people -- the fae -- who had never let one of my kind live this long. Half-fae is a dangerous thing to be. Most have had powers but no ties to the land like the real fae, and that means they have nothing to counter them.

The fae killed those of my kind in the past. Many of them still want to kill me, but so far I'd stay out of trouble.

Well, except for early fall when I helped to save the soon-to-be Queen of the Fae and hundreds of other fae from death. I won my place in my father's clan, and I wear the emerald ring of a member. Sometimes seeing it on my hand still surprises me.

I may be accepted by a few, but I am not one of them. I can't be. Being half-fae and half-human is something too odd. I am genderless. I'm not fae or human, I'm not male or female. I'm just me. It's always been enough.

So I stay clear of the fae and keep my secrets hidden from the humans. That seems the best answer for all of us. I do my work, and I have contact with Darion, who is the Sapphire House Ambassador besides being in love with my human cousin. He's also my guard since he made himself responsible for my life back in that mess last fall. At least he no longer feels obligated to follow my every move. I've seen my fae half-sister Aria twice since the Lacey Weaver trouble, and we have neither kicked nor drawn weapons, so the relationship is on an upturn. I have not gone to Emerald House, and everyone is happy to let it stay that way.

Except . . . I can still sense when something is wrong. Like today.

I leaned back and closed my eyes, hoping for a nap, right there in the chair. Nightmares had plagued me the night before, most of them about being held against my will. Those same nightmares had bothered me last fall. Faris Ruby Day was dead, and no one wanted to pick up where she left tried to go before she died.

I wanted to rest, but the moment I slipped away, an inexplicable terror took hold of me, like something clawing at my stomach, and far worse than what I had suffered during the night. I came back awake with a heart-pounding thump and almost shot out of my chair and had pulled up magic before I even realized what I was doing. I saw nothing to fight and let the power go again, gasping and shaking.

Gods of all people, I had never been afraid of shadows and nightmares. Why now? Why at this moment when everything was going so well? I had broken out in a cold sweat, and not all of it from that call of magic, which I find painful to use. It's another part of not being one thing or the other.

This wasn't good. This wasn't --

The phone rang.

If I hadn't already let go of the magic, I would have blasted the device. I keep an old-fashioned land-line at my place because it's far more reliable around magic than cell phones, at least as long as I don't attack it. I took a breath, and another and picked up before the phone went to voice mail.

"Hello?" My voice sounded a little shaky.

"Skye. This is Ian."

Not the person I would *ever* have expected to call me. Ian had married my mother long after my birth. We lived in the same house for several years while my mother did her best to make certain he guessed nothing about me, including that I wasn't a 'daughter.' Those had been tense years until my mother sent me away.

"What's wrong?" I asked because something had to

have happened. Was this what had been plaguing me for the last couple days?

"Kelly is missing, Skye. She disappeared yesterday morning on the way to school. I wanted to call you earlier, but your mother --" He stopped and took a ragged breath. "We've only told the family. It's been almost thirty-six hours. The police have nowhere new to look. You -- you can help, can't you?"

Kelly was his oldest daughter, my half-sister on the human side. The thought of something having happened to her made me shiver for a new reason. Even so, I had to be truthful.

"Ian, my mother and I don't get along. I'm not sure what I can do. I'll try, but I don't dare come over there."

"Your mother is irrational." He spoke as though he was not talking about his wife and with no emotion in the words. "I don't know what happened between the two of you, and I don't care. I want help to find Kelly."

"Do you have any ideas at all?" I had not even seen Kelly since she was ten, almost eight years ago. She would graduate soon, I supposed. The realization gave me a chill: the child grown up who had always been a little girl in my mind.

"Your mother is at the police department, Skye. I heard. . . ." He stopped and took a deeper breath. "I heard that you're good at your work. We need help. Please."

"How long will she be with the police?"

"I'm not certain. She's filling out reports."

"I'll be over as quickly as I can get there and see if I can find anything. The police don't like private detectives working in their major cases, and my mother will be angry.

I don't suppose we can keep it a secret from her."

"I don't think so. Does that really matter to you?" he asked, sounding lost just then.

"No it doesn't, but you don't need more trouble. If my mother shows up, this is bound to get ugly, and we don't need that right now."

"Skye, I don't know what happened between you and your mother --"

"None of that matters. I'll be there as soon as I can. Can you get me a picture of Kelly? I haven't seen her since she was ten."

"You haven't met Veronica and Little Ian."

"No, but Cherry told me about them, so they aren't a big shock." He was trying to hold on to the conversation so he didn't have to face other things. "I have to go, Ian. I'll see you in a few minutes."

"Thank you."

He hung up first. I held on for a moment longer, wondering what the hell I was getting into this time. I wanted to help find Kelly, and if anyone had hurt her, there would be hell to pay. She had been a sweet little girl, and I'd played dolls with her sometimes. That seemed like another lifetime though I remembered her face with laughing brown eyes and bright smile. She had reached the age where she wondered why our mother didn't treat me the same as her and Mary. She had gone to school while I was (supposedly) home schooled. I had learned everything on my own from their school books and television. My mother wanted nothing to do with me.

As I stood, I caught at the desk as a wave of nausea passed over me. Was that fear? Was it the worry of going to my mother's house and facing her again? We'd met at Cherry's apartment last fall in the midst of all that other madness. She hadn't changed, except to grow more angry and bitter.

What had happened to Kelly?

Blood calls to blood. I might track Kelly if I found a link to her. My abilities gave me opportunities that the police didn't have, and that realization gave me the strength to go over to the door, pull on my jacket, gloves, hat and scarf and head out --

I was on the steps leading down to the alley when Darion and Cherry arrived in his little sports car, even in this weather. I hadn't been expecting them and Cherry hurried out of the car, rushing toward me.

"Skye --"

"Kelly is missing. Ian just called me and asked me to help."

She looked worried and frantic. She hadn't even put on a hat and snow dusted her jet black hair. Darion stood and gave me a grave nod. Missing children bothered the fae. They have so few children of their own that they are instinctively drawn to protect any child, whether fae or human. Maybe that instinct had kicked up for me, too.

"You're going over there?" Cherry asked and looked worried for whole new reasons.

"My mother is at the police station. This might be the only chance I get to see Kelly's things."

"Ah. Okay. Darion --" she said, looking back at him.

"We'll take you, Skye. Come on. You look like hell, and I'd rather be driving than worrying about whether you'd make it that far before piling up your car somewhere."

"I'm fine," I protested even though I wasn't. Then I gave way to my macho pride -- or whatever it would be in my case -- and nodded. "You two might help, anyway. I want to look in a mirror, if I can find one, and to get a feel for her. I can't do that if Ian is there."

"True. Come on," Cherry said and took my arm. They offered me a wall of protection, and I felt safer with them at my back.

The two had the same looks of worry on their faces, which was odd in people who otherwise looked so opposite in all other ways. Darion stood tall, his long golden hair pulled back in a tie, his face ageless in the way of the fae. He might be the age he looked -- which was doubtful considering Darion was a fae Ambassador -- or he might be a couple thousand years old. I had never asked. I wondered if Cherry had breached the subject, or if she wanted to pretend that age didn't matter.

Cherry was very much human -- a petite Chinese-American woman with a bob of black hair, and an overpower presence that belayed her small size. She was a chef and ran a bustling catering service that sometimes served at very prestigious events.

Winter was her slow time, though. Most of the occasions where she worked were summer, spring, and even autumn parties. In winter, all the 'better' people retired to the warmer climes, and Cherry (who didn't like the snow any better than I did) took care of small events and stayed close to home. She made enough the rest of the year not to worry about the downturn, and she paid so well that she had little trouble hiring back her best people each spring.

She bundled me into the back seat. The snow was coming down harder. If it hadn't been for Darion's magic, I doubt we would have gotten out of the alley behind my apartment. A lot of city would soon be impassable, at least for most cars. I suppose people would think something odd when they saw Darion's sports car taking those streets where trucks bogged down in the snowdrifts.

Did I care? No. I wanted to get to Ian's house as fast as possible, check everything there, and then find Kelly. Darion would get me there faster than if I had driven. Then, if I could refine my link to Kelly, I should be able to track her, just as I could find Cherry. I even used Cherry as a tie on the other end of a magical path and go to her sometimes.

"You all right, Skye?" Cherry said, looking back over the seat at me.

"Worried," I admitted and pulled the cap back off my head. Darion kept the car warm. "I haven't seen Kelly since she was about ten."

"It's funny," Cherry said with a tilt of her head. "She looks like you, only not as blond-haired fae exotic."

"That might not be good. Not with my mother."

"Do you suspect her of having a part in her disappearance?" Darion asked.

"I suspect her of being part of everything bad," I replied. "That doesn't mean it's so. Do you know where we're going?"

"Cherry took me by your mother's house a month ago."

"Why?" I asked, startled by the news. "Trying to

torture her or Darion?"

"We didn't go in," Cherry said with a quick smile and then lost it again. "He wanted to see where you had lived."

I wondered what had drawn Darion there. His eyes in the rear-view mirror narrowed at an unpleasant thought. I didn't want to pry, but the house had been part of my world, not his --

"I saw so much of your life when I scanned you that I felt like what I had from you was only a dream, and I needed to get the facts grounded I reality so I could sort things out from some of my own thoughts and reactions."

"Ah. Sorry."

"You have no reason to be sorry." He took a turn and slowed. A truck spraying out sand made slow progress down the road ahead of us, another truck ahead of it, clearing the way with snow shoveled out to both sides, creating a narrow, white corridor. "Damn. We would have gotten there faster without their help."

I leaned back as my stomach cramped. I fought the pain back and took a deep breath. "If the roads are this bad, it might slow my mother too. I don't want to run into her."

"Good thing Darion and I are along, then. We can help out there."

"True. Though if she sees Darion she will react just as badly as she would at seeing me. She knows he's fae."

"True enough. We'll be careful. There's no reason to make this worse," Darion said and quieted Cherry's start of a protest. "This isn't the time to take her on, Cherry."

"No time is a good time," I said and saw Cherry give me a narrow-eyed glance. "What happened between my mother and me is far in the past, Cherry. Don't get into a war with her on my account. I would just as soon forget everything about my past."

"Can you forget?" Cherry asked.

"No. That doesn't mean I want to re-fight that battle. I've moved on."

She relented with a sigh of resignation. "Sorry. I shouldn't push you about her, especially not now. I'm worried about Kelly. She's a good kid and works hard, and I don't want to see anything bad happen to her."

"She was always nice to me. Mary was too young. But Kelly . . . Kelly had figured out things were not right, which may be another reason my mother panicked and got rid of me."

"There is no excuse for what she did," Darion said, a touch of anger in his voice. "Or for how she treats you now. But then, there's no excuse for your father's behavior either. They are both egotistical bastards."

I gave a little laugh and the tightness in my shoulders eased. "I don't need them, Darion, and I would rather not get caught up in something involving either of them, but I'll do what I can to help find Kelly."

Darion nodded and fell silent. So did Cherry. I wondered what they thought. I wouldn't have minded more conversation to keep my attention. Every time my mind turned to Kelly and the trouble -- and the fear of crossing paths with my mother -- I felt a twist in my guts that said something horrible was happening. I hoped it was my imagination.

"Darion, I kept sensing something odd in the air today and last night and thought I caught something fae-related.

Anything going on?"

"Nothing I have heard," he said. "It might be your link to Kelly."

"I wish I had better control to sort this out faster."

He turned down a side street, where we made better time despite more than a foot of snow. "Sometimes being fae isn't the answer."

"Yeah, I know." I slouched back on the seat to hide a sudden bout of cold sweats. Maybe I had the flu. Great timing. "I would just like any kind of answer, to be honest."

He nodded and said nothing more again.

We were getting closer to home.

Oh, now that was odd. I hadn't considered this building as home in a long, long time. I had my *home*, and I loved my place, but there would always be a link to the place where I'd lived the first years of my life, spending almost every single day of sixteen years there. When the ranch-style building came into view, I felt a draw I had not expected. I had grown up here, dressed in pink and frills, and I had left to be. . . . something else. I sometimes wondered what I had changed into in the years since I left this street.

Most days it didn't matter.

Darion pulled up across the street. I stared at the unassuming white house with blue trim, surprised that they hadn't changed the color scheme in all these years. The window to my bedroom sat at the end of the long side. I looked away in haste. Snow piled up in the driveway and along the walk to the door, but there had been many people in and out, trampling out a path.

I took a deep breath and followed Cherry out of the car. When she started to cross the street with me, I stopped her there. "You don't have to go with me, Cherry."

"Yes, I do. And she's my cousin, you know."

"Oh. True. You know her better than I do," I said, depressed at the realization. I should have tried harder. Maybe I could have protected her if I had spent more time with Kelly.

Maybe doesn't get you anything in the end.

We crossed the street. Ian came to the door, looking frantic, his hair barely brushed, his shirt not even tucked into his pants. I had never seen him less than dapper in all the years I had known him. He hadn't aged much. It was odd to come up and see him watch me, judging things.

"You've changed, Skye," he said.

"I got rid of the damned dresses," I said and won a brief, almost bright smile. Then he stepped aside and let us both inside the door.

"Cherry. It's good to see you."

"I was already heading over to tell Skye, so we drove her over."

"Oh. Thank you." He looked past us into the street. "Is your friend there? He can come in --"

"He'd rather not intrude," Cherry said which was true. "I'm sorry this has happened, Ian. I pray she's all right."

Ian nodded and pushed the door closed behind us.

I felt peculiar being back in this house. I experienced a strange resonance with walls as though the house and I belonged together. We passed from the entry hall towards the kitchen. I glanced in the living room and saw three children watching TV -- quiet, frightened children, which made my stomach tighten again. They looked my way, and I thought they recognized Cherry, but even Mary wouldn't remember me. I hurried past, almost running into Cherry, who glanced my way and then at the children, and then gave me a nod of understanding.

The kitchen was better because they'd remodeled. The old white cabinets were gone, the sterile whiteness that I had scrubbed and re-scrubbed every day had given way to rich wood and marble counters. This didn't look like home. I felt safer here in this place I didn't recognize.

Several boxes of cereal sat on the counter, and dirty bowls and spoons littered the sink. Children's drawings covered the refrigerator almost hiding a grocery list. All common, family things. This was *not* my home.

Ian leaned his back against the counter and waved us toward the chairs by the table. He watched me. I met his look, worried --

"I had forgotten how different you are, Skye. Your mother has no pictures of you. She will not speak about you."

I gave a small shrug. "That doesn't matter. We need to talk about Kelly. I can't stay long and risk running into her. Have there been any problems, Ian? Anything in the last year you can remember that of that might have led to this?"

"You mean between her and your mother?"

"No, I mean any problems at all. School? Boyfriend? Girls she hangs out with?"

"Nothing I know about," he said and glanced around the room as though looking for an answer. "Nothing at all.

The police asked the same thing. We went over everything, Skye. She has good grades and is checking out colleges. Kelly and her friends had a sleepover a week ago here at the house, and everything was fine. She doesn't have a boyfriend right now, and the last one moved away. They didn't have a bad breakup and they keep in touch on the computer. The police took the computer to an expert to search, but I don't think they'll find anything." He ran a hand through his hair. "There is nothing that might give a hint. I wanted something, Skye. I don't want this to be random with no hope of finding her."

"What about Kelly and her mother?" Cherry said with a hand lifted to stop me from saying anything. "Skye doesn't want to ask, but I will. I don't trust her, Ian, especially after what she did --"

I grabbed her arm, frantically trying to stop her from going on, but Cherry looked at me and shook her head. "No, Skye, baby. He needs to know because if she did that to you, she could have done something like it to Kelly."

"She had her reasons --"

"What the hell did Tay do?" Ian demanded and stepped away from the counter. His face had reddened, and he looked both angry and dangerous. I had never seen him angry in all the years we'd shared the same house. I didn't want to change that memory now. He and Kelly had been my link to a whisper of a happy childhood.

Cherry touched my hand where I still held to her arm. I knew she was right, but this wasn't a conversation I wanted. Not now, not ever. "He needs to know for Kelly's sake because you can't know that she didn't do the same to her."

"She had no reason --" I said again, protesting.

Cherry shook her head and looked at Ian, who appeared to have lost the last of his patience. "When Skye was sixteen, Aunt Tay took her to the bus depot, gave her a thousand dollars, and told her never to come home again."

Well, there it was out. I saw Ian blink several times, shook his head and stopped again. "Son of a bitch," he whispered. It was the first time I had heard him come even close to cursing. He leaned closer, staring into my face. "This is no time to lie, Skye. Tell me the truth. Did she do this?"

"Yes."

He nodded. Why didn't he doubt? I was a stranger here and didn't even look like the step-daughter he had remembered. I watched him, curious why he would trust this story. He forced himself to lean back against the counter once more and held both his hands together before him, his head bowed. I waited and after a few breaths, he looked up and spoke.

"The marriage hasn't been good for years," he said, his voice neutral. He stared out towards where the other three children were still watching TV. "We sleep in the same bed, but that's as close as we get except for dinner with the kids. We kept together for the children. I never thought she would hurt the children --"

"We don't know that she has," I protested.

"Even after what she did to you?" he asked, confused now, his gray eyes meeting mine.

"She had reasons," I said.

"I believed you must have been into something bad. Drugs and that was why she sent you off to live with your

father. But she didn't, did she? God, please tell me you
went to him. That you didn't live on the street --"

I had not expected to see Ian appalled for my sake. I
hated adding to his emotional turmoil. His voice had risen,
and I signaled him to stay quieter before the other children
heard. "I managed. I'm here. Let's move on to Kelly."

"Why? Why did she do it?" he asked.

I considered lying and saying he'd been right about the
drugs, but I didn't want him to think badly of me, which
seemed odd. I realized he was, perhaps, closer to real
family than I had ever admitted, and I wanted one of my
parents not to hate me. Since he had already admitted that
he was not happy with my mother, I didn't need to cover
for her now.

"It had more to do with my father than with me," I
said, which was true. "I was too much like him. She had to
be rid of me."

"Why didn't you tell me? Even though you aren't my
daughter, I always treated you well."

"You were always kind, Ian, but I couldn't come back
because things would have gotten worse. I didn't want
trouble here for Kelly and Mary any more than you do for
the children, which is why you've stayed. We did it for the
same reason: because the kids didn't deserve to be caught
up in our problems. I couldn't have come back to live here,
Ian. All I could have done is caused problems for
everyone."

He took a breath, his face paler as he nodded. "I don't
know what to tell you, Skye. I don't even know why I
called you. I'm just -- I'm panicked."

"What bedroom does she have?" I asked, glancing at

the hall to the right.

"Your room," he said, and he saw me shiver at those words. "Skye --"

"I'm just going to take a look. I won't touch anything," I said.

He nodded and would have followed, but Cherry caught his arm and shook her head. "We need to talk, Uncle Ian."

I suspected she planned to talk about me, and I wondered what Cherry would tell him. It would not be about the magic at least. I wanted to stay and listen, but I left anyway. I had work to do.

The kids looked my way as I passed and watched with wide, frightened eyes. Had they known about an older half-sister? Kelly would have remembered me. Had she told the others? Should I want to be remembered in this place?

I wanted a family. This place reminded me what it was like to sit at a table with others. Sometimes everything had been normal when my mother didn't stare at me, fear and worry in her face.

The room that had been mine had changed, praise the gods of all peoples. My room had held dolls, a pink canopy bed, and pink lacey curtains. I still have an aversion to pink. Kelly's room looked more like a normal teen's room with a lot of yellow and blue, but no unifying theme. She had a desk in the corner by the window and a still an unmade bed. The closet, standing open, showed normal, teen clothing. She had good taste.

A teddy bear sat on the bottom of the bed. I brushed my fingers over the fur and got my first sense of Kelly and for her, and for her worries. Nothing seemed out of place.

Teen things: grades, friends, summer job.

The mirror still stood on the back side of the closet door. I pushed the door open with my foot since I did not want my fingerprints anywhere in this room. How often had I looked into that mirror myself? If I stood here long enough, could I even pull back a memory of the child I had been?

This was not about me. I bowed my head for a moment before I lifted my hand and reached with magic to pull back the images buried in the mirror's memory.

I hadn't been able to work with mirrors when I had lived here. This was a power that came one day when I was helping someone locate her missing husband. I had looked into the bathroom mirror, wishing it could tell me something --

It hadn't, really. Oh, I had seen her husband shave with a dull blankness to his face like he did every morning before heading to his equally mind-numbing job. The realization gave me a hint of what had happened. Not long afterward I found him wandering through parks, watching the flowers bloom and free from all the things that had so weighed down on him. I found Ike a new job and last I heard, they'd moved out of their dull little apartment and into a house with a lakefront view.

I liked jobs that ended well and held tight to that memory while I reached forward and almost laid my hand upon the glass.

This was a bittersweet experience. I drew the image back to where Kelly had gotten up out of bed and then let the scene roll forward again. She resembled me, without my odd blond hair and green eyes. Kelly also had all the right bumps and curves I lacked. The sight made me self-conscious watching her come from the shower in a big fluffy robe and then dress for school, discarding one shirt after another until she had the right choice. I was right about her good fashion sense.

Mary came in and teased her as she sat, cross-legged, on the bed. I wished I had sound with the mirror and could hear what the two sisters said to each other. I wanted. . . .

I wanted to be Kelly with a sudden, unexpected longing. I wanted to be normal and have a family and --

And I couldn't. Kelly was missing, and my personal feelings would not help her. Nothing here gave me a clue. She wasn't distraught the morning before she disappeared. I needed to search elsewhere, but I was unwilling to step away.

Then I saw my mother come into the room and walk up behind Kelly. My breath caught in sudden fear, but she only put a hand on Kelly's shoulder and gave a quick smile, then brushed down the side of my sister's hair to get a strand in place.

The little kindness hit me like a knife -- that moment when mother and daughter stood together before me. That would have been me if I had been different. This was torture, but I watched anyway and noted my mother's face when Kelly turned away. An emptiness came to her eyes that seemed more like what I remembered from her --

Kelly came back, patted her on the shoulder, and walked away. I bowed my head. Nothing had helped.

I looked back up, surprised to find my mother still there --

Only not there.   *Here.*   I spun just as she leapt, screaming at me.

CHAPTER TWO

With my attention engrossed in what I saw in the mirror, I hadn't heard the altercation when my mother came home. Cherry still yelled and tried to get past the crying children in the hall. I had no way to escape as she rushed in and caught me in the small room. She grabbed me by my hair and screamed so loudly I heard nothing else. I saw madness in her eyes as her claw-like fingers ripped down the side of my face and she threw me to the floor. She kicked once and then flung herself down on me.

I tried to push her away. I didn't hit back, though a great welling of anger in me wanted to strike with hands and magic. I didn't. I tried to scramble away from her, aware that the others came to help me. Ian had her by the arm and dragged her across the room, throwing her on the bed. The children stood at the door crying.

"Get them away," I said, gasping and waving a hand

towards the kids. "Cherry --"

She gathered the three and hurried them back down the hall.

My mother screamed about demons, evil, and me. Darion arrived and reached to help me stand. She spotted him, and her eyes blazed.

"Out of my house. Out of my house! Evil! Out --"

"Let's go," I said to Darion. "This will not help."

He gave my mother one quick glare, a glance that would have silenced any fae. She wasn't that wise and continued to yell and curse. Darion held my arm and steadied me as we left the room. The attack had done one thing for certain: I no longer wished I was Kelly.

She pushed past Ian and came for me in the hall. Darion almost stepped in to stop her, but I held up my hand, and he moved aside.

I didn't allow her to slap me this time. I reached out and caught her arm. She shrieked.

"Shut up," I said. There was no power in my words, but she stopped yelling, her breath caught, her eyes large. "I am here to help find Kelly and nothing more. I would think you'd want anyone to help."

"You. You are part of it," she said and with such conviction that her words felt like the truth, even to me. I can sense the thread of untruths in extreme emotions, but she *knew* I was involved. "You are the reason she's gone!"

"You're crazy," I said and meant those words. Until now, that part had not been more than words. I looked into her dark, merciless eyes and realized there was more at work here than just her hatred and fear of me. "I had nothing to do with Kelly's disappearance. I would never harm the children."

Those words set her off once more though I understand why. She leapt at me, and I shoved her aside and just did my best to get out of her way and out of her house. This place was not a home I had lost and not somewhere I wanted to be.

Cherry had the children in the living room, and their raw, unbridled emotions almost overcame my mother's rage. I wanted out of here and away from them all. Even Ian's anger became too powerful. Coming here at all had been a mistake. I doubted I could help Kelly --

I headed straight out of the door and into the cold which hit me like a blow, the brush of cold flakes and ice on my hot face.

Here I found a different problem. Police. They had the doors open to their two cars, but they must have heard the yells from inside the house.

The sight of them brought me up short though it didn't stop my mother. She still screamed, tore free of Ian and attacked me once again. Ian pulled her off before the police got that far, but they watched me as though they believed I must be part of the reason Kelly had disappeared. This might get worse.

Then I saw another problem. Detective Barber came out of one car and stalked towards us. I saw his glance go from me to Darion to Cherry and back to me as he recognized us all. He'd been working on the case when Lacey Weaver disappeared.

He didn't appear happy to see us now.

"What the hell are you three doing here?" he demanded. The police and Ian had pulled my mother away.

Another stood close by me, a hand on her gun, believing I had to be a kidnapper or worse.

"Kelly is my half-sister," I said, looking at Detective Barber. His eyes narrowed, and he looked back at the woman who shouted obscenities in my direction. "Yes, she's my mother."

Shock touched his features as though that part hadn't registered yet. "Skye --"

I waved away whatever he meant to say and accepted a paper towel from Cherry to put to my face. The cold took me, and I trembled as I fought to get all my rampant emotions in control. I didn't want the police to suspect I was part of the trouble. I wanted to cry though I wasn't even certain why, except I felt as lost as I had that day she shoved me out of the car.

"Arrest it!" My mother shouted the first real coherent words I'd heard since I first saw her. "Arrest it and make it say where Kelly is!"

"I had nothing to do with Kelly's disappearance," I answered, making certain my voice stayed calm. I had winced when she called me 'it.' Barber noticed.

"Why did you come here then?" she demanded. She almost sounded reasonable

"I asked Skye to come over and see if she could help," Ian said and drew her shocked looked. "I asked *her* to come to help us find Kelly because she is good at this kind of work. And if you cared about Kelly, you'd be taking help wherever you could find it, Tay."

"Not from it. Nothing good comes from it." She came a step closer, and I backed away, unwilling to let this go on any longer. None of the police looked happy though

I didn't know if that came because of me or her. I suspected they were mad at both of us for making them stand out in the damned cold storm.

"You are involved in Kelly's disappearance," she said. She must believe those words from the amount of power I sensed when she said them. "I know what you've been doing, spreading lies about me to the family and how you are trying to turn everyone against me and ruin my life. You took her, didn't you? You took her to get even with me!"

"I had nothing to do with Kelly's disappearance," I replied because Barber must be curious and I wanted that out there.

"Skye, I perhaps we should go somewhere and talk," Barber said.

My mother looked pleased and then her eyes narrowed. "You know it? You know them?"

"I do not intend to stand out here in the snow and discuss this matter," he replied and sounded more than a little annoyed already. "Skye?"

"Yes, let's go," I said. I wanted to leave, and I didn't care what happened next. I had nothing to do with Kelly's disappearance, and I realized I could prove it, even without magic.

"Will you ride with me?" he asked and didn't order. He gave a wave to a third car, unmarked, by the curb.

I nodded, though Cherry and Darion both protested. "No, it's all right. Given the situation, Barber would have checked on me anyway. I am related to Kelly."

"I didn't know that part," he said, looking at Tay again. Did I see distrust in that stare? "You never mentioned

Skye."

"I don't want it in my life," my mother said with a lift of her head. The words didn't help her case. Barber took his work seriously. This melodrama would not make matters better for her.

"We're going to my office," Barber said with a nod to Cherry and Darion.

"We'll meet you at the police station," Darion said, snagging Cherry's arm. "Just come on. Let's get away from here."

Relief spread over me when I slid into Detective Barber's car and leaned back, welcoming the warmth from the still running heater. I held the paper towel to my face with my left hand and held the other hand to the heat. I trembled though not from the cold.

Barber spoke to the cops and then came to the car. Darion and Cherry were in the car across the street, and the cops were staying to talk to my mother and Ian, though they did it in two different little groups, Ian going back in the house with two.

"Buckle the seat belt."

I did so, waiting for Barber to ask questions. He wouldn't wait until Cherry and Darion were with us, and I didn't mind. I could deal with Barber, one-on-one.

Barber put the car into gear and forced it through the growing snow bank and out of the driveway. I had forgotten about how difficult driving a car without magic would be in this weather. I worried but then I looked back and saw Darion pull out right behind us, and that meant we'd be safe. He wouldn't let anything happen to us.

"That was quite a scene," Barber said, glancing my way

at the first stop sign.

"I shouldn't have gone there, but Ian asked for my help, and if I could do anything to get Kelly back, I would. Do you have anything at all?" I asked, hoping for any bit of good news.

"Nothing," he admitted, and then frowned again as we moved again. "You and your mother --"

"She hates me. She always has." I shifted; bruises and sore spots where she had hit and kicked began to ache. When I thought about the scene, I shuddered. "We have never gotten along."

"That's why you went to your father when you were sixteen?" he said.

I looked at him, silent for a moment. Then I decided truth might be the better answer. "I lied. I didn't go to my father. She took me across town to the bus depot and dumped me out with some money and said never to come back home again."

He said nothing at all this time as we drove out of the neighborhood and onto a busy crossroad. We reached a red light, and he stopped, his hands tight on the steering wheel when he turned to me. I hadn't wanted to give him that much honesty, but we had told Ian, and he would mention the situation to the police now.

"I want the truth," Barber said, his voice harsh.

"I am being honest. I lived on the streets for years," I replied and shifted a little, uncomfortable with the truth more than the bruises. "I don't tell people what happened."

"Your mother says you are telling lies about her to ruin her. You know this sounds a lot like one."

"I suppose it does," I agreed. "But you can have some

of it checked.   Cops stopped me now and then.   I'm noticeable.   People will have remembered me living in the downtown area for a few years."

"Hell." He stared a moment longer and then noted the light had turned green and pulled out again.   "This is the truth, isn't it? And you not only don't tell lies about her, but you have also protected her by keeping the truth to yourself, haven't you?"

"There was nothing to gain that would change what happened.   It's done and long in the past.   I didn't want what happened between us to be a problem for her or the kids.   There was only Kelly and Mary when I left.   I didn't even know about Ian and Veronica until last fall when I spent so much time with Cherry during that entire Lacey Weaver situation."

"Do you suspect your mother did the same thing with Kelly that she did with you?"

"I hope she did.   That would be something simple, and we can just hunt her down, and put an end to this mess. But I don't think this is going to happen.   The problem between my mother and me was more about my father and me being too much like him." I caught a strand of blond hair.   "She never forgot him as long as I was around.   She and Ian were happy together."

"I understand that's not the case now."

"So Ian told me."

He gave a sigh. "I hate more complications."

"I had not intended to be one and only came over because Ian asked me, and because he said my mother was at the police department, filling out reports.   I wanted to ask Ian a couple questions, try to help him feel as though he had a hand in assisting in finding his daughter, and get out. She came back too soon."

"My fault. The weather looked bad, so we packed her up and took her home. We intended to finish the questions, and some forms there and the police would check out her room again." He looked at me, frowning.

"I touched nothing except the top of a teddy bear . . . well, at least before my mother attacked me."

"You say those words with no more emotion than if you'd tripped over something and fell. There's no hatred in your voice. Why not?"

I considered that one because he was right. What she'd done today hadn't shocked me or made me think any worse of her. "Maybe that's because I survived and I do not want to be like her, who never gave up her unreasoning hatred of me."

"Damn. That's a good point, kid."

"I don't believe what happened between us has anything to do with what happened to Kelly. She had no reason to turn on her daughter. From all I can tell, they had the kind of relationship that I --" I stopped myself, appalled by what I had almost said.

"The kind of relationship you wished you'd had with her."

I gave a quick, silent nod, unable to say the words aloud, though I couldn't deny them, either.

"Hell. When I first met you, I thought you were just some rich kid playing at detective rather than getting a real job. I looked into the work you'd done, and you did well enough. You seem to have a gift for detecting. But now --
"

"I'm still the same person," I reminded him and felt an unexpected glow at what he'd said about my work. "I like helping others find things they've lost."

He glanced my way and then gritted his teeth as the wind caught the side of the car and nearly sent us sideways on the ice. He glanced in the mirror and shook his head.

"That is Darion Wilding back there, right? Best man at the Lacey wedding?"

"Yes."

"And your cousin Cherry is with him?"

"Yes," I said and smiled this time, even though that pulled at the cut on my face. "She likes tall blondes. He likes her. They met during the preparations for the wedding and got together again after Lacey turned up again."

"He handles that little car damned well in this weather, but he's a fool for driving something like that in this kind of snow."

"You're right," I said, though for different reasons. I had been right earlier; the little car drew notice.

The weather turned worse, and Barber paid more attention to handling the car rather than to asking me questions. I suspected, though, that he considered everything I had told him. By the time we reached the police station, he had looked grim. We got out of the car and hurried into the building. Cherry and Darion had to park elsewhere, but they weren't long behind us.

Barber looked from me to them and nodded. "Come to my office. All of you."

Cherry looked worried.

"It's all right," Barber said. "Skye told me about what

her mother did to her. I'm hoping for a few more details. Cherry, have you had more contact with her than Skye has over the last few years?"

"Yes," she said with a little snarl. Then she lifted a hand. "Sorry. Aunt Tay has never been my favorite relative, even before I found out what she did to Skye."

"You didn't know?"

"Not until last fall when I spent that time with Skye," she said. We had started towards the side area and the door to the private offices.

But we hadn't gone very far when I heard a familiar screech from behind us.

"Arrest it! Arrest it for taking my daughter!"

I looked back, appalled to find my mother close behind us and in the company of two rather annoyed police officers. They had caught hold of her arms, and she looked as though she wanted to break free and come after me again. I took another step away and found Darion at my side, grim-faced and angry as he looked at my mother.

"I had hoped we would be out of sight by the time she came back here."

"Why did you bring her?" I asked.

"Because I suspected that we had more questions for her, and I didn't want to ask them in front of her other children."

"You already didn't trust her?" I asked, surprised.

"She's been acting crazy," he said, and in a way that made me believe he meant those words. "I had assumed there was more going on before you turned up. But now I'm sure of it. And I keep getting the impression she's not as worried about what happened to her daughter as she

ought to be." A jab of fear hit the pit of my stomach, and I
felt ill. Barber had been looking at me, and I saw his face
soften. "There, that's it. You're more worried about Kelly
than she is. Come on. Let's go sit down."

Cherry put a protective hand on my shoulder. Darion
walked at our back. My mother yelled about devils, magic
and evil. The words hit me like blows, and only Cherry's
hold kept me going.

Before long we left the sound of her behind us. I
looked back, surprised.

"Sound baffles," Barber said. "Things get far too loud
out there sometimes when we have people complaining
about one thing or another."

"What will happen to her?"

"They will ask her questions. Then I'll ask her a few
more based on what you say. She'll spend most of the
night here after all."

"And me?" I asked as we reached his office door.

"Depends on what I learn from you, Skye. Like what
you were doing when Kelly disappeared."

"Oh. Well, that turns out to be easy. I was leading the
police down in Harverton to a dognapping ring."

He had pushed the door open and stopped inside as he
smiled. "Hell. I saw that report come through but didn't
read it. That was you? Good work."

"I wish I was as good at finding missing people." I
took a chair. Cherry settled in the other, but Darion stood
back by the door like a guard, reminding me again of the
job he had taken on to protect me last fall. I doubted my
mother could get this far without being stopped, but I
appreciated that he stood guard.

The room looked just the same as when I had been here last fall. There were no windows, and the desk sat crowded with an older computer and a lot of papers. Barber threw himself behind the desk and sorted through papers. He looked up, embarrassed. "I have the report here somewhere. It wasn't a real high priority read for me, though."

"I imagine not," I said with a little laugh. "But it was the type of work I can do, so that's good."

"Yeah, I suppose so." He picked up a paper and scanned it. "We have other worries, though maybe I shouldn't be that way, given the combined price of the dogs they found there. Nearly a fifty grand in dogs? Damn, I'm in the wrong business."

"Oddly, I was thinking the same thing," I said.

He laughed this time, which helped to ease the tension again.

He picked up the phone. "I'll call down to Harverton and get this confirmed. Shouldn't take long."

I nodded, grateful to sit and relax for a while. I had always known that someday it would be my word against my mother's, and I wanted this part out of the way. Barber was a good guy.

He squinted at the paper in his hand, then jabbed at the numbers. Cherry took my hand and frowned, probably because my fingers were cold.

"First aid kit," Barber said, reaching into a drawer. "Here -- Hello. I'd like to talk to Detective Presario. This is Detective Barber. Thank you."

He handed the first aid kit to Cherry and frowned at me with a shake of his head. Then his attention focused back on the phone. "Presario? How are you doing? I hear you guys are really going to the dogs down there."

I heard a laugh I recognized and saw Barber grin. I also recognized the familiar sound of yapping dogs, which meant a few of them were still there. They'd found so many that the detectives had taken a few home with them and back to work again while they waited for the owners to claim them.

"Yeah, I had a reason to call other than to give you grief," Barber said. "I need to confirm that Skye McFaelyn was with you yesterday morning between eight and ten am. Yes, I see the report. Now describe her to me." He blinked and then an eyebrow raised. "No really, *her*. Yes, I understand where you can make the mistake."

I blushed. The people in Harverton thought I was male. Barber noticed that reaction, too. Cherry had caught the implications and looked worried, but this part wouldn't matter much.

"Oh yes, blond Orientals with bright green eyes are kind of rare," Barber said with a laugh. "Okay, that settles the matter. No, she's not in trouble. Her half-sister has disappeared, and we needed to confirm where she was at the time. Really? Yes, I'll tell her. Good luck with the dogs. No, no thanks. I've got *real* work to do."

They both laughed, said their goodbyes, and hung up the phone. Barber looked back at me with that eyebrow raised again.

"They take me more seriously if they think I'm a guy," I said with a shrug.

"I suppose so. But you know she's female," he said, looking at Cherry.

"I'm her cousin. I knew her when her mother dressed her in nothing but pink frilly dresses," Cherry said.

"Oh. And now you dress like this because?" Barber asked.

"Because people really wouldn't take me seriously in pink frilly dresses?" I said, but then I raised a hand before he replied. "I dress this way because it is ambiguous and I can be what I need to be given the situation."

He nodded and dismissed that part. "What can you tell me about Kelly?"

"I haven't seen her since she was ten," I said. He looked startled again. "I didn't go back. That was the first time I'd been to the house since the day my mother drove me away and dropped me at the bus station."

"Ah. Reminds me. Hold on."

He made another call though to somewhere within the building. "Tom? Get people down to the bus depots and check again for Kelly Fairbanks. Put out a description of her mother and the cars she might have been driving. Check any video from streets in the areas. There is a slight chance she might have taken Kelly there and dropped her off. Yes, she'd done it before with an older daughter. Skye McFaelyn. She isn't in the report. The mother failed to mention her at all. Yeah, that starts you wondering, doesn't it? Thanks."

He hung up the phone again and leaned back in the chair.

"I don't think she took Kelly there," I said. "I really don't."

"You're probably right, but we have to check."

I nodded and tried to relax, but we were no closer to

finding Kelly than we had been when I first got the call. I wanted the police to look elsewhere, to find clues, to locate her before something happened --

I feared something might already have happened, but I pushed that fear from my head and took a deeper breath.

"What are you going to do now?" Barber asked.

"I will do what I can to help Ian find his daughter," I said and lifted a hand when he began to say something. "I won't interfere with anything you are doing, and if I find anything at all, I'll tell you right away. You can't expect me to back away. I liked Kelly. She was a sweet, fun little sister. She is a rare, pleasant memory from my past."

"Presario thinks you are professional in your work," Barber said. "That doesn't surprise me. But in this case, I'd rather you didn't --"

I looked up, shaking my head. "I have to. I can't walk away, Barber, any more than other relatives would stop looking."

"Just don't make this a problem between us."

"I won't. Thank you."

"Is there anything at all you can tell me? Anything about their home life that might help?"

"I can't. Cherry?"

She knew more than me though not much. She even had a more recent picture of Kelly than I had seen. I took the photo from her hand and stared for a moment, memorizing the face which looked so much like mine. Then I handed the picture over to Barber.

"Good. Thank you." He frowned and then stood. "Come on. I want to tell your mother what I learned about your whereabouts when her daughter disappeared."

"That won't help," I said and panicked at the idea of even being in the same room with her.

"I know. She's unreasoning. This isn't for her; this for the rest of the police working on this case. I want them to realize you were not in the area, and I want them to see her reaction. I don't want anyone taken in by what she says. Can you handle this?"

I stood, forcing myself to stay calm. This was a good idea. I didn't want the police believing her about my involvement. Things could get messy since I would have to hide any magic. Besides, they needed to be looking elsewhere since I had nothing to do with her disappearance.

So we went back out of the room. Cherry and Darion walked with me. I looked at the two. "You can sit this one out --"

"No way in hell am I letting you near that woman without back up," Darion replied with a shake of his head. There was power in those words, reminding me again that he was a powerful fae when he wasn't pretending to be human.

"There will be police around," I said.

"She needs to see you have people who will stand with you when the police *aren't* around," Barber said, surprising me. He was right. My mother and I might cross paths though if I looked for Kelly. She needed to know I wasn't alone in the world.

We walked back out of the office and down the hall, past other people working, and then past felons in cuffs who stared daggers at us. Darion put himself on the side where one brute of a man glared at everyone. I sensed the hatred off of him like the stink of death, and I knew he had killed and would kill again if someone didn't stop him. The brief connection made me half ill, especially thinking about Kelly and wondering if some animal like that had caught hold of her.

Oh gods --

"You all right, Skye?" Cherry asked. "You've gone pale!"

"Ill," I admitted and put one hand against my stomach, hoping it would calm. "Worried. I want Kelly to turn up right now."

I even looked pleadingly at Darion, hoping he could do something that would help. He shook his head with regret. So I stared back down at my feet and just kept moving, taking short breaths, forcing calm back into my body.

We turned a corner and stepped into a larger room filled with desks and file cabinets, the sounds of computers and the buzz of people talking. I had just lifted my head when I heard her speak.

"Why isn't it arrested? Lock it up! Make it say where my daughter is!"

When I looked at my mother, I felt revulsion for the first time. Before this, I had gone through anger, pain, hurt and betrayal. Now . . . Now I felt something different. The harridan who stared at me was not anything I wanted to be associated with any more than she wanted to claim me. I had done my best to stay out of her life but damned if I would stand back with Kelly missing. I wouldn't have turned my back on a missing stranger, and I wasn't going stop looking for Kelly just because I wanted nothing to do with that woman.

"Officers, this is Skye McFaelyn. She is the missing girl's older half-sister. Yesterday, at the time when Kelly Fairbanks disappeared, she was with the police down in Harverton, working on another case. I have it confirmed by Detective Presario."

"Whoever he is, he lied," my mother said, a snarl in her voice.

"As it happens, Presario was a part of this department for fifteen years before he transferred two years ago," Barber said, looking straight at my mother. She almost said something, but he continued. "He didn't lie. Skye was nowhere around when your daughter disappeared. She is not under arrest. However, we have several more questions to ask you, Mrs. Fairbanks. When was the last time you took one of your children to the bus depot and dumped them out and said never to come back?"

"I didn't --" Her face went livid, and her breath caught. The others glanced from her to me and back again. Barber had been right; their reaction to her was already changing. Then she blinked, and something more calculating came to her eyes. I didn't like to see the change. She was easier to deal with when enraged. "I didn't do that with Kelly. I did with Skye since I wanted it out of the house before its unholy ways spread to my other children. I had to protect them. Skye is turning everyone against me. You can see that now."

She believed those words just as firmly as she assumed I had some part in Kelly's disappearance. I saw calculation in the eyes of some people, and I realized that my mother had gone from being a worried mother to a potential cause of the entire problem.

"You can go now, Skye. I'll contact you if we need to talk. Oh, and here." He reached into his pocket and pulled out a card. "Call me if you learn anything at all."

"I will," I promised. Cherry still had hold of my arm and pulled me away. Darion walked at my back. My mother yelled, but I didn't listen, grateful to be going away from her.

We stepped out into the cold, late afternoon. The snow fell in a white cascade, but I didn't shiver this time. Instead, I stood there breathing in the fresh air. That place reeked of death, hatred, and evil, and it all had crept into my soul.

"Hey," Cherry said. "You two all right?"

I looked over at Darion, who had been doing much the same thing as me.

"That was a bad place for fae," Darion admitted as he hooked his arm in hers. "So much bad concentrated in one location. I'm glad we didn't have to stay longer. They've had a bad week in there. Hard work."

"Ah. Well, if you two don't mind, can you get your asses moving before I freeze to death here?"

Darion laughed and led her down the stairs. She still held my arm. I feared I'd have to pry her fingers off to get free. I was grateful for her support, though.

A snow plow went past, clearing the way as we got into the car and Darion pulled out into the street.

"You need a more formidable car," I told him, leaning forward from the back seat.

"This one doesn't give me any trouble."

"I know, but even Barber noted that it shouldn't be getting around in the snow so well."

"Ah." He looked startled. "Yes, you're right. I'll pick up something with a plow. That way I cannot only get around 'better', but I can also clear the way for others if need be. Thank you, Skye."

I nodded and leaned back again.

"What are you going to do now?" Cherry asked. She looked back at the police station as though she expected someone to follow us. "You two will not give up on this."

"I'd like to check things out at her school."

"Do you know where it is?" Darion asked.

"I do," Cherry said. "I went there for a talent show they were putting on. Kelly has a lovely voice." She sighed and leaned back, a wave of sadness touching me.

"I didn't mean for the two of you --" I began.

We were at a stop sign. They both looked back at me, saying nothing.

"Fine. Let's go."

I looked back at the police station as we turned the corner, but my mother would not follow us. I was safe.

And I shivered at the thought.

CHAPTER THREE

They'd closed down the schools early in the day because of the weather. Even in a city used to snow, a storm of this magnitude was more than they could handle. Besides, you didn't take chances with kids, even the older ones.

The parking lot sat deserted and knee deep in snow, which didn't stop Darion, who turned in and whipped the snow away from us. When I looked back, I saw the snow fall in behind us again, covering the tracks we made.

"No one will see the car," he said as he stopped. He lifted a hand, and a whisper of a message came to him. "My people will search for information. We've found lost kids before. We might help. Skye, I'm going to ask something stupid. You can find Cherry with your link --"

"I needed more of a connection to her. That's why I went to the house. Let me see what I can get." I leaned back and closed my eyes, but found what I expected: a swarm of lines and connections that were all dull except for the bright star of Cherry beside me. I gave a frustrated sigh and let go. "All I get is a jumble of all my other relatives out there. If I have to, I'll sit down and sort each one of them out but that will take time and magic and a lot more energy than I think I can afford to spend on something I fear won't help."

He nodded. "You might be right. We'll hold off and see what else we can do first. What do you hope to find here?"

"Something about her life outside the house." I patted Cherry on the shoulder since she had to open the door and get out before I could leave the car. "You two can stay here. I can do this myself."

"I'd rather be in there with you," Cherry replied. "It worries me more when I don't have you in sight."

"Must make it hard to sleep at night," I said with a grin.

"Yes, it sometimes does," she said and laughed. "Okay. Let's go."

She shoved the door open and got out, bracing herself for the worst. Darion had already put a magic shield up around the car, and it kept not only the snow away, but also the cold. Cherry stood there as I got out and she even smiled.

"The snow is beautiful when you don't have to suffer for it." She looked around the lot. "This is really lovely."

I agreed, though my mind wasn't on the weather. Still, I appreciated Darion's help even in this. The shield stayed around us, pushing aside the snow so it might as well have been summer for all the trouble the weather gave us. It would have taken me far longer to get to the door with the help of Darion's magic. I would have been in agony half way to the door if I had tried to create such a shield and frozen if I hadn't.

"Careful," I said when we reached the large, double doors. The overlay of emotions from all those students piled year after year atop each other. They were distracting. I had to pay better attention. "They have alarms. I can get us past them."

"You've broken into this school before?" Darion asked, looking curious as I pulled a lock pick out of the inside of my coat.

Good thing Barber never had a reason to search me though a little magic could have hidden it. I had learned not to go out without the proper tools years ago and kept this case in the inside pocket out of habit. I pulled off my gloves and shoved them in my pocket.

"Not this one, but they were almost all redone to the same specifications," I said. I touched a bit of magic to the pick and ran the tip along the edge of the door until if found the little spark of power where the alarm wires ran under the metal casing. I diverted the power and then opened the lock. We slipped into the dark but warm hall, and Darion shoved the door closed behind us. His magic shield went down, and he took a deeper breath. Even a full fae can't do as much magic as he had the last few hours and not show sign of it. Just getting that car through town had been draining him.

"It wasn't like this when I went to school." Cherry shook her head as she waved a hand towards the metal detectors just inside the door. "Damn hard world we live in when you have to worry about kids bringing guns to school."

"It is," I agreed. I made certain the devices wouldn't sound an alarm, and we went down the hall. A sign pointed us straight to the office. I headed that way, and the other two tagged along behind me. I started to bring up a magic light, but Darion did the work faster and smiled.

"Let me do this stuff since the magic isn't pleasant for you, Skye. You don't have to suffer when I'm here."

"Thanks," I said and tried not to be embarrassed. "I can handle this stuff most of the time, but I'm . . . I don't know. Almost disconnected. Here we go. I want to see her records. And then check her locker."

"Good idea," Cherry said. "The police will have checked already, though, right?"

"Yes, I'm sure they did, but they won't tell me what they found, and they can't sense what she felt."

"Oh, true." She looked around as we entered the office and then sat on a bench by the door. "I'm getting far too used to this stuff. It doesn't even bother me that we've broken into the school."

"Kind of sad when even this stuff gets to be commonplace, isn't it?" I said with a laugh.

"I'll have to come up with something exciting for us," Darion said with a grin at her.

"Oh, now that sounds like fun," Cherry smiled in return.

I shook my head and crossed to the computer behind the counter. I called up the password with a tiny spell I had perfected -- very neat since it worked with technology. Kelly Fairbank's records proved easy to find, and I read through them. She was a bright girl, did well, but had a couple marks for being rude to a teacher. A little more digging showed the teacher had an unmistakable bias against anyone oriental and had not been rehired this last year.

In the file cabinet, I found a few handwritten notes, including those from a couple teachers who thought she was an excellent candidate for what sounded like a good scholarship. The notes made me happy and all the more determined to find her.

I closed the cabinet and found Cherry and Darion sitting on the bench together, both of them watching me.

"What?" I said, startled by the stares.

"You're really very good at this," Cherry said. "I saw how careful you are not to leave your fingerprints anywhere, and how you know where to search. How did you learn?"

"Just seems natural I guess," I said.

"Have these kinds of records helped in the past?" Darion asked.

"Oh yes. A couple times I found friends of someone I was looking for, and through them discovered what I needed. I doubt it will help this time, but I always like to check the obvious stuff first. Kelly isn't in any kind of trouble I can find here. Let's search her locker and then I'll try places around town -- and no, you two cannot go with me there."

Cherry began to protest, but Darion touched her shoulder and shook his head. "Skye's right. This is the work he does well and we need to let him do it and get out of the way."

She sighed and agreed although she was not at all happy.

"I'll call you when I get back home," I promised as we walked along the hall with Darion's light bouncing along like a well-trained dog. I got her locker open and just touched the metal since the police had taken everything to go over it. All I caught was someone anxious to do well in school. I sighed and closed it again --

And sensed something odd and then used a little magic --

"Ah. Sharlyn's locker, next to hers. They're close friends. There's something of Kelly's here."

I opened the locker, let my hand hover over the items, and then nodded, reaching down and pulling out a fancy writing journal. It even said Kelly on the cover.

"Oh," Cherry whispered.

"She lets Sharlyn read it. I don't sense anything purposely hidden, except she doesn't take it home," I said as I held the journal.

"We can take this and bring it back later," Darion said. "I'll make certain none of our fingerprints are on it. This might help, and I don't believe we want to stand around here reading it, right?"

"True. The two of you take the journal. You can go over it while I check out other things. I have my cell phone. You can call me if you learn anything."

Darion grinned, probably at the thought of using a phone, but Cherry nodded, grateful to have anything to do. She put the journal inside her coat. I closed the locker, and we headed back out, past the office, past the metal detector and out into an even worse storm. The night had gone dark as the wind kicked up sending a frozen white fog over the landscape. Darion frowned, and Cherry caught my arm as though she feared I would leave them right then.

"Skye, baby, you shouldn't go wandering around out there tonight," she said, panic in her voice.

"I have magic, Cherry. Magic might not be pleasant for me to use sometimes, but I can to get out of danger, including storms. How do you think I survived so long on my own?"

"I know," she said. "But this -- what can you do in weather like this?"

"This is great weather for what I want," I said, surprising them both as we headed towards the car, once more under his protective shield. I was going to miss that one. "People will hold up in places, and I won't have to hunt them down. I know where I'm going, and I won't wander out into the cold much at all."

"Where can we drop you?" Darion asked as we reached the car.

"Downtown," I said.

Since Darion didn't argue, Cherry stopped, though I could tell she wasn't happy about what I planned to do. I wasn't thrilled when I got out of the car and the snow and wind whipped around me. I pushed Cherry back in, waved to Darion, and walked away without looking back. My toes were already getting cold, the snow drifts were up to my ass in places, and I wanted nothing more than to leap back to the car and find a place nice and warm. Any place.

I heard them drive away.

I started moving from one place to another.

And the annoying thing was that I spent the next seven

hours on the street, half freezing to death, and didn't get a single thing from anyone except for a warm bowl of bean soup at the Mission. I wasn't hungry, but the soup was warm. I sipped the broth and sat at the table with a couple old guys who argued about how bad the storm was getting.

No one had seen Kelly or heard about her abduction except for information in the news. The closest I came to learning anything helpful was that there had been another girl, about her age and build but not oriental, who had disappeared a couple weeks ago in the area. They'd found the street kid later, beaten and drugged. She was in a hospital somewhere.

That was all I had, except for the journal in Cherry and Darion's hands and I hoped they had found something helpful there. I left the Mission and stepped out into the storm despite the protests of those who thought I shouldn't go back out.

"I don't have far to go," I said with a bright smile, though face felt raw from the cold. "It's okay. Thanks!"

I hurried out and into the alley, pausing while I tried to decide what to do. Go back to my place, I decided. It was late, and there wasn't anything on the streets tonight. Maybe I'd have better luck tomorrow.

I wondered if I should call Darion to come and get me. I walked away from the area so no one saw me standing around like an idiot. I gave myself little surge of warmth, the little magic no real trouble. Besides, walking alone had always helped me work out problems.

There had to be something more I hadn't done yet. I walked one block and down another alley, out of the wind. How could I find a link to Kelly? I might have a better chance without Cherry so close. I tried, but with no better luck. The attempt only gave me a sudden blinding headache, and I stopped as I caught hold of a trashcan, hoping the pain eased.

I took a step forward -- and found a man standing barely four feet away and between me and the end of the alley. I didn't know where he had come from, and it scared the hell out of me that someone had come this close when I might have been doing magic. He stepped closer and at that moment I sensed something unworldly about him. Something not human, and not fae either, and that didn't make me feel any better.

"You must find something for me," it said. The voice had an odd, echoing property, and I took another step backward, already shaking my head. "You will find what I seek."

"No," I said and saw the head lift, and the eyes glitter with golden light that didn't come from the snow-covered world where I stood. "No, I'm already working on something and I will not go work for someone else."

"You will." It took another step forward. Anger radiated from this creature like a new wave of cold in the already frigid night. The human shape melted and change, which made me half ill to watch, my headache growing worse. What stood before me became far taller and wider than human though part of that might have wings. "I have chosen you. You will obey, little half-thing."

Whatever the creature might be, he was not winning any points in attitude. I detected power from it in ways that made me think I would not get away if I turned around and tried to outrun him. So I tried something else.

I mirrored him.

I have an innate magical ability that allows me to mimic what I see. This has worked well with angry dogs to scare them away when they face something just as fierce. It sometimes even works with angry people who are not ready to face something as big and dangerous as they are.

It *did not* work with the gargoyle. The creature let out a bellow and snapped huge teeth at me, so I dropped the mirror. If I'd had a chance, I might have tried a different tactic that would have allowed me to mirror the area around me and hide. No time. I faced an enraged creature. Hell. I took a step out of the thing's reach and lifted my hand, but he swept forward with unnaturally long arms and hit me. His long claws caught at my glove as he ripped it off my hand.

We glared at each other.

This was wasting time.

"Tell me what you are looking for," I said. "When I'm done, I'll --"

"Now. You will do this *now.*"

"I don't know who or what the hell you are, but --"

I stopped at the sound of a car barreling down the alley behind me and glanced back, very much relieved to see Darion heading my way. He threw himself out of the door before the car had come to a full stop and charged to my side. He had magic in hand already.

"Get away from Skye," he ordered, his voice dangerously soft and without a hint of humor. I didn't feel any safer when the creature drew his lips back to show long, dagger-like teeth.

"You do not order --" the creature began.

"I am the Fae Ambassador, Darion Sapphire Wilding,"
he said, and yes, there was considerable power in that name
and title. "I *command* you to go."

"You cannot command me, little fae Ambassador.
Not you alone."

"Then I shall call others in," he said. A wave of
messages went out so fast they felt like gnats swarming past
me.

This must be serious, and the new complication added
pressure to my already pounding headache. Winter winds
blew harder in around us, fueled by the magic they were
using. I did not understand what this trouble meant.

Neither, apparently, did Darion. "Tell me what you
want, gargoyle," he said.

Gargoyle. I'd heard of them. They were big and
dangerous, and they did not get along with the fae. They
had a strict hierarchy in their society, with workers and
those who were in command, layer upon layer. Only the
strongest ones reached the top -- and this guy had to be
high ranking for this behavior. I realized that was why
Darion worried about the encounter: a gargoyle of this
much power might call on hundreds of others to back him.

I saw the creature in the glow of Darion's magic and
the lights from his car. It stood almost twice as tall as me,
the head stretched forward with a long muzzle and those
damned sharp teeth. The eyes still glinted gold with
diamond-like black pupils. The skin appeared to be lizard-
like in scales, though metallic in shine. He had a tail and
wings, the last folded across the back, twitching now and
then which probably indicated his irritation.

The arms were long and ended in wide hands with four

long fingers sprouting in claws that glittered in the light. I wasn't stupid; I took another step backward, but the gargoyle looked at me, the lips pulled back in a snarl. Darion moved between us. I didn't like that much either, so I moved up to his side to help if it came to trouble.

"What is it you want here?" Darion again demanded.

"I lost something," the gargoyle said, the words slurred by the new shape of the mouth since he had cast aside the shell that made it almost look human. "It finds things."

The 'it' rankled this time, having heard that term too often from my mother in the last day. Then I reconsidered when I looked up at the creature. The gargoyle had an attitude that meant he labeled anything not one of its own kind as an 'it.'

"I told you I don't have time --" I stopped when Darion touched my shoulder, and his fingers tightened, an obvious sign for me to be silent.

This meeting worried Darion, so I made no more protests. When something bothered Darion this much, the situation must be worse than I imagined or understood. I stood still and watched the gargoyle, wondering how *it* had found me and why it had chosen me for this work. I was not well known. Though maybe that wasn't true across the Veil. The idea made me a little more nervous.

"What did you lose, gargoyle?" Darion asked, his tone steady. "Where did you lose it?"

A few other fae appeared behind us with little snaps of magic, which again fueled the storm. I glanced back and found Darion's people. None of them looked happy. This was much worse than I wanted to know.

"I lost a stone of power," the gargoyle said. That won

hisses of surprise and worry behind us though Darion only shook his head and looked disgusted. "I wandered alleys, watching the humans -- dark creatures, bloodthirsty. The stone in such hands --"

"How big of is the stone?" Darion demanded.

The creature's gold eyes flashed towards Darion and the clawed hand lifted, but then fell back to his side. The gargoyle reached towards the wall and pulled up a staff and touched the top part, shaped in a claw the size of my hand.

"The stone rested there," he said. "I was in the alleys, by the docks, studying these human things. They are not to be trusted with such power."

"A big stone," Darion said and sounded worried for new reasons. He glanced my way. "If a stone of power that size fell into the hands of a human, it would give him some magical power just in the touch, but the power would warp him and the people near him since no one would have any protection. These stones are very dangerous, and they should *never* be brought across the Veil where there is nothing to temper their power. They should not be taken into an area with humans."

"Do not lecture me, fae," the gargoyle said with his sharp teeth showing again. "It will find the stone for me. Now."

"Your own people --" Darion began.

The creature hissed in anger, and I figured he didn't want his people to realize about being this stupid because he would lose his place in the hierarchy. The gargoyle grew angrier, and I had the odd feeling that if I didn't agree, we would all soon fight. The fae would win, but someone would get hurt.

"I'll look for the stone," I said. Hell, why not? I would be out on the streets looking for Kelly anyway, so I might as well ask about odd stones. "I'll search for the stone and my sister."

The gargoyle nodded, accepting the compromise, praise the gods. I relaxed a little. Darion looked relieved as well and lowered his hand, the magic he'd held drifting away.

The gargoyle leapt forward and ran a long sharp claw down my chest, ripping through jacket, shirt and skin. I gave a startled cry of pain and went to my knees, incredibly ill. The white world seemed to go red and then dark. I didn't want to be unconscious on the ground with that creature above me. Blue grabbed hold of me, and I heard shouting, but there was no battle yet.

I got back to my feet to make certain Darion knew I wasn't dead. He almost leapt in and attacked right then, but the Gargoyle had backed away by several steps.

"Marked as mine," the gargoyle said with a satisfied sound that came almost like a purr. "Will do my bidding now and the others will wait. Find the stone."

He backed up, and again and then disappeared in a flash of light and snow.

"Damn!" Darion shouted, and the word echoed up and down the alley like something alive. He turned and took hold of my arm, magic rushing down through the wound. "I'm sorry, Skye. I *never* expected him to do that. I've never known a gargoyle to mark anything but one of his own."

"I don't feel well," I said, half sagging into Darion's hold, even after the magic.

"Hell. The marker normally isn't poisonous, but this

has affected you that way."

"Of course," I said. I shivered, despite the warmth of the fae all around me. I looked back at Darion. "What were you doing here, anyway?"

"Came out to find you and take you home so Cherry would stop worrying," he said. I glanced at the car, worried. "No, she's back at the apartment. I said I'd get you home and that you'd call her. Hell, maybe I should take you to her apartment --"

"No. My place," I said. I started towards the car. Unsteady steps, and weak, but I moved, and the others stayed close beside me. I felt protected as I always did when Sapphire Clan people were around me. "Just to my place. My plants."

"Yes. Good idea," he agreed. "The rest of you can go back home. Say nothing out right about the damned gargoyle, but see if you can find out about him, okay? I want to know what the hell one was doing here and if there are more gargoyles we need to chase back out of this realm."

"They hate humans. They would never come over here in numbers," Sand protested.

"I hope note, but we need information, people. Go. I'll get Skye to safety."

"We'll be listening if you need us," Blue said. He opened the door and all but lifted me inside the car.

"Thanks," I said as he closed the door. Darion slid in the other side.

"Damn mess," Darion mumbled as we pulled out. The others had already gone quickly and quietly back to Sapphire House. I was glad they'd slipped away without running into trouble with the gargoyle.

"I can't search for the stone," I said -- but a sharp pain rushed up through my heart at those words and I gasped --

"Skye!" Darion had stopped the car and leaned over, taking hold of my shoulder. "Skye!"

"Oh hell, that hurt," I said, opening my eyes and looking at him. "What the hell --"

"Magic, in the wound. I'll do what I can but --"

"But the mark makes certain I do what the gargoyle wants. Why didn't it mark me to begin with?"

"He needed your agreement to search first," he said. He sat back on his seat. "Don't worry. I'll help you. We'll find the damned stone. And we'll find Kelly."

I didn't want to doubt him, but right then I wasn't any closer to either of them, and things had just gotten a hell of a lot more complicated.

DAY TWO:

CHAPTER FOUR

We went to my place, Darion dealing with the snow still piling up on the streets without a problem. As we pulled into the alley, I spotted a big SUV, the windows steamed over and the engine running. Darion frowned until Ian got out. I wondered what had made him drive here in this weather. Desperation, I supposed.

Darion looked relieved as he came around to help me. By then Ian had come close enough to see the rip on my coat and the blood.

"What happened?"

"Nothing serious," I said, trying to sound steadier than I felt. "Just the wrong alley at the wrong time. I'm sorry, Ian. I haven't found out anything."

He helped get me up the steps to my apartment. My friend, the squirrel, came chattering at us and knocking snow everywhere, which made me smile a little. He had a personal little squirrel house up by the wall near the heating duct so he stayed warm in winter.

We went inside though Darion stopped long enough to drop food out for the squirrel before it followed us and complained more.

I moved over to the chair across the room by the window and sat there with a sigh of relief. Ivy plants trailed down to brush against my head, and I pushed them gently aside.

Ian looked around with that shock everyone gets the first time they step into my jungle. Another time I would have enjoyed watching him, but I only wanted rest for a few hours. It was already five in the morning. I hadn't realized how long I had spent out on the streets.

"Ian --"

"When you left home, I assumed it was because you were into something bad," Ian said. He took a chair across from me and leaned forward, intent on seeing my face while we spoke as though he expected to read there. "I asked, but she never wanted to hear your name again. I thought -- I thought it wrong, but she said you went to live with your father, and though I tried to find out who that might be, she would never say. I wanted to make certain you were all right, Skye."

"Thank you," I said and meant those words.

"You should have come back. I'm not your father, but --"

"I stayed away because that was the best thing to do.

My mother and I would never reconcile, Ian. You saw her reaction, even years later."

"I never realized she was this vindictive. This *dangerous.* The police brought her back, and she stopped ranting when she realized you were not anywhere around."

"She'll get over all of this when Kelly comes home," I said and looked him in the face.

"You believe she'll come back."

"Yes," I said the word with a little power, though I didn't have enough to make much of a difference.

Ian nodded, but the belief never reached his face. If I hadn't been so ill, I might even have attempted a little more magic to help him through this horrible time. I had done so for Ted Weaver once. Unfortunately, I hadn't the strength to even lift my hand now.

"I suspected you were into drugs," Ian admitted. "I had to find a reason for her attitude, though I couldn't imagine how you managed any trouble, the way she watched over you. I wondered if you had fallen in with a cult, especially when she brought home books on magic and voodoo and stuff. ,"

That caught my attention. I glanced at Darion with worry, but he shook his head. No, she didn't have any magic of her own. I took a quick breath of relief and looked back at Ian again. He was staring at his hands now and hadn't noticed the interplay. Good.

"She had a few of those books at home again about a month ago," he said. "And that made me think it was about you again since I'd heard you were in contact with Cherry."

"I am not involved with anything of that sort," I said,

which was the truth, though he might think differently about the fae. "However, she might think I am, and you won't be able to convince her otherwise."

"True. She is unreasoning, and once she decides something, she never does let go." Ian shook his head. "After this -- I can't see how I can stay with her. But the children --"

"You can hold on for them," I said. "And when Kelly comes back, it will be much better. Then is the time to consider the future, not now."

"What if she doesn't come back?" he asked.

I shook my head. "No. I won't think that way. It doesn't help you or me. You must consider the children, Ian. You have to do what you can for them."

"I'm going to call Cherry and say we're here," Darion said, walking over to the phone. He looked like he didn't want to be pulled into the personal, family conversation and I didn't blame him. I wasn't comfortable with this discussion, either.

I desperately wanted rest.

"Ian, I'll do all I can to find Kelly. I have contacts and help that might do something more than even the police. You have to go back home and be with your children because right now all they have is their mother."

He looked up, startled and even afraid. "I shouldn't have left her there with them. She's dangerous --"

"She will not hurt them, Ian, but your children need you because she doesn't understand the emotional needs of others."

"Damn," Ian said. He looked startled. "You nailed her, right there. I have tried to figure her out for years, and you did it in one sentence. She's so self-absorbed that she can't see that others have needs at all."

"She's always been that way," I said with a sigh and tried not to wince at a little movement. "Go home, Ian. Be with her and the kids. This might change her once she gets over the idea that I'm involved. I'm not, you know. I had nothing to do with it."

"I know. Detective Barber came in and told me personally when he brought your mother home. She was livid that he'd spoke to me, which was why I had to leave. I'm going back."

He stood and ran a hand through his hair this time and looked, if not saner, at least a little calmer. "Be careful, Skye. I don't know what I'd do if something happened to you, too."

"I'm not --"

"You are part of the family, Skye. I'm sorry I failed you --"

"You didn't!" I protested, and started to stand, but I changed my mind. Hell, it hurt. I wanted to go rest, but I didn't want Ian to leave believing he had had done something wrong on my account. "I made my choices, Ian. I could have called you knowing you'd take my side. My mother would have been out so fast it would have made her head spin. But I couldn't do that to Kelly and Mary -- or to you. I was the problem, Ian. I wasn't into anything dangerous, but I was still the problem."

He frowned. "Is that cut serious? Do you need to go to a hospital?"

I did my best not to shiver at those words. Doctors, of a sort, had gotten hold of me once. It would never happen again.

"It's not serious. The jacket took most of the damage. I was stupid. I've had worse," I said and even gave a wave of my hand adding a tiny touch of reassuring magic. "Go on home."

He headed for the door, but before he went out, he turned back once more. I tried not to sigh in frustration. "Thank you, Skye -- for helping now, and for what you did in the past for the children and me in the past. Thank you."

He stepped out. I heard him going down the steps and in a moment the SUV pulled away. I looked at Darion, who gave a nod.

"He's a good man. And he's safe. I gave the car a little protection, just to make sure he gets home."

"I shouldn't have let him believe the kids might not be safe with her," I admitted.

"What you said might be true, though," Darion replied. He sat where Ian had been a moment before and looked at me. I was about to get lectured. "You keep taking this all into yourself, but the real trouble has never been you. She was the one who did something wrong, and having done so to you, for whatever reason, means she can't be fully trusted again. We needed to send him back home."

"Home." I brushed my hand over a plant and looked back at him. "You can go --"

"I'm staying here while you sleep because I don't know what the hell that was about with the gargoyle, but there's no reason to leave you unprotected right now."

I didn't argue and even let Darion help me up and out of the jacket and ruined shirt. There was an ugly, long red cut from my collar bone to my waist and Darion used a little more magic to help stop the bleeding. I took a shower and crawled into my bed to sleep knowing I wouldn't be there for long.

I didn't sleep well, plagued by nightmares of being called and never seeing who was there. When the light of day came through the windows, I could hear the howling wind of a full-fledged blizzard outside, so I burrowed deeper into the blankets. I slept and woke again. Maybe Darion was getting magical calls from his people, and that was what I had heard in my dreams. He might have more information. I got up and dressed, having slept fitfully for a few hours.

We left a little while later. He didn't even argue. Snow still fell, covering over paths shoveled clean once or twice already. Darion wasn't any happier about the weather than I was.

As we drove away, I realized the roads were icy beneath the snow which made them all the more treacherous. The wind had died down, but the snow fell harder again, a white curtain against the world. Darion, with a quick flash of fingers and magic, stopped one accident about to happen with a bus and a van. Those people would never realize how lucky they were, and I hoped they got off the road soon. No one -- at least without magic -- should be out in this weather

"Thanks," I said to him.

"For what?" He looked at me, surprised.

"For stopping people from being hurt. They can't tell you thank you, so I will."

"You would have done the same. You had your hand up and ready, but I was just a little faster."

"Yes, but that means nothing. You still did the work and very well. I still am too showy and rough."

"Magic is harder for you. But you do it anyway, to help people."

"Yes."

"Is that because you are human or because you are fae?"

"It's because I am who I am. I lived out there on the streets, and I know how easy it is to get hurt, to get lost and forgotten, and for no one to care. If I can save some of them, I will. Now you tell me why you do it."

He looked at me for a moment. Then he did something unexpected; he pulled over and parked.

"Don't worry. This is a story that needs attention, but I'll be fast. A long time ago when I was . . . well, younger, if not young, I got bored and did something stupid. I went wandering to different realities, and I went too far."

I looked at him, shocked by the confession. He'd told Cherry and me about how fae sometimes wandered to other realities looking for excitement and how, if they weren't careful, a fae might go to places where magic doesn't work, and they couldn't get back.

"The place I went to had so little magic I could barely breathe for the lack of it. The world was dark and cold, and I expected to die there. I curled up in a ball, and I didn't move -- and magic came to me. Just a little at a time, just a whisper. If I held on and did nothing, eventually I would have enough to retreat to somewhere safe. I had a damned long time to think, Skye, my friend. Far more time than any person should have. I couldn't turn my thoughts off because if I did, I would lose my hold on the magic."

"Oh hell." I tried to imagine what that would be like and shivered.

"I thought about everything I had ever done and looked at each action from every angle. I imagined what it would have been like if I did something different instead, and sometimes those were the worst thoughts. I saw how much I should have helped others and how self-centered I had been. This was not a pleasant revelation, but I vowed to change. I kept that pledge, though it was tested before I even left the dark world. I was gaining power and saw more of the world around me.

"There was life not far away. I hadn't expected it. An odd life form, dark as the world, living in holes. Four legs, long arms. Heads that peeked out from the shell covering sometimes. Not bright and intelligent, but entertaining to watch. I enjoyed studying them far more than I enjoyed reliving my own life.

"And then disaster came. Storms rushed over the land. This was natural, but it didn't happen often. I watched the weather coming and sensed the dread from the little creatures. They tried to reach higher ground, but there weren't many such places. The storms began with a horrible acid-like rain that gathered in rushing streams and tore at the world, destroying everything. The creatures would die. They would all be wiped out, and this was natural -- but I didn't let it happen. I had seen all the times I'd turned away in every world I'd visited. So I saved them. It used almost every bit of magic I had, but I tore the storm apart, and I gathered the creatures to a higher ground I made for them. Then I sat down, and I waited again -- a long, long time -- to get my power back. I watched them go back to their lives. I think they might have, on some level, understood what I did. I even fed them a little protection before I left. And when I got back home, I kept my vow. I will not turn away, Skye, and I will never say it's not my problem."

I stared at him in awe. He had done more than keep his vow, he had made the promise his whole life. We were akin, the two of us.

"So you tell me why you help them," he said.

"Oh, nothing as dramatic as your story," I replied and glanced out at the cold world. "It's just that I've been on the other side too often and watched people turn away when even a little thing could help. I don't want to do the same to others. And I want to help. I want to believe that what I am can count for something."

He nodded and drove away again, and I felt as though we dared fate in that drive. I felt as though danger lurked at every corner, but we reached her parking lot without trouble. Walking from the car to the apartment reminded me yet again about how much I hated winter.

I was glad to get in out of the cold. Cherry's apartment had been my refuge too often of late. I should have remained at my home, but Darion would want to see Cherry, and right now I needed him to help figure out this mess.

We found my cousin sitting on the sofa. She looked up and nodded before she turned away. I feared she had been crying. Darion saw as well and hurried over to her while I took off my coat and hung it on the rack.

"What's wrong?" Darion asked, sitting beside her. He took her hand in his. They looked delightful there, together. I hated that I was intruding again.

Had she learned something about Kelly? The fear kept me rooted halfway to the chair, afraid to go farther and wanting time to stop --

"I've been reading her journal," Cherry said with a wave of her hand to the book on the side table. I went to the chair and dropped into it, drained again by the rush of emotions. "Mostly girl stuff: the new dress she really, really wants. The concert she wanted to go to, but her mother wouldn't let her. There were a couple times she talked about her mother reading weird books, and once where her mother acted oddly, and she feared it was drugs. She debated talking to her father, but her mother was fine the next day. But then . . . but then I found this page."

She held the journal out for me instead of Darion. I didn't know what I'd find. The date on the page took me by surprise though not nearly as much as the words.

Today is Skye's birthday.

I always remember her birthday. I used to buy her cards after she'd gone, but mom found them and screamed and yelled how I was never to even think of Skye again, that Skye was evil, and Skye is gone so we can be safe now.

I remember her, though. I remember how she used to help me with my homework. I don't know how she got so smart since mom wouldn't let her go to school and didn't really try to teach her anything. Skye was kind and gentle and helped me with any problem I had. I won't forget her no matter what mom says.

Mom used to make me promise never to mention Skye to anyone.

*She said that if I did, people would come and take her away and then
they would take the rest of us, and we'd never see each other again. I
used to cry at night, for fear that someone would take her. And I
never said anything at all, not even to my best friends. I don't even
talk about her now, but it's for a different reason.*

*I asked dad once, but he admitted he didn't understand what
had happened. He said that I reminded him of her and showed me a
photo of Skye that he kept hidden away. I look like her. He said
never to tell my mother about the picture, and we kept silent afterward.
I loved him more, though, knowing he cared.*

*For a long time, I feared she was dead and suspected mom had
killed her. But a few days ago I heard my mother and Aunt Mei
talking about her being back in town. She's all right! I was so glad!
After all these years, to hear anything at all!*

They were mad, though. I didn't dare ask anything.

*Happy birthday, Skye. I hope I get to see you again someday. I
miss you.*

I put the journal down, stunned. Cherry must have
told Darion what it said while I read. I hadn't heard her
speaking, lost in the words there on the page.

Kelly *remembered* me. Kelly had missed me. I looked at
Cherry, stunned by what I had read.

"She didn't forget me." I held the journal tightly in my
hand, a link to something I had never expected to find. "I
thought -- I didn't expect her to remember me."

"Of course, she remembered you. We all remembered
you," Cherry replied and looked astonished at what I'd said.

"Did you think that after your mother sent you away that we'd all forget?"

"Yes."

"Skye --"

"It was unfair to all of you, I suppose," I said, trying to stop this conversation from getting any more personal. I closed the journal and sat it on the table by the chair. "But I had never left that house more than twenty times in my entire life, Cherry, until the day she took me to the bus stop. It's why I couldn't go to any of you, even if I figured out how to get there. Did you even remember I existed? You never came to visit, either."

"Your mother never wanted any company at her house. She made that plain." Cherry sounded angry now, which was a better than crying. I didn't like to see her sad, and the tears had bothered Darion. Now he held her hand and listened, learning more about me and my upbringing. He'd been polite enough not to ask too many questions. "I heard mom talking to dad a couple times about how your mother acted and how she hid something. We didn't realize the secret was you, but I remember how much mom worried about your well-being. We didn't know until you were in your teens that she never let you go to school. That was the point where my mother stopped talking to Aunt Tay. She said what her sister had done was unforgivable, keeping you locked away. Mom didn't go to the authorities about it, though."

"Just as well," I said. "It wouldn't have been good if someone else got hold of me, Cherry. At least I was safe in that house."

"But not loved and not wanted."

"Not by my mother. Ian and I got along, though. My mother rarely left us alone for long, though. Kelly and I were sisters. I blocked most of that from my mind, you know. I let myself believe that once I left all of you would forget me because I had never been one of you. If I didn't return home, the others would be fine. I thought she would be a better mother. And you know what? I was right. It was only after I turned back up that this happened."

She nodded. "But it was never your fault."

"I should have gone far away and come nowhere near here again."

"I think the trouble would have drawn you here anyway," she said.

"Cherry's right," Darion said. "Part of what kept you here was that draw of family, even while you denied it to yourself. It's the same reason you can travel to Cherry through magic. Blood draws to blood."

I nodded and winced, my hand to my side at a sudden pain there, but this one passed quickly. Darion started to ask, but I waved his words away.

"I want to find Kelly." I tapped the journal. "I owe it to her, for never forgetting me."

"We will find her."

We went back out not much later. This was the futile part of the work, but we had to go to all the places the police already knew about, on the off chance we might *feel* something they had missed.

The city looked like a ghost town with most of the streets unplowed and no one wandering around except for us. The snow still came down in a thick white blanket.

Huge mountains of snow stood here and there where the plows had done some work, but even they appeared to have given up on all but the main roads needed for emergency routes.

"We will be real conspicuous --"

"No. They won't see us at all," he said and touched the door. A wave of magic slipped up around us. We were now in stealth mode. "That will do it. Sit back and relax. You can even sleep if you like. I'll be right here."

We spent hours driving from school to houses of her known friends. The day wore on, and I became increasingly tired. Darion wandered around the area where she had disappeared, and he left me in the car to nap. I didn't even argue.

I had a dream again; vivid, frustrating and frightening. I wanted to reach a person huddled in the dark, cold and afraid. Trapped.

Darkness covered everything. Sometimes a slight flash of light seemed to bring part of the area into focus, but the more I tried to move through it, to grab the other person, the more it hurt, and I came awake with a gasp of pain as Darion slid back into the car.

"Skye?"

"Damned nightmare again," I replied. I hid how the fire spread through the wound in my chest once more. "This is annoying."

"You don't look well."

"I suspect I'll continue that way until we can get these problems figured out. I need to work on the damned stone, Darion. That's a big part of the problem."

"Yes. I was testing to see if we could slip out around

the spell," he admitted. "Which is why I didn't mention it to keep it off the radar if the gargoyle's command of you would lessen."

"That worked for a while," I admitted and moved to ease other pains. "But it's back. Do you have any suggestions?"

"Let's go to the area where he lost the damned stone."

So we drove down towards the docks and spent the rest of afternoon and into the night wandering around that area of town. Darion kept us hid, but sometimes I would move out where others saw me, on the off chance someone would come over and talk. It didn't happen, and I suspected the magic itself was keeping us from learning anything.

Sunset and long ago passed. We sat in the car and tried to figure out what to do next. Darion tested for magic. "Nothing I can find that's specific, but I sense there has been something at work here. Let's get back to your place. You can sleep for a while."

"And you don't intend to leave me," I said and frowned. "Darion --"

"I will rest, too. All this magic to fight the snow and to stay invisible has drained me. Let's go and take advantage of your lovely little jungle."

"You could go back to your Clan House --"

"Not if I want to rest. I put everyone to work, Skye. They'll report what they find."

"Ah." I supposed there was a reason to go with me, besides the fact that I had a gargoyle who wanted answers from me, and nightmares that were making sleep increasingly difficult. I glanced at the clock and saw we had only a few hours until dawn again. I didn't complain about the company that kept me safe.

DAY THREE:

CHAPTER FIVE

I went to bed, pulled the blankets up around me, and forced my eyes closed. I had to be tired enough to sleep this time. Going longer without a good sleep would make matters worse. Sleep. . . .

The nightmare started almost immediately as something caught hold and dragged me, against my will, into --

An abyss again. Darkness, and pain, and I heard a voice crying. The sound tore at me. I tried to find the person, to take hold of her. For moment, I thought I saw my own face staring back at me, tears running down my cheeks --

"Damn it, Skye! Wake up!"

I came awake with a gasp and a curse. Tears streamed

down my face, and my hands still reached for something. Something lost. Something I wanted very much --

Darion had hold of me, and he looked white-faced and worried. I blinked at him, trying to come back to here again.

"What?" I asked. The Abyss was still there, holding to the edge of my attention so I couldn't even clearly see my bedroom. The crying faded to a whimper and disappeared.

"What the hell happened?" Darion demanded. He sounded frightened, which drew me out of my sleepy stupor.

"Sorry. Nightmare," I said. I winced when I tried to move. Everything ached now, far worse than when I'd gone to bed.

"More than a nightmare. Something caught hold of you. Something magical, but I couldn't find a link." He sat down on the edge of the bed. "I suspect this has to do with the gargoyle, but I'm not sure. I don't like this at all, Skye."

"Does that mean I can't even sleep now?" I asked, more annoyed than afraid.

"I don't know. Damn! I hate that his is getting worse."

"Look at it from my point of view," I mumbled. I sat up, pulling the blankets around me. "What do I do now?"

"I need to go back over the Veil and talk to people about gargoyles," he said. "But I will not leave you here alone. Someone can come over. I can call Cherry to head over here as well since she'll be worried."

I shook my head at the sight of the storm. "Take me to Cherry's. There's no reason for her to come over here. I want your people working on other things, rather than babysitting me."

"Good point," he said. "Get dressed."

He didn't baby me and gave me privacy. I'm never more aware of how different I am than at a time like this when I'm weak and unsteady. I dressed and found an old coat to replace the one the gargoyle ruined. Although it wasn't as heavy as the other, it was good enough for a quick trip over to Cherry's place. I put out food for the mice and Darion helped me down the stairs outside and into his car. He had fed the squirrel again, I saw. He'd be spoiled.

We were on our way before I could change my mind.

"Tell me about the dream," Darion said as he navigated out of the alley.

Snow stood piled up everywhere. The street beyond wasn't any better. The night was still dark, but dawn was near, which meant I had slept -- if you could call it that -- a few hours. The snow would have been impassable for most people, but magic took care of that problem for us.

"Skye? What do you remember of the nightmare?"

"It was a strange, like being pulled into an abyss. I could hear crying --"

"You were crying," he said and glanced my way.

That brought a welling of embarrassment.

And then I sensed something strange. I looked up as a cloud of black floated over us, blocking out the gray of the clouds. "Darion --"

And the cloud swept down at the car.

"Trouble!" Darion swerved to the right and straight into a parking lot, going over the curb with more of a bump than usual in this car. I looked back and saw the thing coming at us again.

"What the hell is that?"

Darion lifted one hand from the steering wheel while the car dashed through snow banks that stood taller than the hood. Magic swirled up around us.

"I don't know. Powerful magic, though," he admitted. He had hold of the wheel again and maneuvered us back to the street rather than going straight through a building. I was sure he could have gone through with enough magic, but he needed that power for other things right now.

The dark cloud switched direction when we did, even when we were out of direct sight.

"It can trace us by magic," Darion decided. "Which means it will follow the car even if we don't use any other magic."

"Seems likely," I said and twisted, despite the pain in my chest. "I don't see it!"

"I'm putting down the top." Darion gave a little flick of a button on the dashboard and the cloth top flipped back like a giant wing. I felt the cold and wind for a heartbeat, but Darion set magic to keep us warm. The scent of lilacs from his magic seemed out of place in the snow. I played scout while he kept us moving. I twisted around until I found the black cloud sweeping at us from over a building.

"There to the right!"

Darion hit the brakes, lifted both hands, and sent a bolt of lightning at the creature that caught the thing in the middle of the elongated black shape. The creature tumbled into the snow.

And stood up again: a humanoid shape but taller, with huge black wings, spread out. It looked our way though I saw no face. The darkness lifted into the sky once more and came towards us.

"Oh hell." Darion hit the gas, and we darted into an alley and kept going so fast that we left a plume of snow in our wake. The thing still chased after us though not as swift as it had been.

"We're heading for the Clan Houses." Darion turned at the next corner, heedless of snow that blocked the street. I saw people at the corner and then reminded myself we were in stealth mode though they couldn't miss the wake of flying snow we left as we passed. I feared they would see our pursuer, too. "If this thing can take a full bolt like that one, I can't stop it. We need help and safety."

"What is it?"

"I have no idea," Darion said and dared a glance back at the sky.

Darion darted this way and that through alleys because the narrow confines appeared to slow our pursuer. Whenever we crossed open areas, the thing would gain on us then. I glanced at the speedometer and saw that Darion was doing well over one hundred miles per hour, and we were not getting clear of it.

"It's gaining again!"

Darion snarled under his breath, the words lost in the sound of the car and the wind. We were close to the alley that would lead to the Veil. My clan ring would lead me to Emerald House, far stronger now that we were so close.

The creature swept down between us and the alley and stood guard as though daring us to go past him. I saw Darion try to call for help with a wave of magic, but he couldn't get through to the others.

"Cherry's place," he decided, backing up to the corner

and hitting the gas again.

"I don't want to take trouble there --"

"Neither do I, but her building has the best wards of any place on this side of the Veil, Skye. Far better than your own. My people know to find me there, too. Someone on the other side will soon realize there's trouble and come over. I want to be somewhere safe when they find us. As long as it believes we will try to get in again, it will give us a head start. The thing is fast, though, and we will be in the open too much. I want you to drive. Can you?"

"Yes," I said. "Good plan. Far better for you to be ready with magic."

He turned the car at the first secluded spot and stopped. He leapt out, and I slid over and got the car in gear and moving before he had even settled. I had driven his car a couple times in the past, but never over the speed limit. The power in this magical car scared me, but not so much as the huge thing coming after us.

I put my foot down on the gas, and we went faster. "Freeway?" I asked, both my hands tight on the wheel and without daring to glance his way.

"Yes. It's mostly straight, and we can go faster, but we'll lose the tall buildings and alleys for cover. Speed seems to be our best plan."

I aimed towards the nearest on-ramp, ignoring that it was barely plowed. I didn't dare try to watch for the creature at these speeds and trusted Darion with the work as I raced past one snowplow. The driver never saw us although the plume of snow must have surprised him. I didn't like being out here where others had begun moving and might get in the way.

I went up the first ramp I found and hit the freeway at well over a hundred miles an hour, the car surging *through* the gate that closed the road in bad weather and leaving it intact behind us. At least that meant there would be no other cars. Snow covered the lanes, but Darion's little car never slowed. I kept going, my hands tight on the steering wheel and intent on the road. I didn't even glance up when the black cloud swept over the car once more though I sensed the creature sailing above us.

Darion sent out a flash of magic that filled the world with the scent of vanilla for a moment as the black cloud tumbled down not far ahead of us. I snarled as the thing stood, a huge black shape we would hit --

Until I swerved and went down the off ramp, sensing the anger chasing after us on the wind.

"Damn good work, Skye."

I slowed on the side street where I couldn't clearly see. I didn't cut across and straight up the ramp again because we wouldn't be past the creature yet. Instead, I followed the surface road along the edge of the freeway, ignoring red lights and holding my breath for the next three miles before I took another ramp. We came close to hitting a car abandoned along the edge, but I reacted in time. Then I was back up on the freeway

Maybe we would outrun the thing. All the magic Darion had thrown at it had to have some effect. I dared a glance at Darion, who had been quiet. He looked almost dead white, and I saw a sheen of perspiration on his face. Hell. If he lost consciousness, neither of us would survive an encounter with this thing.

I kept going. Then, in the rear-view mirror, I saw the creature on foot and running along on the freeway. He must have tracked us along the road, but he wasn't taking to the air this time.

"He's not flying, but he's back there, Darion."

"We're not far. Just get us there, Skye."

I stepped down on the gas pedal and even fed a touch of my magic into the car, despite the surge of pain. I didn't use enough to make the ploy dangerous for me because one of us had to stay conscious. We sped up another twenty miles an hour. The thing fell behind by almost a mile. We were closer to Cherry's place now, but I feared the creature would have a better chance of catching up once we were on the side streets. I didn't dare go this fast once we left the freeway; I wouldn't risk hurting others.

I took the off ramp. No one ahead. I kept up our speed, straight through three red lights before I eased the speed back down again. I checked the mirror. Nothing --

"In the air again," Darion mumbled. He took another deep breath, then turned and reached upwards, though he trembled. "I'll take the damned thing down one more time, but I will be out of it afterward, Skye."

"I'll get us to safety."

"I know you will. Be careful."

I nodded.

I had slowed. There was a car ahead on the road, and another at a stop light. The streets appeared to be cleared better in this area, which helped. I went through an intersection, passed a car, and saw nothing ahead all the way to the corner where we'd turn to get to Cherry's apartment building. Speeding up once more, I took the corner faster than I would have liked, but the car held tight, and we went around with no trouble. The parking lot to the apartment building sat on the right --

The shadow fell over us.

Darion sent up another flash of lightning as powerful as the first one and I felt the pain as Darion slumped against the seat, blood at the edge of his lips. *Oh hell, oh hell.* But the thing went down, tumbling behind a building. I hoped no one else saw it!

This was our only chance.

I hit the gas and did almost one hundred miles an hour on that last three blocks and turned into Cherry's parking lot, sliding to the side and hitting a car with a distinct bump that sent us spinning, but we came to a stop with no real damage.

Darion was unconscious. There was blood athis mouth and nose, and his skin looked almost pale blue. I dashed around the car and pulled Darion out by brute force. I used magic to get him to the stairs.

"Careful. Quiet. Let's -- let's not scare her," he mumbled and pulled away from me halfway up the steps. He wiped his hand against his nose and grimaced. He looked at the sky, but neither of us could spot the creature. "I didn't want to draw it here. That thing is damned powerful. I don't know -- even with the wards --"

"We are not going back out on the road." I took hold of his arm. "Come on. We have to get up there and out of sight. Maybe it won't find us."

"Cherry -- I don't want to put her in more danger."

"Neither do I, but she would want us to come here."

"I know. Let's go. It's cold out here!"

Neither of us had any magic left to combat the weather. We went up the stairs, slipping on the ice and snow though we finally reached the safety of Cherry's door. It was still too damned early in the morning. I started to knock and then remembered I had keys to the apartment and fished them out of my pocket while Darion stood with his back to the door frame and watched the sky.

"Anything?" I asked.

"Not that I can see. Not that I'm sure about."

"Let's go in." I turned the key and pushed the door open.

I did not expect Cherry to be awake. I especially didn't expect her to have company, and the moment I saw who was there, I realized we had a whole new set of troubles. Mei, Cherry's sister, sat in the chair, drunk and weepy -- and in the next breath enraged when she saw us.

"It's them! It's both of them! You said they wouldn't be here!"

"I told you that they weren't here *now* -- Damn, Darion, what's wrong?" Cherry leapt to her feet and came to him. Yo-Yo, Cherry's cat, had been on her lap and now gave a blistering glare to Mei before she hurried to the bedroom. Safer there, at least. I remained standing with the door a little open and caught sight of a shadow moving through the clouds above us. I showed the door closed and looked at Darion, shaking my head.

"What are you doing here?" Mei demanded, rage growing in her face. She got to her feet, swaying so badly I thought she would fall. Her words slurred, but I had no trouble understanding "Your mother says you took Kelly! You should be locked up!"

"I didn't take Kelly!" I all but shouted. The reaction from her didn't surprise me. I didn't need another round of trouble now. Damn! "Even the police know I didn't take her, Mei. Just sit down and shut up."

I had never talked to her that way. I rarely talk that way to anyone at all. This time, my outburst worked, and she dropped to the chair as though I had hit her and stared at me with a look of shock and fear. Maybe what my mother had told her helped, and the woman believed me to be so dangerous that she didn't dare stop and argue when I turned on her.

Fine. She shut up.

Darion stumbled to a chair in the little kitchen. We couldn't tell Cherry about the trouble with her sister present. I couldn't imagine what Mei would do if she heard the tale, but I knew it wouldn't be good.

Mei wasn't quiet for long. Soon she yelled about devils, me, kidnapping and the gods knew what else. I didn't listen, at least before she came stumbling into the kitchen and tried to grab hold of me.

I backed away and lifted my hand. She froze, her blood-shot eyes gone wide and her mouth open. I could smell the liquor, an unpleasant addition to my growing unease. "Don't do that. Go sit down and don't bother me, Mei. I'm not in the mood for this today."

"You shouldn't be here. You're dangerous. Aunty Tay told me about you and these people. Devils. Evil. You should be all killed --"

"Shut up!"

I panicked, but not because of Mei. I saw a shadow pass over the window by the front door. Darion sat up straighter though he still looked pale. Mei still kept shouting about evil and devils and everything we had done to her -- apparently everything was about Mei, which didn't surprise me. She made my head ache, and I needed to think clearly.

"Shut up!" I put a little power into the order because I had heard something on the outside wall. We needed to trace the moving enemy.

Mei still tried to yell, but she made no sound now, and it scared the hell out of her. I had a fear she would have a stroke the way her face went red, and she clutched at her throat.

"Skye --" Darion said, looking worried.

"There. Hear it? The thing is coming down the wall by the door!"

"Oh hell." He stood, caught hold of the table and then straightened with a force of will. He looked at Mei, who had fallen onto the sofa. "Skye --"

"Yeah. I know."

I let go of the little spell.

She screamed at the top of her lungs, and she didn't stop when she heard herself. Mei scrambled to her feet when I crossed the room, grabbing a book from the end table to throw at me.

"Devil! You are a devil! Stay away from me!"

"Just be quiet!" Nothing Darion had tried so far had more than inconvenienced the thing for a couple minutes. When I turned towards Mei and lifted my hand, she fell silent.

Relieved, I moved towards the door. Darion moved to help me, just as worried. We were in for trouble --

Mei dashed past me and grabbed the doorknob, yanking it open.

And that broke the ward that would have kept the creature out.

CHAPTER SIX

Darion and I shouted and created enough magic to send the huge creature flying backward and over the railing. The thing didn't stay down long enough for me to even reach the door and shove it closed again. Mei screamed, gone far beyond reason. She had seen the thing outside, and she went crazy.

It did not help.

I was trying to get the door closed and fight the creature back while Cherry grabbed Mei before she got herself killed -- or more likely got all of us killed. If I'd had an ounce of superfluous magic, I would have put her to sleep and saved us all from the screaming and chaos she created. I didn't dare try. Darion and had troubled holding back the blackness that had come through the door like a shadow come to life, and one with enough physical power to counter our magic-enhanced shove to keep it out of the apartment.

The thing that had looked like a cloud in the air was solid but jelly-like, with a faintly bitter smell. It moved in ways that a rigid form -- or one even with bones -- could not. I tried to grab the black oozing past the door with my hands, but the touch burnt. I grabbed my gloves out of my pocket and shoved them over blistered fingers and tried again, this time adding a magic shield at my fingertips.

The creature didn't like the touch and where my magic brushed the black surface, I saw streaks of red and gray that peeled away like dead skin and oozed a pale substance. Magic applied directly to the skin was a weakness. I took comfort since this was the only thing we'd done that had any immediate effect.

I was never good at sustaining magic and couldn't do it much harm. I hoped Darion saw because I didn't even have the breath to tell him. The thing backed up as it grew weaker. It had tried to come in with odd limbs growing everywhere, reaching for us, burning against any exposed skin. Now the thing pulled away, and I heard almost a keening sound like something hurt. I didn't let go. I kept pushing.

"Mei! No!"

I heard her coming. Darion tried to reach for her, and the creature took advantage of the moment to shove him into the wall with enough force that he started to slide down, stunned. I turned, hoping to stop Mei before it got her --

She shoved me straight into the creature, screaming as she tried to get past us.

The malleable surface wrapped around me in a covering of burning black. I put my hands up to protect my face, palms out as I called up magic while the thing burnt through my clothing. I was suffocating in the dark, and burning, and losing hold of my power --

A sense of timelessness came over me as I became nothing but thought and . . . I heard crying again and tried to reach, but something held me back this time. I would die like this, wrapped in the burning dark that had gone beyond pain.

I regretted that I couldn't help find Kelly and that I had failed in that one job of helping someone who had meant something to me. I prayed to the Gods that she was safe --

But the crying, the crying --

The blackness let go. More than let go: I flew out from it, staggering backward a few steps, gasping for breath, blinking back the red and black spots in my sight. I went down to my knees, my hands still raised, trying to fend off --

Something else had come to the doorway and grabbed the dark. The gargoyle.

"Mine," he said in a hiss of anger. "Mine, and you shall not have it."

He dragged the darkness out of the doorway, and it withered, caught in the gargoyle's long claws, his wings spread. He jumped into the air and away, the gargoyle flapping, flapping -- and gone.

Safe? I got back to my feet and went to the door, limping and hardly able to move at all. I hurt everywhere and found blood on my hands, and I could taste it in my mouth. Mei was still cursing and shouting, but I didn't care. I was ready to shove her out of the door and into the hands of whatever monster waited out there.

I heard sirens. Coming closer.

"They're coming here!" I said, seeing the lights nearly to the parking lot already. "Darion!"

"I have a little magic left. Illusion. We can fix and heal things later!"

He swept the magic up around us. A shine of magic swept over me, and I couldn't see the blisters on my hands. A broken table righted itself and stuck back together though it wouldn't stay that way long. Other things flew back into place.

The only problem left was Mei, who continued to scream about monsters, even though she was hoarse. Cherry grabbed her arm when she tried to throw herself out of the doorway again. She was so unsteady she would have tumbled down the stairs, and I couldn't tell if that came from liquor still or just fear.

"I can quiet her --" Darion lifted his shaking arm --

"No," I whispered. "No. She needs help, Darion. Right now magic would only make her worse."

And the police arrived at the still open door. Dawn had just started to gray the world outside They looked inside with trepidation, but we must not have looked dangerous, though Cherry was still trying to hold back her sister.

"We have a complaint about the noise," one said, standing in the doorway. "And we heard her down in the parking lot --"

"Monsters! They're evil! Magic!" Mei shouted again.

That would not help her, I realized. She looked and sounded delusional.

"This is my sister." Cherry shook Mei while trying to get her attention, but Mei fought and slapped and got away --

"Too much to drink?" the man asked which was obvious the moment he caught her. She still stunk of liquor. When Mei fought, he expertly passed her on to someone else. Mei stopped fighting for a moment.

"Yes, she's drunk. I'm sorry about the noise. She was so drunk when she showed up that I wanted her to sleep it off. She wanted to leave. I couldn't get her to quiet down." Cherry had given the bare truth of what had happened without all the magical parts to muddy the waters. "She needs help. She needs more help than I can give her anymore."

"You are with them!" Mei shouted. The two officers who had hold of her now took her down the stairs, which wasn't easy. She kept getting louder and fought them, shouting again about monsters. I winced and didn't understand why she put up such a fight since she was getting away from us. I was glad to see her go. My head pounded with each sound and breath, and Darion looked like he would fall over if we didn't get this cleared up soon.

"What do I need to do?" Cherry asked, still sounding upset.

"Just some basic information," the policeman said. "This is pretty straight forward. You did the right thing."

Cherry didn't believe those words, but she gave names, addresses, ages -- whatever else he asked, but by then I wasn't paying much attention for fear that one or both monsters might return. Cherry closed the door after the policeman left. She leaned her back against the wood and looked at the two of us, saying nothing. Fear and worry played across her face, and she took several ragged breaths, unable to speak.

I stood by the window and watched as they fought Mei into the police car. The snow came down harder, and no one wanted to be out in the weather this long, so she was not making any friends. People stood by their open doors, heads shaking and looking toward Cherry's apartment. I feared Cherry would move soon, which made me sad because some of this trouble was my fault. I knew she liked this place.

Maybe she could find one closer to the area where the Clan Houses were. We wouldn't have so far to drive to get from one to the other. Now there was a selfish thought, but I would consider suggesting such a choice to her. Hell, at the rate I was going, I should find a little place downtown to move into with my business and my jungle-like home. Then we could all be close together and only run from hiding place to hiding place when we needed to take cover.

Right now that sounded like an excellent idea.

I looked up into the sky. Snow fell on my face, ice cold against the flush of heat that came from using so much magic. I felt ill with fever, and I wasn't going to hold on for much longer. I watched, fearing the return of either the monster or the gargoyle and had expected to see him sitting on the roof across the way.

Down below they got into the police cars and pulled away into the cold, slick morning. I sent a little wave of protective magic towards them all so they had no accidents on the way back to the police station. I wanted nothing to make any of us feel guilty about this.

When I pushed the door closed and looked back at Cherry, I knew it was already too late. She looked frantic -- more so than she had during the fight. The anger had given way to new fears that had nothing at all to do with battling magical monsters. Cherry had always worried more about others than about herself.

"She's gone?" Cherry asked. Yo-Yo brushed against her leg, and she grabbed the cat up, holding her a little too tightly. I thought about Kelly's teddy bear just then, and imagined her holding it in the same way.

"They're taking her where she'll get help, Cherry. She needs help," I replied and tried to sound steady.

Cherry either didn't believe those words or didn't understand them. That disconnect came from shock. Too much had happened too fast. I wanted to comfort her. Instead, I took one step forward and then went to my knees. Darion slid down where he leaned against the wall, and the room went back to the chaotic mess it had been. My hands showed the blisters, and I feared there were more elsewhere. I wanted to lie down, but that would hurt --

"What should I do?" Cherry said, frantic as she reached for me but looked at Darion.

"Just leave me. Don't touch me!" I said, frantic because it would just be more agony. She backed away a step, looking afraid.

And then help arrived, praise all the Gods. I looked up to see Blue and Sand come through a portal straight into the room. The ward didn't keep fae out, and especially not ones from Sapphire House.

"We couldn't come in with the others here." Blue

dropped to the floor beside me and reached out, but didn't touch. Instead, he wrapped me in a field of clove-scented healing magic that swept through me and eased the pain in a heartbeat. I looked at him startled --

"I've been taking lessons for Ambassador Peren," he explained with a soft smile. Sand had gone to Darion, and he looked better. "That was scary. We sensed the thing chasing you two, but you were moving far too fast for us to get a clear link. Then I figured out where you were going, and we tried to get here, but the creature makes some kind of field around itself that we couldn't get near. And then the police arrived --"

"Quiet Blue," Darion said. "Calm. You did well."

Blue took a deep breath and nodded. He still looked panicked.

"What was that thing that followed us?" I asked, glad I could breathe and speak again. The blisters on my hands had faded already, and I pulled off the ruined remnants of the gloves while the magic kept working through the rest of my body, healing whatever injury it found. Clothing that had felt like fire against my skin didn't rub against the burns. I trembled, but that came from relief and cold.

"Something up by magic on the other side," Blue explained with a glance at the window. "Something that has no name and no real shape, only a goal. We think it was to get you, Skye, though it may have been after Darion."

"Why?" I asked, confused and unhappy, and still too weak to stand.

"We don't have that answer. We're trying to find out." He offered a hand and helped me to my feet and then over to the sofa. Darion stumbled over and sat down beside me. Cherry didn't sit next to him as I expected. Instead, she went to the chair across from us and sat with her hands in her lap, staring down at them.

"Cherry?" Darion asked. He seemed worried about her continued odd reaction.

"I let them take her. She wasn't lying about what she saw -- about the monsters -- and they think she's crazy --"

"No," I said and drew an angry glare. "They won't think she's crazy: they'll think she's *drunk*. And they're right, you know. She was too drunk to drive home, and that's why you had her here. You didn't lie about that part. She should never have been driving in that condition. It's a wonder she made it this far without a wreck. Cherry, she needs the help."

She looked at me and then at Darion. "Could you fix it? Could you make her right?"

"I could make her stop drinking, at least for a while," he said. He did not remind her of how that had gone with her last boyfriend. "But I'd have to change her to make it permanent, Cherry, and that's not something I will do. It's dangerous to play in people's brains and minds that much. I can help people forget little things that have just happened. I can make them believe something else entirely, but doing something that fundamentally changes who they are is far more delicate magic and not something I -- or any reasoning fae -- would ever want to do. Earis did that kind of thing with her followers, and they all died fighting us because they didn't have the sense left to stop. That's what happens. You try to change a little thing, to warp the person in a certain way, and it becomes far too important to them. They can't let go, and it makes them irrational in whole new ways."

"Oh. I just want -- I want this to go well. I want her to get better."

"That part is up to her, Cherry. She has to decide that she needs to change. She'll get help to start down that road. You did the right thing. She'll get the care she needs in their hands. I can make certain of that much, at least."

"Thank you, but don't. Let it go. They'll take care of her." She pushed both hands through her hair. "It was a horrible night before you showed up. I don't understand why she came here, weeping and whining and drunk. She knows you are both around here sometimes. She started out by lecturing me about the two of you, in fact, but she was so drunk, she couldn't even keep that up."

"It's good you got her help," I said. I leaned my head back, too ill to stand and my chest ached. "We were lucky about the gargoyle."

"Gargoyle. That was the other thing?" she said, worried again. "It's like the entire night is a blur of one nightmare after another."

"And that reminds me of other problems," Darion said. "Blue, I need information about the gargoyles and how they mark their own and if that's the reason Skye is having dangerous nightmares."

"That doesn't sound good," Blue said. He looked over at Sand, who nodded. "I'll go straight back to Sapphire House and see what I can find out. I'll listen for trouble, though. The others are still on the other side trying to find out about the gargoyle, anyway. I can get word to them to check for more information."

Darion sat up straighter with a look of calculation in his eyes as if he sensed something happening. I knew I would be involved far more than I wanted to be. I wanted to push that part away because I hated the type of problem where I was the focus. It had happened with the Lacey Weaver kidnapping, and I had been far too much in the middle of the trouble. I had almost screwed up everything beyond all hope of fixing, too. I didn't want to be in that position again.

The fear made me feel ill as I worried about things heading my way. Hell, they were here already. That Gargoyle had come looking for me. My sister was missing. I was caught up in two little dramas and messing up either of them would mean something seriously bad.

"Hell," I said and glanced around with growing panic.

"Skye?" Cherry said and looked worried again.

I looked from Darion to Cherry and to Blue. "I don't want to be the person who does something stupid and gets people killed --"

"You got no one killed the last time," Darion replied. "Granted, you should have called to us right away or let me go with you, but you will not make that kind of mistake again, will you?"

I didn't want to drag anyone into my trouble, but I stopped myself from saying that stupidity aloud because this was not *my* trouble at all. Both cases dealt with others and problems I might need help to solve.

"I won't unless I have to," I said because I would not make an unequivocal promise to a fae and be held to those words at the wrong time. Darion's eyes narrowed, but I shook my head. "No, I won't tell you I will *never* do

something again. I don't know what might happen next.
What if we're in a position where it's more important that
you stay behind and fight while I go? If I promised you, I
couldn't leave."

"He's right," Blue said with a nod of appreciation.
"You understand how things work better than some fae
do."

"True enough," Darion agreed with a little sigh of
frustration. He relaxed, though. Cherry just looked
worried, holding Yo-Yo in her lap. The cat had purred
now that we were all calmer and creatures were not coming
through the door. "You are wise, Skye Emerald
McFaelyn."

"Just comes from being in too many dangerous
positions and dealing far too much with the fae," I said and
grinned when he looked up at that last line. I made him
smile, which helped.

"I have to go," Blue said. Sand had been putting the
place to rights, and it no longer looked as though we'd just
had a battle for our lives here. I wondered what had
happened to the darkness and where the gargoyle was or
how long would pass before something came to drag me
off into more trouble.

Darion patted Blue's arm as he started past to where
the portal had been and would be again. I caught a hint of
spring scents in the air. "Go, but be careful," Darion said.
"This is getting dangerous, and we don't even why or who
the target might be."

"You don't think it's you or Skye?" Cherry asked.

"Maybe we were just the only two fae out there,"
Darion said with a wave of a hand towards the window. I

hadn't considered that possibility. " And our magic drew it, which means any fae might be in danger. Spread the word, Blue, and find out anything more you can about that thing. It was powerful. I couldn't take it down, even with full blasts. You might mention that to the others."

"What do we do if we see it?" Sand asked with a nervous glance at the door. Realizing Darion couldn't handle it worried her.

"Run like hell. Come to here if Cherry doesn't mind --"

"Of course, I don't! But why here?" she asked glancing around the room.

"I've put so many wards around this building it's a wonder the place doesn't glow," Darion confessed. "I've added to them a little each time I come by. This is the safest building in the city right now. So if fae can't get back to the Veil, this is where they should head. The shadow blocked the alley to the Veil, which is why we ended up here."

"But it got in here anyway," Cherry pointed out with a wave of her hand towards the door.

"Mei opened the door and broke the ward in that place," I said. "Don't open the door and let fae in. They might not be what they appear to be. Fae can get inside without using the door, right, Darion?"

"Yes. True. This is dangerous, Cherry. If I could make somewhere else as safe -- but I don't have the power to do something so elaborate right now. I don't want to leave any fae out there with no safe place to run to."

"Send them here," she said with a quick, decisive nod of her head.

"Spread the word to Sapphire and the other clans," Darion said looking back at Blue. "Tell them to come here and port in if they have to. Also, tell them they will answer to me for anything annoying they do within Cherry's home."

Blue nodded, took a step away and disappeared into the portal he had created. I saw the building at the other end. Sapphire House. I needed to learn that magic, rather than relying on mirrors all the time.

"I need to call Mei's husband. He'll be wondering where the hell she is."

She stood and crossed to the phone, walking like someone who had a job she didn't want to do. I wished I could call him myself to save her from the bother. At the last moment, she straightened her shoulders and jabbed in the numbers. The phone rang only a couple times.

"Tom? This is Cherry. Mei was here and so drunk she couldn't drive home. She got loud and dangerous. The police just took her away."

I heard Tom yelling obscenities all the way across the room. Cherry held the phone out from her ear and listened for a moment. Darion got to his feet, but she hung up.

"Sit down. It's all right. I expected that reaction from him. He's not any better than she is and they suit each other even if they both snarl about having made a mistake getting married. I need to call my parents."

She wasn't as slow to do that one. "Mom?" she said after a moment. "Sorry to wake you up. Mei was here drunk. She got too loud and dangerous, and someone called the cops. They took her off a few minutes ago. Yeah, I shouldn't have let her go this long, but it wasn't easy to give up. I'm more worried about the kids, to be honest. I called Tom already, but he didn't take the news well. I would go over, but I don't think Tom would be happy to see me. Yeah, thanks. I'll talk to you later. I'm just bushed. I was up all night with her. And there's the problem with Kelly. Okay, I'll get some rest. I'm sorry -- Okay. Thank you."

She hung up and looked relieved this time. "It's sinking in that this is for the best," she admitted. "That isn't what Mei or your mother will say, Skye --"

"But it's done," I said. My mother's reaction wasn't something I wanted to consider. "I am so tired, Darion. I need to sleep."

He looked at me and nodded. "Here, in Cherry's apartment. If something is trying to get to you, the wards might keep it out."

"Come on," Cherry said and stood. She caught my arm to pull me up, but I put a hand to my chest and winced. "You all right?"

"Cut. Gargoyle."

"The same kind of creature that just saved us?" she asked.

"Same creature. Wants me to find some damned stone."

"Damned indeed," Darion agreed. He stood, looking steadier already. Good. We needed strong people. This was not all in my hands, and I needed to stop pretending I was the only one involved. "The stone is something very dangerous to lose out on the streets and it will cause trouble without a doubt. I have my people already looking, so don't worry. We can still concentrate on Kelly."

I nodded agreement and then doubled over in pain.

"Damn!" Darion grabbed hold of me and magic swept up through the pain and pushed it aside a little. "That's magic, and it must be linked to the gargoyle's mark. Every time you decide not to work on finding his stone --"

I looked at Darion, shocked and worried. "Then I have to find it. And fast. I can't rest, Darion. I have to get that job done so I can search for Kelly --"

"Four hours of sleep," he said. "You have to sleep. You've lost too much energy. I might have an answer by then, so in fact, you will be working on the case."

Four hours seemed a long time, but I nodded agreement and let Cherry take me by the arm, helping towards her room. She pulled me close and held me. "Be all right," she whispered. I nodded, too tired to answer her.

I sat down and kicked off my shoes and let her help me with the blankets. She stood there for a moment, looking lost.

"You did the right thing," I said.

"She was different when we were children. She was quiet and careful, but we used to play together."

"I played with Kelly, too," I said and remembered the times we had sat quietly together in her room, dressing dolls that were, at least, a lot like me. "Sometimes, when my mother wasn't glaring at me, it was like -- like I was a real child. Like I was one of them. But I wasn't. Cherry, you want to know a real truth and one I've never even admitted to myself? Once I stopped panicking, I felt relief she kicked me out. I didn't have to go back to the lies again."

"God, Skye. Here I am all worked up about Mei, but

there's Kelly out there, lost. Mei got what she deserves and what she needs. We need to focus on the real problem. Can I get you anything?"

"No," I said. "I just want to rest."

She leaned down and gave me a soft hug. "I wish we had known, Skye. I wish we had taken you away from her."

"She wouldn't have let you. She would have feared that you'd find out what I was. A monster."

"You are not --"

"She thought I was, Cherry. That's why she was so afraid. That's why she still is. I can't change what she believed, Cherry. I am not a monster. But I'm not like you, either."

"No, you aren't," she agreed. "You are Skye. That should be enough."

I didn't understand what those words meant, and I didn't need to be confused. "I'm tired, that's all."

"Sleep. Sleep well."

I pulled those words around me, and used them like a magic shield, hoping they worked as I closed my eyes. . . .

CHAPTER SEVEN

When Cherry opened the door and came back into the room, I remembered why I don't go to her place to sleep. It's because before long something or someone disturbs me.

"What?" I said and sounded surly. I heard quiet voices in the other room.

"Detective Barber is here, Skye," Cherry said with a sigh. "He wants to talk to us. And then you can go back to sleep."

I glanced at the clock. I'd had an hour and a half of sleep. It had been deep, restful, and without a nightmare. I woke up to a nightmare instead. Barber. What did he want this time?

I sat up and grunted at the pain that ran through my body. My clothing looked rumpled, the shirt blood-covered and torn, which was not the way to go meet with a police detective. I could have used magic to fix things up, but my hands shook, and I feared to expend any power. The pants weren't a problem.

"Shirt," I whispered.

She went to the closet and drew out a simple blue pull-over sweater, tossing it to me. She went out the door and pulled it closed, and I changed. I ran a hand through my hair, which felt like it was ready to stand up in spikes all on its own. It might be a good new hairdo for me. Less work.

The snow still fell outside the window although not as hard as it had during the long night. The wind gusted as I watched, plastering more white against the windowsill. I saw the tip of a building a block away, but snow swirled around and blocked the view again. The weather was not much better.

I didn't bother with my shoes. I was only going out to talk to Barber about whatever he wanted and then back to bed and hope to sleep as well again. Besides, the rug was soft beneath my toes, a pleasant sensation when everything else hurt.

I limped to the door and then forced myself to stand up straighter and stop looking so churlish. I stepped out into the other room and found the rest of the group in the kitchen having coffee and rolls. My stomach growled. I wasn't certain when I had last eaten, and I wasn't certain this was the right time to do so, but I didn't complain when Cherry put coffee and a cinnamon roll in front of me. Just the smell alone was enough to put me in a better mood.

"Is there a problem?" I asked, looking at Barber.

"I saw a report go across my desk about trouble here," he said. "With everything else going on, I decided I had better come and check it out. I didn't expect to find you two here."

"Darion is often here," Cherry said. She gave a little shrug and reached out and to touch Darion's arm.

"I figured that was the case," Barber said. "And you?"

He looked at me. I grinned a little. "They need a chaperon."

Darion coughed as he snorted coffee, which won a smile from Barber, but as quickly gone as he turned back to me --

"I was out looking for Kelly most of the night. It was quicker to come here and sleep than to go back to my place, especially in the weather."

"Besides, I wanted to make certain she did rest," Cherry said. "Skye has a habit of trying too hard. I want her where I can see her sometimes."

He nodded and accepted the answer.

"I can take care of myself, and I've proven that by now, right?" I said, looking at her.

"That doesn't mean I don't worry. With Kelly missing -- and you out there, going to dangerous places just because you can -- doesn't make waiting any easier. At least when you rest here, I can rest."

She was right, I supposed. "Well, I didn't find out anything last night. Except about some other girl, about the same age." I looked at Barber. "Found a couple weeks ago. The minister down at the mission told me she's in the hospital now?"

"Yes, the Cheshire Case." He shook his head with worry and regret. I wondered about all the missing people cases he might have to handle. He had even been working somewhat on the Lacey Weaver case. "It might be related and it might not. They disappeared from different areas. Besides, Anna Cheshire was a street kid for a couple years and got hooked up with the wrong people. The drugs ruined her mind. We can't reach her. We don't know what happened."

He left out the part about her being tortured. I didn't bring it up, either. Cherry had enough to worry about, and it wasn't as though she wouldn't have thought the worst already, anyway. I only nodded, and I'd tell Darion later.

"What happened here this morning?" Barber asked. "Why were the police called in?"

He must have known the answer, but he wanted to hear our version. For a moment, I feared that something had happened to Mei, but I didn't get that impression from him.

"My sister, Mei," Cherry said with a shake of her head. "Mei Davis."

"Yes. She has a problem, Detective Barber. She drinks, gets upset, and she comes here to complain about it because she blames me for all the problems in her life."

"Because?" he said.

I wanted to say it was none of his business -- but then I realized he needed to get a handle on the family, and not just my mother and her husband. Cherry had paused for a moment, but then gave a shrug and continued, and I suspected she had come to the same thoughts as I did.

"Because she married the man I had been dating and walked away from when I realized he was a big loser. Because I have a nice life, a good business -- which I have to go check on this morning if the roads are clear -- and a nice boyfriend. I have what she wants, and that's always been the problem. This morning -- all night, in fact, since she showed up about one-thirty -- was worse than usual. It's the stress from Kelly disappearing. Darion had gone out to find Skye and bring her here, and Mei exploded when they got back. The police had to take her away. Now she's forced into getting the help none of the rest of us can convince her she needs."

He looked at her, blinked a couple times, and then nodded. "She has a record for being picked up drunk. She had her license revoked a few months ago."

"Damn. I didn't know it. And she's still driving around? Sometimes Mei is an idiot."

"And her husband?"

"Let's just say I wasn't stupid enough to marry him," she said, her eyes narrowed. Then she stopped and sighed. "I tried to tell Mei, but she wasn't interested in listening."

"And you believe her marriage troubles are your fault because you didn't try hard enough to stop her, and that's why you let her come to you and blame you."

She looked at Barber, startled.

"You hit that one right off," Darion said. He leaned back, sipping coffee and not looking much better than I felt. I feared Barber would ask about what we'd been doing to look so rough.

"We don't need to discuss my family dynamics," she said with a little scowl.

"Actually, considering the situation, we do," Barber said. "I had to come and check because we're checking out everything unusual with anyone connected to Kelly. The FBI will be in on the case today, but I can't expect they'll find out much more than we did."

"I'm sorry to hear that," I said, hoping for better news and for an easy and good answer. I was looking for a fairytale answer. I had been spending far too much time around magic and thinking it could fix anything.

Cherry looked at her watch. "I need to go if I need to get to my kitchen and get the work done before noon," she said. "Do you need me for more?"

Barber looked at her and then shook his head. "No. I would like to talk to Skye though, about what she might have seen on the streets last night. Not about your half-sister, Skye. I'm sorry, I wish I had something more for you, but I am hoping you can help me with something else."

I had nothing better to do except sleep, and that would not return now. I agreed with a nod and Darion planned to stay. Cherry put on her coat and hat and grabbed her purse. She nodded to us.

"Stay out of trouble," she said, as she headed towards the door.

The looks both Darion and I gave her at those horrible, ill-omened words, won a brighter laugh from Barber than I had expected. He didn't understand that Darion and I were bound to find more trouble.

Cherry pulled the door open, hunching her shoulders against the cold as she headed into the storm. The blast of cold air made me wince, but the snow had eased, and the sound of snow plows drifted up from the street. I wished Darion would have gone with her, but he stayed with me as a guard.

I turned to Barber as soon as the door closed. "What kind of things are you looking for?" I asked, knowing we'd all be out in the cold and snow before too long.

"We're having gang problems downtown and out along the lakefront docks. It's come up just in the last week, and it is bad. I saw reports about you, from years ago, that said you had gang contact, but you didn't get caught up in their troubles."

"I wasn't that stupid," I said. He didn't laugh. "Last night I heard about the problem. Some gang has suddenly gotten out of control, and a couple people are already dead," I said with a nod.

"We've kept quiet about what's going on down there," Barber said. "It's gotten vicious out there, and people are getting caught in the middle of it --"

I heard someone rushing up the outside stairs and the sound of something larger and louder not far behind the first. Darion and I were both on our feet so fast that the chairs fell. Barber had stood. I hadn't known he had a gun until then --

Cherry came in the door and slammed it shut behind her.

"Something -- some *thing* is coming back in *again* --" she said and frantically looked over at Barber.

Darion rushed forward and got her out of the way. I headed towards the door just as it snapped open and banged against the wall.

The gargoyle come through the ward using the link the thing had with me as a key of his own. I sensed that much above the shock of what he did. He bowed his enormous head and nearly ripped the frame free when his wing caught. The thing was uglier than I remembered: tall, the metal-like scales a dirty brown color, and the face narrow with dark slits of eyes that glittered with an unnatural light. He stank, too, which I had not noticed out in the cold.

Anger came from the gargoyle; rage and hatred so intense that the emotions felt like power. I almost brought up magic to keep him from hurting anyone as I rushed the last few steps to confront him.

The gargoyle snarled as I came closer, but not as much as I did. I glanced back once to see Detective Barber frozen with that gun in hand and staring wide-eyed at something that could not be real in the world in which he lived. Damn. This created all kinds of trouble. More trouble.

"What the hell do you think you're doing?" I demanded when I turned back to the gargoyle. Its head snapped back in surprise at my words and my anger, but the glittering gold eyes stared in rage. I didn't care though that was probably part of the creature's own rage slipping into me. "Are you stupid? You have no right to burst in here like this!"

"I --" it began.

"I don't want to hear what you have to say!" Where did this courage, or insanity, come from to make me face this thing as I stalked forward the last few steps? Darion made worried, panicked noises. I had gone crazy, but I didn't care. "You should *never* have come in here like this. Are you trying to make my life more difficult? I said I'd find the damned stone for you. You've made certain I have no choice. Now get the hell out of my life until I find it!"

I had pushed the gargoyle too far. He growled, lips pulling back to show huge, dark dagger-like teeth before he took a swipe at me. I avoided the claws as I got out of the way -- but I didn't back down this time. Instead, I brought magic up into my fingers and held the ball of powerful magic in front of the creature.

He took a step backward.

"I'm not helpless."

Another step back. What I held in my hand in a ball of the bright blue and red light would have punched a hole through the wall, and I suspected it might have done the same to him, though I couldn't tell for certain. The gargoyle still growled with a deep, ominous sound. I saw the eyes watching me with enough hatred and intensity that I hoped it would go off to find someone else for this stupid quest.

"Others are after you," he said. "I will guard while you hunt."

He backed out of the apartment, though never turning his back, and pulled the door closed. I heard wings as he flew off though not far.

"Son of a bitch!"

I dropped the magic which disappeared in a quick flash as I gasped for breath, almost going down to my knees. I fought against that reaction out of sheer perversity and anger. That show had required a lot of power for me. If the gargoyle had stayed much longer, I would have passed out, which wouldn't have helped at all.

"Are you crazy, Skye?" Darion exclaimed. He had let go of Cherry and hurried over to catch my arm before I fell. Darion even shook me, which won a little gasp of pain, my hand going to my chest. He relented somewhat, but there was a wildness in his face that would have either amused or frightened me at another time. Right now I was still in the throes of the same madness that had sent me against the gargoyle. I didn't care how Darion reacted to what I had done. "Are you crazy? That creature could have killed you with one blow!"

"Hell yes, I'm crazy!" I pulled free of his arm and faced him down with much the same glare I had given the gargoyle. Darion didn't back away though he appeared startled. "Who wouldn't be crazy by now? But that's not why I did it. The gargoyle sees me as weak. I can't let him run me, Darion."

"Damn. Hell. You're right --" And then he stopped what he was saying and turned his head, a new worry in his eyes. He had just remembered Detective Barber was with us, and I wondered how we were going to explain this!

"I'm not going to work after all. I'll call my people and tell them to stay home for a few days. The weather's bad anyway," Cherry said. She sounded calm and sane, which bothered me more in a way. I didn't want things like this to be commonplace in her life. She took off her coat and went back to the kitchen, grabbing the phone.

Barber still stared though he blinked. He still had the gun in his hand, which I didn't like to see how it kept waving a little to the right and left, alternating as it pointed at Darion or me. "What the hell is going on?" he said, his voice flat and calm, but that came from training.

Darion started to speak. Stopped.

"Let's sit down." Darion led me back to the table and picked up the chairs. Cherry spoke on the phone, promising pay for the days off -- such mundane things to worry about in the real world. I should go feed my mice and squirrel. I should make my life normal again.

Normal? My life had never been, and never would be,

normal.

I sat down, glad to be off my feet. Darion dropped into the other chair, looking exhausted and worried. Barber sat back down. He put the gun on the table in front of him, but at least it was out of his hand.

"Before we start -- it got past the ward, and that's because of his link to me, right?" I asked, looking back at the door with trepidation now.

"Yes, the link it made to you," Darion agreed. "I'm sorry, Cherry --"

She waved her hand in a gesture of dismissal and went on talking on the phone.

"Ward. Magic. What was that thing?" Barber demanded. His hand moved towards the gun. I turned to Darion, uncertain what to tell him.

"That was a gargoyle," Darion said. He sat forward, both his hands on the table. "He came from over the Veil, which is a magical wall between your world and mine. I'm fae."

"Fae."

"Elf. A being of magic."

Barber shook his head in denial.

"You saw what came through that door," Darion said.

"Drugs. Tricks. What the hell games --" He stopped himself, even as his hand went towards the gun yet again. "This can't be real."

"It is," I said. "I'm sorry the gargoyle came in here as he did. He was way out of line and just made matters complicated for the work he wants me to do."

"Gargoyles don't give a damn about humans," Darion reminded me. He leaned back. Cherry settled in the chair next to him. She looked worried now, but Darion took her hand. The normality seemed to help Barber relax. Then he got a different look.

"Your sister was screaming about seeing monsters. She did see them, didn't she?"

"Yes," Darion answered.

"And you let the police take her away, anyway? Even though it was true?"

"It was true she saw the monsters," I said, trying to forestall Cherry's guilt. "But it's also true she was falling down drunk, she wouldn't take any help from us, and she was a danger to herself and to others. There was no way she should have driven home that drunk. Trying to help her with magic was not an answer, either. The monsters were just coincidental, and that's the real truth, Detective Barber."

He sat still for a moment and then nodded. "If she hadn't already had those DUIs, I'd be less apt to believe you. God in heaven, what is going on? You -- I saw you do magic. Are all of you --"

"No," Cherry said with an emphatic shake of her head. "I am not. Darion is. Skye is half fae."

"Do you think Kelly Fairbanks' abduction was by something like that thing?"

"No, we don't think so," Darion said. "I have people looking into this trouble with Kelly, and whatever happened, and as far as I can tell, it is nothing from across the Veil."

Barber blinked and looked back at me again. "This is the problem with your mother. You got into magic --"

"She had an affair with a fae," I said. "I was the result.

I had no choice and the evil she assigns to me is just her guilt over her past actions."

He blinked and heard far too much of the anger in my voice. I tried to keep that buried, and I didn't need the extra baggage with everything else. Barber looked as though he wanted more answers, but he didn't ask me more questions yet. He turned back to Darion instead.

"How much of this shit goes on in town?" he said, waving a hand towards the door again.

"Not much. It's just that Skye is a magnet for trouble right now. He is unique and being recognized by his father's clan hasn't helped. I don't understand why the gargoyle chose him for this job, except that Skye is the best one for it. The gargoyle just has bad timing besides being incredibly rude. As far as I can tell, there's nothing from the other side that has to do with Kelly's disappearance. I have people checking to make certain, but so far there's no sign of magic involved at all with Kelly. I wish there were since I could trace magic to find her."

"This is crazy. This can't be happening."

Darion leaned forward and stared into the man's eyes. "I can make you forget about what happened here. You'll leave the apartment with no knowledge of the gargoyle or anything else that's going on involving magic and fae. That would make things a lot easier for you, Detective Barber. If you know things are going on that you can't control -- because you simply don't have the magic to do so -- it will not make life any easier for you."

Barber stared, his eyes narrowed and his finger tapping on the table. The shake of his head didn't surprise me. "I'm a cop for a reason. It's because I don't look away, you know. And knowing this . . . I might not be able to help, but if I see something, I know who I can turn to, right?"

"Absolutely," Darion said with an emphatic nod. "And here is the first lesson about messing around where there is magic involved. Don't fire a gun if you see fae or others doing magic. The result is often chaos, and not good for either side. Magic is very tricky, and anything that interferes with it is dangerous. Shooting a magical creature itself might at least slow it down, but might not kill it. And lesson two: not all the fae are friendly towards humans, but those others mostly stay on the other side. We aren't happy when something like a damned gargoyle thinks he can just walk in on humans. His kind should never be over on this side, and he's already screwed up with his stone of power -- "

"Explain that one."

I was just glad to have everything moving away from the focus on me and on to something I wanted to talk about anyway and Darion gave me realized my lack of knowledge. I gave a nod, hoping to encourage him to go ahead with the story which would save me asking the questions and looking stupid.

"Gargoyles, and some other creatures across the Veil, carry particular stones that have magical power stored in them. Fae don't use them because we have enough innate power of our own. The stones are very dangerous, particularly when brought over to this side, where nothing protects humans against them. Falling into the hands of humans is much worse, and regrettably that's what has happened. The damn, stupid gargoyle was prowling around alleys and shadows and lost the stone he carried. He's marked Skye to find it."

"As if she doesn't have enough to worry about already," Cherry said.

I saw Barber's frown, his head turning from Darion to Cherry and then back again. He glanced once at me and knew the conversation was about to turn back to questions about me again.

He looked back at Darion this time. "You call Skye 'he' and Cherry calls Skye 'she.' Why?"

They both looked startled and blushed, and I felt a moment of amusement, which surprised me. I should have realized that this part would come up soon. How should I approach this one?

"Skye Emerald McFaelyn is unique, Detective Barber," Darion said. He sounded solemn which took me by surprise. "He is the only Fae-human half-breed alive, and the first one born in over two hundred years. Fae and humans don't match up well as far as DNA and genes are concerned."

"I'm not male and I'm not female," I said because it was just as well this part of the story came from me. "And I'm not both. I'm neither. Neutral. In a magical sense, I am what people perceive me to be. I can influence them sometimes by the way I dress and the way I act. But sometimes the way others see me has an influence on me. That's part of the innate magic that surrounds me."

"That has to be hell."

"Sometimes it is," I admitted, surprised by how he picked up that part. "It's hard sometimes when people aren't sure of my gender and knowing matters to them. It doesn't matter to a remarkable number of others. I do my best to avoid crowds or to be the center of attention in larger groups where people haven't met me. It can give me a hell of a headache, and it makes the people brusque because they can't tell how to treat me. They don't like the experience any better than I do."

"Which do you prefer?"

No one had ever asked that question before, which made me like him. "I don't care which one. It doesn't matter as long as the person is consistent."

"Ah." He nodded and was more comfortable with 'he' than 'she' which didn't surprise me. He'd only shifted when Cherry had tagged me as female. He was also taking the news about magic in the world pretty well, but that came from having seen it with his own eyes. The gargoyle was dangerous, and that gave him something for a focus point. "Okay, let's get back to something important. This stone. What should I be looking for?"

"I suspect we can't locate the stone itself. I've been testing out areas with magic, and even I can't find it," Darion said. "They're tricky. They have so much power that they get smart about how to use it."

"Like the stone is alive?" Barber said, looking worried again.

"Yes, in a way." Darion looked at me, and I remembered the little plate I had accidentally awakened in the Ruby House a few months ago. That had been during the trouble with Lacey Weaver -- and I *did not* want to bring that case up right now. I'm sure Barber would remember how he had met all of us, and no doubt realize the magic involved in that mess. "Anything that holds magic for hundreds of years develops an awareness of the world and often manages a touch of cunning, which can make the object dangerous. A stone made by gargoyles will be worse. They're coarse and uncaring about others, and that translates into their magic. I fear that a stone like this will warp whoever takes hold of it. It will make the person --"

"Cruel," Barber said. "And powerful? More than one person?"

"Yes," Darion replied. "Anyone who handled the stone or is close to it for a while would be affected. That much magic and unprotected humans -- this is not good which is why I have people out searching for the stone, even though the gargoyle only tagged Skye for the work."

"How long would this reaction take?"

"Not long, I suspect. We have no idea how long this stone has been out there, anyway. The gargoyle came to Skye last night while he was out trying to find something about Kelly and told him to search for the stone."

"Why you?" he asked, looking back at me.

"Because I'm half fae, so the magic part didn't surprise, shock or frighten me," I said. "And I find things, you know."

"Yes, that's true. And you agreed to find it."

"The gargoyle trapped into it with magic." I put a hand on my chest, but I didn't pull down the shirt to show the cut that didn't heal but at least didn't bleed. "This wasn't what I wanted, but I must hunt for the damned stone, anyway."

"I think I can help," Barber said. He lifted a hand when Darion started to protest. "No, I think I can help because I believe I already have information for you. The trouble I was talking to you about, Skye . . . there has been a big change in a little gang, and suddenly they're taking on people with a lot more power -- normal human types of power -- and they're winning. They're mutilating the bodies of their foes. They tear arms off, twist heads clear around, crush legs with their hands. We've been trying to figure out how they're doing this. Everyone is afraid of a new drug that gives them super powers of some sort. This, I think is the answer, especially since they changed their gang name to Stones."

"Where can we find them?" Darion asked, already standing.

"Sit down. They are since they keep moving around. We are tracking them."

Darion leaned forward. "These people are very dangerous, Detective Barber. They are changed by the magic. Police going up against them with guns may not help at all."

Barber leaned back and thought about those words. "The other gangs had guns. Hell, just about everyone has guns, and nothing has stopped them yet. I don't want to see good cops killed taking on something they can't win against." Barber looked towards the door as though the gargoyle still stood there. He paled, and I felt sorry for him. Life as a cop hadn't been easy before and this just made things worse.

"You keep talking about your people," he said, looking back at Darion.

"I'm a high-ranking member of the Sapphire Clan," he said with a wave of his hand and the ring he wore, which meant nothing to Barber. "Not the Clan leader, but I still have full control here. Skye is under my protection, even though he is from the Emerald Clan. At first, his people wanted nothing to do with him, but some have since changed their mind. Others have not. Skye needs a guard."

"Well, at least you didn't say I need a keeper," I replied.

Barber smirked as he stood. "I'm going back to the office. I'll ask info on the gang be passed by me because there might be a connection to the Kelly Fairbanks disappearance. Hell, there even is, since Skye is working on both."

"True," Darion agreed. He stood and held out his hand. "I'll give you whatever information I can. I trust you, Detective Barber."

Barber didn't pause before taking the hand. "I still have to sort this out in my head, but I'm glad you trust me. I realize you could have made me forget without my permission. I will want to learn more."

Darion nodded. "When you're ready, when you have questions, and when we have time. Right now, though --"

"Right now Skye needs sleep," Cherry said. She caught my arm and got me up before I protested. I hadn't realized, but I had been almost asleep where I sat.

"Yeah, sleep," I agreed. I looked over at Barber and held out my hand. He took it as well and shook, man-to-man. I could tell from the touch that he was the kind of person who, once he made up his mind on something, stuck with it. Good. This cooperation would make things easier for all of us.

I went off to bed, curling up under the blankets again and hoping I got a couple more hours of sleep before the next round of trouble. There was more coming; I could feel it in the air.

But I closed my eyes, ignored everything, and slept.

CHAPTER EIGHT

I slept, though this time when the nightmares started, they ended abruptly. Darion worked to keep me safe, and I would thank him later. I got a lot more rest than I would have without his help.

About noon I had the start of a nightmare where I heard not one, but two people crying. I sat up, gasping and decided I'd had enough sleep. Blue sat in the kitchen and said Cherry and Darion had headed to the store to get more supplies. The image of the two of them shopping together made me stop and stare at Blue with a shake of my head.

"I know, I know. It sounds so domestic," Blue said. He sat at the kitchen table nibbling on a cookie. "On the other hand, if it means Cherry will keep feeding us this really good food, I don't mind."

"They left you here to babysit me," I said with a sigh and tried not to show my annoyance.

"They left me here in case there was more trouble,"

Blue corrected, and pushed a plate of cookies in my general direction. "You don't need someone to watch over you."

I suspected he was being kind and didn't want to annoy me. "I'll shower and see if I am marginally alive. Any word? On anything?"

"No," Blue replied with a frown. "Detective Barber left a message saying they may have a lead on the gang, though. Darion told me about that problem. You know -- the one with the gargoyle and the detective. Gods, are things just trying to be difficult?"

"Welcome to my life," I mumbled and turned to the bathroom, almost tripping over Yo-Yo.

Blue gave a little chuckle, but he didn't argue the point.

The shower helped. I was already out and drying off when a sudden influx of magic filled the apartment, along with excited and worried voices. For a panicked moment, I feared something had happened to Darion and Cherry, but I held my breath until I heard them both, so they were safe.

Darion knocked on the door. "Skye?"

"Almost done. Be right there." My hands shook as I put on the blue sweater.

I sensed worry growing. Something had gone wrong, and I feared to learn the worst about Kelly. I glanced into the mirror as I straightened my clothing, and for a moment I even saw the Path Guardian, a hint of green and human-shaped, looking back at me. She bowed her head and moved away again. The Guardian has helped me in the past. I couldn't guess what had brought her here, and I suspected her presence meant nothing good.

I bowed my head and then slipped out into the other room.

Rose stood by the door. She shook her head as she looked at me. The others had gone silent.

"Your youngest fae sister is missing, Skye," she said.

I blinked and stopped as one single truth hit me. "This can't be random. It has to be linked and to me."

"Yes," Darion agreed. He still had his coat on and so did Cherry. Sacks of groceries sat on the counter. "I don't understand what this means, though."

"Except that everything has to be pointed at me." My legs went weak, knowing others were in danger because of their connection to me. I took a couple steps forward and caught at the edge of the sofa and stood there, stunned. "The two have nothing else in common, and this can't be a coincidence. Damn. What is going on!"

"No one knows," Blue replied and took my arm, guiding me to sit on the sofa. I had trembled. "No one at all understands what is happening, Skye. This isn't only your problem. The people on the fae side are no happier about this than you are. A child should never go missing in fae, and yet she did, and no one even knows how it happened."

"Child? How old?"

"The same age as your other missing half-sister on this side," Darion said. "Or at least about the same, as those things go. Lily is your father's youngest child."

I winced at the mere mention of my father and realized how he would react with my unwilling involvement in this mess. I didn't want more trouble with him. Then I pushed away my own emotions and all the baggage that came with them. I needed to pursue this as a job like other detective work, or I had no chance at all of helping. I took a breath.

My hands steadied. "This isn't a coincidence, which means something has to have had access to them on both sides of the Veil. That can't be easy, can it? We still haven't found magic where Kelly is concerned."

"Perhaps someone heard about Kelly's disappearance and has worked to make more trouble for you," Blue offered.

"Maybe. But --" I stopped and closed my eyes for a moment. "In my last nightmare, right before I got up, I heard two voices crying where there had only been one before this. My feeling is that the nightmare is linked to what is happening."

"Yes," Darion said, trusting my intuition. "You are also right about the difficulty -- I would say impossibility -- of a non-magic using human to grab Lily. This must be more magic-related than we first assumed, despite finding no clues pointing that way. We're trying to track that part as best we can. I haven't sensed magic in it on this side, but then there's been other odd things going on, so I haven't found the right link. I'm sorry."

"You have no reason to be sorry." I leaned forward, anxious. I wanted to do . . . something. I didn't care what now, just as long as I helped rather than slept. "We have to --"

"Donal Emerald McFaelyn has asked that you come to Emerald House," Blue said as he sat down by me.

The news shocked me. Donal was the former King of the Fae and now served as head of Emerald Clan. I looked down at my hand where I wore the ring he had given me, which made me a full member of the clan. I had not gone back to Emerald House since my last visit when I was working to find Lacey Weaver, which was before I officially belonged there.

"I'm going with you," Darion said. He shook his head before I spoke; I must have looked ready to argue. "I want to talk to Donal, and we need to find out all we can about Lily. You need to eat something, though."

"Something quick," I said. "And light. I'll be nervous. I don't want to be ill."

Cherry moved sacks aside, rummaged through things, and made me a quick sandwich. I took it with me and left with Darion.

He didn't lead me to the usual car. This time, we went to a black pickup with a scoop on the front. I smiled, and he noted my reaction.

"It was a good thing to point out about what I drove in this weather. I never considered something so obvious. Most of the time I would just hide the car so no one even noticed, but there were times -- like following Barber -- when that was not possible."

The truck was so big I had to climb up into it, and we sat high above the other cars. It was comfortable, too. I expected no less from a fae vehicle. Fae didn't appear to be masochists.

"Eat the sandwich. How did you sleep?"

"Well enough when you stopped the nightmares."

"They shouldn't have gotten through the ward. I'll figure out why -- or better yet, find out how to stop them."

He put the truck in gear, and I wouldn't have ever guessed that he was more comfortable in his little car than in this one. He drove well, and I relaxed again, wondering if many fae picked up the ability. I had not seen cars in the driveways around the other Clan Houses. "Any idea at all what's going on?" I asked even though I knew he would have told me.

"None. I hate this, Skye. Not as much as you do, but I still hate what is going on. And add this trouble with gargoyles and it is bound to spill over into the rest of fae. Right now --" He stopped and said nothing for half a block.

"Right now they think this trouble with the girls is my doing," I said, filling in what he hadn't wanted to say. I shouldn't have eaten the sandwich.

"Some of them do. The Queen, of course, doesn't, and that counts for more than anyone else on the other side. Don't let that part bother you."

"Even though it bothers you?"

"I hate injustice, Skye. It's a personal quirk."

He made me grin. I kept silent as we drove through town, getting closer to the alley that would lead somewhere not part of this world. I had the ring that would open the way for me now, and I didn't need Darion to take me there. Still, I hadn't gone back. I would never go as a beggar to the door of Emerald House, even if I were a clan member now. A poor member, the country cousin no one wanted to discuss. Base born, and half-breed --

"Do you have to look that glum and angry?" Darion asked, glancing at me. "It won't help to antagonize them, you know. Besides, Donal likes you."

"Ah. True." Fae sensed emotions sometimes, and they wouldn't even have to see my face to pick up on my bad mood. I didn't need to bring my old baggage to them when I needed their help.

I had never met Lily and knew nothing about her.

Until they told me she was missing, I hadn't even known she existed except as a vague part of a group of half-siblings I had across the Veil. I'd only met one of them, and that was Aria. We were getting along a little better now. I'd seen her twice since the Queen came to rule and it hadn't gone to blows either time.

"You haven't been back to your Clan House, have you?" Darion asked.

"No."

"Why not? Donal made you welcome."

"True, but others wouldn't, and I didn't need that kind of pressure, Darion."

"I want better for you," he said.

"I appreciate it and the help you've given me. However, there's one thing you need to understand: I don't *need* to go to Emerald House, Darion. I am glad Donal gave me the ring, but I don't have to use it to prove that I can. If I use the ring, I want there to be a better reason than walking in to find out what's for dinner. I don't need to flaunt that I am one of them. It's enough not to have them hounding me all the time."

"Ah." He kept silent for a little while. "The Clan House is so important to fae that even I, who spend a lot of time on the other side, have trouble comprehending that it isn't important to you. You realize that we've made Cherry's apartment much like another Clan House. There has never been one in the human world, but Sapphire Clan, who spend considerable time on this side, appreciate having a place that is easier to reach than Sapphire House sometimes."

"I hadn't thought about it, but I see what you mean.

You people tend to just drop in and out of there a lot."

He nodded with a little smile. "Cherry likes it, too. She's odd, you know. A gargoyle breaking into an apartment would annoy most people, fae or human. She takes it in stride and bakes cookies."

I laughed agreement. Cherry baked when things unsettled her, and I was sure Darion had figured that out by now, too.

The day looked frigid outside the truck, and I didn't want to get out there at all again. We drove through town, swerving past piles of snow where the plows had left it, sometimes with cars buried underneath a blanket of white. The alley stood empty, except for a hint of fog ahead of us and some boxes, but I knew they weren't real.

We drove through the Veil and into spring. I looked around, shocked to see green leaves, bright grass, and a plethora of flowers blooming.

"The last time I was here, it was autumn," I said. "Just like the other side. Why is it spring now?"

"That was only chance the last time," he said and pulled the truck into the driveway at Sapphire House. "The autumn season had to do with the final days of the King of Fae's rule. We have a new Queen. It's spring now. There can be which sometimes comes from frustration, anger -- disagreements between the king or queen and the clan leaders. Summer rarely lasts long."

"Is it ever winter?"

"Yes, and it means things have gone drastically wrong somewhere."

That sounded unpleasant. I got out and took off my coat and scarf, tossing them back into the truck. I had expected to feel nervous here, but instead . . . I thought I had come home. Not like a place where I lived or grew up, but rather more like visiting the family's hometown. There were ties here, and they were warm and friendly and not at all like the last visit when most of the time I had felt like a whipped dog, slinking from house to house.

I looked down the street to the rainbow colors that marked the veil. We were in a little pocket of fae that bubbled out of the fae lands into this reality, and which the fae clans kept going so anyone who had business in the human world could reach a safe haven. All of them had connections to the human world, and I would have to ask Darion more about what they did, but later, after we had all this other trouble settled.

"You want to go right to Emerald House or stop at Sapphire House first?" he asked, waving a hand towards the Green door of the house where my clan held power.

"Let's go to Emerald," I said, hoping this wouldn't be a problem. "I want to find out what Donal has and what I can do to help."

Darion agreed, and we headed for the Emerald House. Others had to be watching us. No one came and went on this odd street without people in each of the houses taking note which spiked my paranoia.

We did not have to knock since Aria met us at the door. She looked at me with a frown, worry in her face.

"I'm sorry to hear about Lily," I whispered and just for her. She gave a little nod, the pain in her face. "Is there any word?"

"Nothing at all," she said. "Anything on your side with Kelly?"

"Nothing," I said with my own painful shake of my head. I had not expected her to take the time to learn my human half-sister's name. Aria had changed over the last few months, and I suspected her dislike of humans had lessened. That might have been something she had acquired from our father. She no longer followed him.

She led us down an entry hall. I had been into the building once before, but the place seemed different today. Darker: that came from worrying over the fate of one of their rare fae children. We went to the dining hall where Donal Emerald McFaelyn sat sipping tea. He nodded when we entered.

"Sir," I said, with a bow of my head.

"Come in, sit down. Both of you. I see you still have your Sapphire guard. Good. You might need him."

"Darion isn't --" I began and then I looked at Darion. "You aren't, are you?"

"I took you into my care."

"That was before -- with the Queen and --" I stopped and thought back through everything that happened. "Oh, don't tell me this is one of those things that's permanent. Is that why you keep following me around? You're the Sapphire Ambassador! Don't you have something better to do with your time?"

Donal laughed. I looked at him, startled, and realized I had just been a little over the top. However, the idea that Darion had somehow pledged himself to keep me safe for the rest of my life was more than I could deal with right now.

"My apologies, sir," I said, taking the seat Donal indicated. "I still get surprised by some of these fae things."

"It must make life interesting," he said and nodded to Darion. "Do sit down, Ambassador Sapphire. And you, too, Aria. Share tea with me while we discuss this problem. I assume that you don't know why this has happened, Skye."

"None sir. I'd have sent word if I found anything. If I had known that something would happen to another child --" I stopped and thanked Aria, who had handed me a cup of tea. "We thought this was something human-related, sir. Children disappear there all the time."

"I know. It's lamentable, the things that can happen to children in the human world. We save the ones we can, but we can never do enough."

I wanted to ask about how they saved children. Later, I told myself again. There was much we would talk about later. I wanted to know more about this case.

Case, as though this was something another hired me to do. I didn't want to treat the matter that way-- or maybe I did. If I stopped taking this as something personal, I might see the clues without being panicked and afraid. It might be a good thing to keep my emotions in check.

"What can you tell me about how Lily disappeared?" I asked.

Donal saw the difference in me or sensed the change in my emotions. He appeared to approve. He held his cup in his hands, though not lifting it to sip, as he looked across at me. I had mimicked the move and waited, hoping for anything that would help. Facts sometimes linked with other facts when you gathered enough of them. I needed to know everything so that when something matched, I could see it.

"Lily was living with her mother, of course," Donal said. He must have seen the blink of my eyes and the almost question that part. "Ah. Your father is not popular, and he's not making things better for himself, so the younger child went to live with her mother again. They'd always gotten along well, Lily and her mother, while your father. . . . Forgive me for saying this, Aria, but --"

"But he's been an egotistical fool," she said and with a little snarl of anger. "You need not worry about my sensitivities. I've gotten over my worship of him. I saw him clearly after the problem with Earis. He was no help. In fact, he was worse than no help, and since he still claims Skye was part of the trouble, instead of helping us --"

"He says that?" I asked. The idea didn't shock me. I grimaced, though. "Do others listen to him?"

"He's popular with Lord Topaz," Donal replied with a wave towards the window. "That's where he's been staying since most of the people of Emerald House are tired of him. It's no surprise that Topaz listens to him."

Lord Topaz was an old, bigoted monster, and the two making common cause against me came as no surprise. I also had not made friends with a group of younger Topaz when they tried to kill me -- and I survived. Remembering the web of bad relationships brought up another question and one I hated to broach.

"I don't like to ask it, but --"

"We have checked," Aria said. "We can find no link between Topaz and the trouble, either here or across in the human lands. I kept watch on the two myself. As far as I can tell, neither they nor any of the people around them, are involved."

"Thank you."

"I wish it had been them. I wish I had found such an easy answer. But -- we suspect something from the human side, Skye. And that's dangerous. Really dangerous."

"How could a human get hold of a fae child?" I asked.

"By magic. Humans have acquired magic now and then. Sometimes it comes to them naturally," Donal explained. He sipped his tea, his eyes half closed, as though exhausted. What did a clan leader do? "A human with magic is like they're born with some link to the fae though they remain human. You have had your wizards and witches in the past, and your world is filled with magic for those who can manipulate it. That darkness that chased you and Darion did not come from our side, my friends. It came fully formed in the human world."

"Oh hell," Darion said. He leaned forward this time. "That's bad. I don't want to deal with a human mage."

"None of us do. They're dangerous and unpredictable, and they don't know the rules or care to learn them," Donal explained. "And most of them will take power anywhere they can get it."

"Like from a fae child?"

"No. Lily was too young to have come to more than a whisper of her power. She would have put up more of a fight, otherwise. She was out visiting friends and riding back home. Her mother felt the rip in the world and heard her daughter's cry for help. Half of fae heard the shout. Whatever took her moved rapidly and left no trail behind at all. It was as though the magic used disappeared with them."

"No magic," I said and looked at Darion.

"We have been assuming that Kelly disappeared in a solely human way because we found no magic link," Darion explained as worry grew in his face. "With the disappearance of Lily, I suspect this may not be so, Lord Emerald. I don't know where to turn next."

"The entire situation is troubling and more so since this is aimed at Skye."

I nodded, having already guessed that part. "Does something want my powers again?"

"Perhaps. Whatever this thing is, it knows about the fae and knows enough to grab one of our own who is related to you. I'm glad -- and grateful -- that you have your Sapphire guard, Skye. You are not safe."

"I realized that the moment they told me about Lily -- but I have to keep looking for them." Donal frowned. I suspected he had brought me here to keep me safe while others looked. "Sir, this is what I do. It's what I do well and why the gargoyle even came to me."

"Yes, there is that problem," he said with a shake of his head.

"We already have a lead on that one," Darion said. "It may be cleared up soon, though I suspect dealing with the stone will be messy. Something will have to be done on this side, though. I would like to believe this is only one gargoyle, acting on his own. But if it isn't --"

"Yes. More problems." Donal looked at me and shook his head. "Gargoyles are hierarchal and protective of their positions, but sometimes they form brotherhoods for a single cause, and then there is hell in fae while we get them beat back to their own place. They dislike dealing with us at the best of times, though, so I can't say if there is something more going on or not."

"Everything is a complication," I said. "The darkness that came after us . . . Darion, it attacked after your people began searching for the missing stone. People down there have access to magic --"

"Oh, I don't like to think they've figured out how to use the power already," Donal said. "But it would, at least, give us a definite clue."

"We'll need to go over everything," I said to Darion. "Maybe we tripped something and didn't realize. We had better get right to work on it."

Donal agreed with a weary nod. "I wanted you should stay here, Skye. However, I am reminded of how you have done well in the past. I cannot, in good conscious, hold you back when your own life may be in danger."

"Thank you, sir --"

I looked up as someone came into the room and blinked in surprise to see my father.

He saw me.

The others never realized he meant to attack me, but I saw the rage in his eyes and had already stood. He moved faster than I expected. Darion and Aria both moved, but I was closer to him than either of them, and he caught hold of me --

I had not expected the knife. I would have fought him, hand-to-hand, but the blade changed things; I tried to slip to the side, and I caught hold of Aria and pulled her out of the way.

"Knife!" I warned just before he came at me again.

The knife caught me across the side. At that moment, before the pain hit, I knew he had stabbed at almost the same spot where Aria had pushed a knife into me, though not of her own free will, back when Earis had control of us. I gasped and staggered back, but only far enough to get one good kick at my father's knee. He howled and almost fell. Darion viciously twisted his hand, and the knife fell to the floor, though my father tore free of him and came back at me. He pounded me with a fist, and when I went down, he kicked. I mirrored that one back to him, and he grunted in pain and stepped away.

"What did you do with her? What have you done?" he yelled, even as others grabbed him and dragged him away.

Those words had been a strange near-echo of what my mother had said. I gasped, trying to sit up --

"Be still!" Donal ordered. I obeyed in shock and then realized he spoke to my father. "You are banished, Cedric No House. You are forbidden from claiming ties to this house and clan."

My father went silent and pale. Darion let go of him, although he remained close by, ready for another attack.

"You cannot -- for it --"

"You broke the covenant of Emerald House," Donal replied with such a snarl of anger that I wanted to crawl away. Donal grabbed my father's hand and yanked off the ring. I had never seen any fae so enraged. I glanced at Aria, who glared at our father. "You attacked a guest who had come at *my request*. Even if Skye had been the worst enemy of the clan, it would have been unforgivable. Be gone from this clan. Never come back."

Cedric backed up a step. He shook his head. "You can't. It is evil. It stole my daughters from me --"

"Something we don't understand took Lily," Aria said

as she leaned closer to him, her eyes blazing. "And you drove me away."

"No --"

"Be gone or I will have the others throw you out," Donal said.

He turned and fled.

Donal turned and looked at me as I started to stand, and then he looked startled and worried. "Someone get Peren Ruby Day!"

"Oh hell, Skye! I didn't realize he had stabbed you!" Darion rushed over and caught hold of me. I was about to fall flat on my face. "Damn! I didn't expect --"

"None of us did," Donal said. "Can you carry him? There is a sofa in the other room. Peren will come quickly, I'm sure."

He was right. Peren had arrived before they got me to the sofa. He looked angry.

"What happened?"

"His father -- who is no longer of the clan," Donal said.

That caught Peren by surprise for a moment, but then he nodded. "Probably long overdue. He's been over the line a long time, and no, that is not a reflection on you, Skye."

Darion had already stopped most of the bleeding anyway, so I wasn't in any real danger this time, but Ambassador Peren Ruby Day took the wound seriously enough. He did good work, too, and when he stepped back, he nodded.

"Please sit down," Donal said to Peren. "Rest in our house. Thank you for coming to my call."

"I owe you a great deal, Skye."

I shook my head because I had been the one who killed his daughter, and someone must have told him what happened by now. I liked Ambassador Peren Ruby Day. He had been kind from the start. And this wasn't the first time he had helped heal my wounds, either.

"Sir," I said, looking at him.

"I try to remember Earis as a child," he said, his head tilted for a moment as his eyes looked elsewhere and he called back another time. Then he shook his head and focused on me again. "I saw little her, to be honest. I was already an ambassador. Her birth came at the start of the Age of Change, and she lived with my Ruby mother, who tried to bring her up to understand the duty that might fall to her. She was always willful and capricious, Skye. We knew she would not be the one long before the initial sorting. She, however, became convinced she was the better person than all her cousins. Better than everyone else. She made wrong choices at every turn, my young friend. I'm sorry for everything she did and for the number of people who died -- both fae and human -- by the end. I cannot feel the same pain for her death because she had chosen her path. You did what you had to, Skye Emerald McFaelyn, and in doing so, you saved us all. You did what I would have had to do myself if I had been there instead. I'm not sure any of us could have because it was your uniqueness that stood against her."

Everything he said was true, and I felt some of the guilt about killing his daughter ease. "Thank you." He had lifted another weight from my heart.

"You need to rest, Skye," Peren said. He accepted a

cup of tea from Aria with a nod of thanks. "You need to rest because this healing takes as much from the body as it gives. At least three hours of sleep. There is more trouble going on in your body, like that gargoyle wound that doesn't heal. I'll study the poison he used now that I have touched it. You must rest while you can, though. I insist."

I was not one of his clan, and part of me wanted to test that order but knew better than to even attempt it; if a Ruby Ambassador couldn't order me, the Emerald Chieftain could and would. I sighed and relaxed a little. The sofa was very comfortable, at least.

"Good," Peren said. "Sleep while you can, Skye."

"The girls are missing," I said looking at him. "I can't rest for long."

He agreed with a solemn bow of his head. "Three hours. And while you sleep, the rest of us will do what we can to find more information. This matter will not rest and wait for you."

"Thank you," I said. "I need help. I don't know what to do."

Peren stood. He looked tired, and I realized the magic he had used to so quickly heal the wound was no easier on him than it had been on me. I was lucky to have such friends. I looked at them, wondering what I could do to repay them. They were getting ready to leave the room, all except Darion, who would not leave my side.

Donal put out a hand and stopped her at the doorway.

"I name you the new Emerald Clan Ambassador, Aria Emerald McFaelyn. Serve in honor."

She looked at him, startled. He held out the ring he had taken from my father.

"I can't -- I'm *his* daughter --"

"And Skye is also his child. The blood you share with Cedric is no more reflection of you than it is for Skye," Donal replied. "Take the ring and serve as you were trained to, Aria. He brought you up to be the next Ambassador."

"But he was bad at the job."

"He was *lazy*," Donal corrected and patted her arm. "I intended to replace him, anyway."

"We all knew. I suspect every clan out there knew."

"True," Darion said. "It's not like anyone thought you'd be stupid enough to keep him on, sir. This is a crux time with Ruby House in control, and the fae having more contact with the humans again. An ambassador with such prejudices wouldn't help Emerald House. You were always a wise king; this wasn't the time to keep someone so self-centered and biased in such a position."

"And me?" Aria asked, looking not to his clan leader, but to Darion. That seemed odd, even to me.

"You are not your father. You and I never got along well, Aria, but that has nothing to do with how good you will be at the work. And besides, you've changed."

She nodded agreement at his last words. "Yes, I have. My father would have joined with Earis Ruby Day. I never want to be that stupid."

"Then take the ring," Donal said.

She accepted, bowing her head and holding out her hand so he could slip the ring on her finger. The clan had a new ambassador. She still looked shocked when she, Peren, and Donal left. Darion took the chair where Peren had been sitting and looked at me. "Sleep," he said. "Sleep now, because all too soon we'll be out there again. You'll need the strength."

I agreed and closed my eyes. Sleep came quickly this time -- fast and deep --

And filled with nightmares. Darion's magic couldn't reach me. Frantic, I tried to grab hold of him. I sensed Aria as well with that whisper of fae-related blood calling to me, but when I tried to take hold, I realized the mistake. Not Aria.

Lily.

And she dragged me deeper into the nightmare; I saw only black, but I felt the cold, and the bounds -- both magical and metal -- that held her in place. I heard crying, crying -- two voices --

Darion yanked me up out of the nightmare. I came awake with a cry of dismay and my hands to my chest where my heart labored too hard --

"Look at me!" Darion ordered, his voice harsh. I saw Donal rush back into the room. "Skye! Look at me!"

I blinked, trying to bring myself back into this place. "Nightmare," I said. "Or not? I think -- two girls. Lily pulled me in --"

Darion shook his head, panic still apparent. "Something took hold of you and would not let go. This wasn't fae magic."

"I could feel her, Darion. I could have found them --"

"It had to do with the gargoyle magic." He took hold of my arm because I shook my head, still confident of the connection. "The cut broke open again and bled both blood and magic, Skye. I had to get the wound closed. There was nothing else I could sense in the magic."

"I can't sleep." I looked from Darion to Donal. "I

can't sleep if this is going to happen every time. Let's see what I can find on the damned rock and get that trouble cleared up."

Neither argued which told me my problem had become far worse.

Chapter Nine

We left the little pocket of the fae realms and drove back out into the winter lands. I shivered, even in the heat of the truck and looked back to see the spring world disappear behind a haze of fog and falling snow.

"Will it be a long spring?" I asked with a hint of hope.

"I suspect so. Lacey is too bright and filled with joy to give way to an angry, heated summer or to the melancholy of autumn."

"And then the rule will pass to Sapphire House," I said, startled with the realization.

"That's a long way off. No children have even been born to the choices of that age," he said. "We have worries enough without looking towards that trouble."

I didn't look forward to whatever adversity we faced out here in the human world. I was not up to any exertion and Darion knew it.

"We're going back to Cherry's," Darion said. "For a couple reasons, so listen before you protest."

I grunted and pulled my jacket closer around me still cold from the dream. The covering of what snow everywhere didn't help. "Why Cherry's place?" I asked.

"First, so Cherry can see you're all right. Do try not to look as though you're about to fall over dead, all right?" he said.

"Ha, you think that will work? If I look well, she'll suspect magic and that we're hiding something."

"Damn. You're right. Okay, then I'll settle for 'don't fall over dead' instead."

"I'll do my best. What's the real reason we're going there?"

"Blue, Sand, and Rose are there. They've been working with Barber to find out about the street gang and the trouble. It will be easier to go there and hook up with them than to have them use magic trying to reach us. We have no power to waste this time, Skye. We need to know what they've learned."

What he said made sense. I wanted to see Cherry, too, and to know she was safe because people related to me . . . . "You left some of Sapphire Clan there to make certain she isn't taken," I said. He gave a quick nod. "Thank you. And I won't tell her, either."

"She'll have figured it out. There are other reasons to gather there. Her apartment makes a convenient place on this side of the Veil for us. The place is already warded, and Cherry makes us welcome. I think she rather likes having such unusual things going on in her life."

"Apparently so. After all, she had already accepted

me."

"Good point. Rest a little, Skye. Don't sleep, but rest while you can. I'll get this figured out --"

"How long are you going to be my guard?" I asked since we had a little time alone. "And don't you have better things to do?"

"I put no limit on the time I would be your guard," he replied with only a glance my way. "And I did so on purpose because I didn't want there to be questions from anyone else, or assumptions on their part. I won't sever that tie now or in the near future, even if we figure this out, so don't even ask."

"Can I order you to stop being my guard?" I asked.

"No, you cannot. You accepted me as your guard. We can only sever this by mutual agreement, and that's not going to happen, friend. And no, right now I don't have anything better to do. Between the stone of power and the missing girls, there is no other place I would do more good."

He was right, so I obeyed and rested. If we ran into trouble, I didn't want to be weaker than I needed to be, just because I was stubborn.

If we ran into trouble? Of course we would. We would even hunt for the problem.

I had not put everything together. There were pieces of the problem bouncing around in my head. Everything was a distraction. The closer we got to Cherry's place, the more I wanted quiet time. I began to fidget.

"What is wrong?" he asked.

"I need time alone, Darion." I waved towards the park on the right which was only a few blocks from Cherry's house. "Let me out here."

"Skye --"

"Gods, Darion! I spent most of my life alone. Now, I can't get five minutes to myself. I need to be alone to sort some of this out and hope for something that will help."

He gave me a worried glance as he pulled over to the side of the road. I opened the door and slid out and then looked back at him. "Go spend time with Cherry. She needs you. I'll be there soon."

"Don't be too long."

I smiled and stepped away, closing the door. Darion drove away.

It was trust, I suppose, leaving me alone. He would have a link and know if there was trouble -- but still, this was a few precious moments alone. I watched him drive away as the wind whipped around me. Was this stupid? Should I go be back at the apartment with Cherry and him and the rest of the fae --

I needed to sort out my thoughts. When I spent time near many fae, their emotions seeped into my brain, and I had trouble sorting out what was me. Besides, I needed to think about things that were painful for me and that I didn't want to share with the others. My father's attack had triggered other memories, and I couldn't hold them at bay much longer. They were nothing that would help us with the current problems and I needed to calm.

People moved throughout the park, laughing despite the weather. An ice rink sat off to the right, and I heard music and more laughter in that direction. I thought people were crazy to go around skating on ice and purposely do things out here in the cold. I like the warmth, and I remembered the spring-filled street with the Clan Houses with a whisper of longing. Then a little pang in my side reminded me that it wasn't such a good place to go. Both of my visits to that area had ended with people trying to kill me. And yet, and yet . . . it wasn't the call of spring that made me want to go back. It was the longing to belong there.

To belong *anywhere.*

That old pain hit. I had buried those emotions a long time ago, even before my mother turned me out on the streets. I had not belonged with her and her new family, and she'd made that plain for years. Why had she kept me around so long and didn't just kill --

A memory came to me of something so long ago that I couldn't have been older than three or four. She had taken me to a lake-side park. The night had been cold and foggy, and I wanted to go home. We walked out on a jetty, the wind sharp and a touch of ice in the air.

She grabbed me by the arm and threw me into the lake water and walked away.

And I -- not knowing any better -- I somehow got out of the water and had followed her home. I don't understand how I had found the house again since she had gone back by car, but I somehow had known where to go. I remembered the horror on her face when she found me in my room that next morning.

The memory made me so ill that I staggered over to a bench and sat down, ignoring the snow piled up on it. How could I have forgotten such a thing? Did I only imagine it? I wanted to believe so, but the memory felt real in a way my fae side could not deny. She had tried to kill me. I now suspected that hadn't been the only time. I assumed she could not get rid of me, so she had waited until I was old enough that I would not come back on my own.

Odd. That meant I must have had magic from birth, even if I didn't know what to do with the power. The magic had protected me from her and from being killed by my father and his people. I might have to ask Darion later after we handled everything else and I could tell him what I remembered without making this current problem worse. My past was not important.

Kelly was missing and so was Lily. That meant something. Something about me, but why? Who?

Maybe I knew something without realizing it.

Like the fact that I was freezing my ass off sitting here in the snow.

Idiot.

I stood and walked again, heading towards a stand of trees midway in the park. Even in the dead of winter, the trees drew me. The scent of the evergreens was heady with the essence of life. Little birds flew in and out of the branches, and I saw bird feeders nearby. I was glad the humans took care of these little creatures of the wild and the sight made me happier about my human half again. Sometimes I felt so completely cut off from humans that I forgot what we shared.

Despite the painful memory of what my mother had done, the walk here still helped. I pushed away all the thoughts of my past, which had been playing at the back of my mind for the last couple days. Hadn't the incident at the lake been right after she met Ian? Had she wanted me gone before they married? I supposed that made sense.

Not an excuse, but a reason at least.

I wouldn't forget what she had done this time, but I forced myself to make the memory less important. My emotions had been taking a roller coaster ride, and I needed better control. I didn't want to mess up just because --

My father stepped out from behind a tree and moved right in front of me.

"I knew if I waited long enough, I'd find you without that Sapphire dog at your back."

I took a step backward. He waved his hand and put a wall of magic around us -- one I couldn't get through and one that kept the humans from seeing or hearing anything we did. Good. I didn't want those people to get caught up in my stupidity. He used powerful magic, and an overpowering scent of apples filled the air, odd in the midst of winter.

He didn't have a weapon in hand this time, but he had more magic building in him like a storm about to break over a mountain top. Power flashed in his eyes, and I watched as his hand lifted.

I brought mine up first -- a hint of vanilla almost lost in the other scent -- and hit him with a bolt of magic that burnt his chest and sent him flying. He landed hard while his own magic dissipated in a flash of light.

"It won't be that easy." I stalked towards him. Anger grew in me and came from memories of my mother mixed with the knowledge that he was no better. "I didn't take Lily or Kelly --"

"You turned Aria against me --"

"You did that yourself, you pompous, stupid bastard." I waved my hand and sent another burst of power that knocked him down again as he started to stand. It must have hurt even though I did no real damage. "You can't blame me for your own stupidity."

"You should have been killed at birth."

"You tried and couldn't do it."

I had made a guess, and I saw the way his eyes widened with panic. "You are unnatural. You're evil. You should never have lived --"

Those were my mother's words coming from his mouth, and I felt a strange chill hearing them, as though he and my mother were --

Were linked?

Did I tie them together or did the hatred of me fuel the bond made possible by the magic he held? He wouldn't have let me live since I would be a black mark against his reputation. I stared down at him as he tried to get his breath and pull magic back up and use against me. I waved his power away again, although the fiery pain of what I had done took hold. I didn't dare show the weakness to him.

He surprised me: Instead of calling up another round of magic, he rolled over and kicked me in the knee, much as I had kicked him earlier. I went down with a grunt of pain, but he'd already moved out of the way and came back to his feet, kicking again so I went face down on the icy walkway. I rolled just as a flash of fire hit the sidewalk, melting snow and leaving a hole all the way through to the frozen ground. I got back to my feet before he could react. He wasn't very fast. Probably too much of the good life.

He had lost the good life, and he lived in disgrace because he had attacked me. Did he think he could get back what he had by killing me now? Maybe he thought that no one would know what he'd done, here in this realm. Or did it not matter anymore? Probably the last. I saw nothing hopeful in his dark, hateful stare and that made him dangerous. With no hope of redemption, he had no reason to hold back. I watched him pull up magic again, fueled by an unquenchable rage. The surge of magic was strong and would kill me this time. I wondered when I'd lost the protection I'd had as a child --

I charged at him, hoping to get so close he didn't dare release the magic. It almost worked. Fire burnt across both my arms as I reached, but I deflected the worst of the power out and away -- sorry that a tree to the right took the brunt of the attack, several branches breaking away and flung to the ground. He struck not only with the power of his fist but also with magic. I struck back but not hard enough and --

We were not alone.

Aria spun him around and hit him so hard he crumpled. She kicked for good measure. I winced, having been on the receiving end of one of her kicks once. The feeling passed; I had no sympathy for the man who laid on the ground, hands to his chest and looking at her with shock.

"I knew you'd do something stupid like before long," she said looking at her cowering father. *Our father.* She leaned down and caught him by the collar, jerking him half up so he came to his knees. She didn't use magic either; Aria is strong.

"Aria --" he started and then yelped in shock when she slapped him. Her anger even surprised me. She was in no mood to listen to anything he had to say.

"*Leave Skye alone.* You've done enough already to ruin his life --"

"How can you stand up for it!"

She slapped him once more, and I saw his anger surging into power again. I feared I might have to step in to help though Aria would not appreciate the gesture. She was just as stubborn as he was in most ways. So I lingered nearby, trying to maintain control of my emotions (again) and to regain my power.

"Listen to me: *leave Skye alone.* If I find you are trying to hurt him again, I will call you into a blood feud."

"Aria," I protested, even though I didn't understand the full implication of what she said. I knew it couldn't be good.

"You wouldn't for that thing --"

"That *thing* is my sibling. Besides, in case you missed it, Skye has done more to help the fae in the last few months than you have in your entire life. I know where my loyalty rightfully falls." She looked at me and even grinned. I had not expected that reaction. "I know the difference between right and wrong."

Cedric Emerald McFaelyn pulled free of her hold and got back to his feet. He did not attack her, and she had moved to put herself between our father and me. He glared at us.

"You have made me an enemy, Aria," he said, his voice a growl of anger.

"And I should care?" she asked.

He stepped away. "This is not over."

"You're far too melodramatic," she said and waved a hand. Did he see that she had his job now? I thought so, the way he glanced at his own hand where the ring had been for so long. "Go back to fae and hide, Cedric No House."

He blanched at that title, and then he turned and disappeared through a portal that looked rather shaky in power. I wasn't certain he would reach the other side, and apparently neither did Aria. With a sigh of disgust, she sent a little power to help him on his way.

She turned back. "You all right?"

"Yes, thank you." I felt new bruises, but I hadn't been seriously injured, except for burns along my hands. They stung, and I glanced at them, surprised that it wasn't worse. "It was stupid to go out here alone."

"Maybe so," she said and surprised me with a shrug. "But he would have come for you at some point, whenever he found the chance. You couldn't hide from him forever."

"And he will try again."

"I don't know. He doesn't like to do anything difficult. You were more work than he liked, but be careful. Let me help you with your hands."

I almost said no, but then I held them out, trying not to shiver when she came close and put her fingers over mine. She looked into my eyes and what she saw must have troubled her.

"I know trust can't come easily to you, Skye," she said with a soft rush of words. "I'll have to work to win it."

"I try," I answered. Her magic brushed over my hands, a far gentler touch than I would have expected from someone who had always seemed so rough. "It's not easy. Especially right now when I'm worried about the others, and this has to do with me --"

"But you are not doing it," she said and sounded sincere in her belief. She took my hands in hers now that the burns had healed. "You have helped the fae. You have done things for us while our ever egotistical self-righteous father sat back and watched. Whatever is going on with Lily --"

"Is my fault."

"No. It is *aimed* at you, but that doesn't make it your fault." She let go of my hands. "I have to go. Skye, don't go walking in the park alone again."

She turned and walked away, disappearing down a portal towards another place. I saw a green land somewhere far from the snow. I wanted to go there, too.

With a sigh, I turned and found why she had been willing to leave me. Darion and Sand were rushing down the path towards me. My father's shield had dropped when he left, but no one else had come this way yet.

"Yes, it was stupid," I said before either of them spoke.

"I felt something and thought it was you at first, that shield. Then I realized it was your father. That was Aria, right?" Darion asked.

"Yes. And my father was here before her. He thought we had things left to settle."

Darion nodded. "Let's go back to Cherry's place."

"Yeah. I can sort out my feelings in the bedroom by myself," I said.

He grinned. "Good idea. Don't worry. We'll get this worked out, Skye. We will find them."

The new problem with my father added another level to the ongoing trouble. I thought it through while we walked back to the truck.

"Somehow my mother and father are linked. They keep saying the same things and I don't think it is chance. I believe they both tried to kill me as a child and couldn't."

Both of my companions stopped and looked at me.

"I assume you don't mean they couldn't because they had a change of heart," Sand said, her face already dark with anger.

"Couldn't because I wouldn't die. I remembered her throwing me into a lake when I was about three, but I got out and walked back home. I had the impression from him that he wanted me dead when I was born, but couldn't do it. Not that he didn't want to, but something stopped him."

Darion stared at me. He lifted his hand, and magic washed over me again. He frowned. "I think you might be right. That's odd. Some outside force protected you because you wouldn't have had the ability as a child."

"I don't need more complications," I said.

"No, you don't. Come on."

As we walked away, I looked back at where my father and I had fought. My anger towards him had disappeared by the end of our encounter. So, remarkably, had the feeling of betrayal. Maybe I had needed to face him, and this had been a good idea.

I didn't mention that one to Darion. He already thought I was crazy.

CHAPTER TEN

I felt worse by the time we got back to Cherry's apartment, but that came as much from anxiety as anything else. The afternoon had slipped away too towards night and dark, dense clouds blunted the last of the sunlight that should have lingered another couple hours. We would face a cold, miserable night.

I climbed out of the truck and slipped on the ice but righted myself with little more than a mumbled curse. The stairs looked like a mountain we would have to climb up to Cherry's place; a mountain covered in snow and ice. And why? We would come back down again before too long. I stood there staring at the steps while Darion and Sand came around to my side. They looked unhappy, but we said nothing as we started forward --

Wings swept down, wide and darker than the early twilight. The gargoyle landed in the lot in front of me. Darion caught hold of me, both of us nearly falling on the treacherous ice. Sand moved to stand on my other side.

"What the hell do you want?" I demanded as anger darted past my good sense again. The gargoyle was something where I could vent my frustrations -- but even so I knew this wasn't wise.

"You have not found the stone."

"I am working on it!"

"You are not. You try to hide in the clan house, but you are not safe there from me. I will drag you out."

"I was not hiding. The way to find things is to ask questions -- which you are not willing to answer. Get the hell away from me. I'm working on the stone."

His golden eyes glittered as anger surged through the creature. Hands came up with those long, sharp claws. I did not back away.

"There is no time," the gargoyle said, leaning down into my face. "It is loose upon your world, and you do not care."

"I do care," I said. But I didn't, really. Odd to realize, but right then I didn't give a shit about the stone and the gang bangers who had found it. I wanted my two half-sisters safe. I wanted out of that nightmare --

No. I couldn't look away and let others suffer just because they were an inconvenient problem right now. I cared about them as well, even the strangers. Even the damned kids in the gangs.

"I'll find it," I said.

"Soon." The creature spread wings and lifted, more with magic than with the power those beats. He disappeared over the apartment roof, but he hadn't gone far.

"No one saw him. I made certain this time," Darion said. He took hold of my arm and moved me more briskly towards the stairs as though afraid of what else might arrive. Blue stood at the door, waiting for us. "The thing is right. It's damned dangerous for that stone to be loose out there."

"I know." We went fast up the stairs with magic to deal with the ice and reached the door with no more trouble. Blue stepped aside, letting us into the warm room. The place smelled of chocolate chip cookies.

"What did the gargoyle want this time?" Blue asked.

"The same he always wants: for me to perform some kind of miracle and find the stone he can't even locate."

"Oh, now there's a part of this problem I hadn't considered." Darion stopped, blocking the door until Sand sighed and pushed him aside. "If this is his stone, why can't he find it? Why can't he even give us a clue?"

Blue frowned and nodded agreement. I didn't care. I went to the kitchen and sat down across from Sand, who settled in front of a street map and traced lines with her finger. The lines stayed on the paper, glowing with blue or red eldritch light. I watched, entranced, and trying to figure out what she was doing.

Cherry put cookies in front of me, and a glass of milk, and took another chair. Cherry noted that I'd had a bad time, though she didn't ask. I decided not to mention being stabbed by my father and then having an altercation with him in the park. It wouldn't help her mood. She'd heard the gargoyle had just been down in the lot again.

What the hell did it expect me to do?

Darion studied the map and nodded, patting Sand's

shoulder.

"What is it?" I asked.

"I am tracing out spots where there might be magic," Sand explained. She sipped water Blue brought her. "I have sensed several spots down by the docks. Detective Barber pointed me in that general direction. He says there's been more trouble in the area this afternoon, and I get a bad feeling everything will be worse tonight if we can't get hold of that stone and stop it."

"We will try. Skye, I don't think you're ready for this work --"

"Then make me ready, because you aren't going out there without me. The gargoyle put this in my hands so I have to be there, Darion. Being here won't help since he is apt to show up where I am. He won't be happy if I am not out there, and I can't fight him without you guys. You can make me strong enough to work tonight."

"That kind of magic isn't often a good choice," Darion replied with a shake of his head. He had a cookie in hand but wasn't eating. "It only glosses over what's wrong and doesn't --"

He stopped speaking before I protested. Cherry shook her head, but she didn't argue at all. We could both tell that Darion, despite his worries, realized I was right. I couldn't stay here while he and the others went off to help settle the problem. The gargoyle would come for me again. I wouldn't be able to stand up to him alone and leaving too many to protect me would make their own work all the more dangerous.

Darion ate his cookie and then came around to the back of my chair. I hate having people right behind me,

and my body tensed as he put his hands on my shoulders
and massaged for a moment. I relaxed again.

"Better," he said. He gave me no warning as his magic
swept down through me, warm and strong. The power
brought a touch of fire with it because all magic hurts. The
strength that came with this rush magic was worth the pain.

"Thank you," I said when Darion pulled away.

He went back and settled on the other side of the table
with Sand and stared at me, still unhappy. "There's some
kind of magic gnawing away at you, Skye. I've sensed it,
but I can't get hold of the link. This may have come from
the gargoyle and that mark he put on you, and that is part
of what's making you ill. I blocked what I could, but it
won't hold forever."

"Then we better move quickly." I stood, feeling as
though I had the energy to walk from one room to another.
"If we find the stone, I'll be free of this part."

"True," he said. He patted Cherry on the shoulder.
"We'll be careful. Blue, Sand --"

"I'm staying here," Sand said. "I'm already worn out
from trying to track this stuff, and that might make me too
dangerous on something like this. Take the map."

Darion took the paper and nodded.

"I don't need a guard," Cherry protested.

"Yes, you do," I said, and surprised her.

"Besides, I'm not lying," Sand added. She lifted her
hand, and it trembled a little. "That took a lot of magic,
and I don't have enough to help them. You three be
careful. I'll try to keep a tag on you, just in case things get
out of hand."

Darion agreed with the plan. Blue was getting his coat

and looking towards the window with obvious misgivings. I had barely gotten my fingers unthawed. I grabbed a couple cookies, which won a smile from Cherry.

We went back to the truck. The interior was still damned comfortable, and I wanted to rest and sleep. Odd how feeling better let me relax enough that if I hadn't worried about nightmares and magic, I would have closed my eyes.

"I like the truck," Blue said, patting the dashboard. He had the spot in the middle this time. "Good choice."

"Still conspicuous, though in a different way." Darion handed the map over to Blue and started the engine.

We pulled out of the parking lot and into the heavier traffic as people tried to get home for the night. Despite the continuing snow, they had still been out -- but many had no choice. I wished them well on their quest to get in out of the weather. The clouds looked ominous, and the wind had already struck with enough force that even the truck bounced.

"Anyone check the Weather Channel?" I asked, leaning forward to glare up at the sky.

"It's going to snow. It's going to snow a lot," Blue replied with a snort of laughter. "And I don't need to check the television to know it."

Blue directed Darion down the streets towards the area Sand had mapped out for us. I didn't like the place as we moved along the barely scooped road. I soon realized that driving in this truck was a problem because something this big and shiny drew looks for a whole new reason. The buildings here were ragged, run-down, and the people who walked along the sidewalks looked our way with both dislike and greed. It was not a typical reaction to a car passing through this part of town.

"Something going on," I said. "Could it be that the stone, just being in this area, is making these people surly?"

"Maybe," Darion agreed, and Blue nodded. "That will not help."

"We should dump the truck and go on foot," I decided. "Otherwise, we're going to draw the kind of trouble we don't want tonight."

"I could hide it with magic --" Darion began. Then he stopped. "No. That might draw other attention."

"So we go out walking," Blue agreed.

Darion didn't look happy, but he was already turning around on the narrow road. "Yeah, we'll have trouble here if we draw this attention, though being on foot might not be much better," he admitted. "I suspect magic might have found an easy hold here."

"Angry people," I said. "But I lived here for a while, and I can understand their reactions."

Darion nodded towards a man with his laughing daughter on his shoulders, while a young boy danced ahead, obviously pleased. "That man makes less money than many of the people here, but he has a family and he's happy, and he's working to make things better -- but even if he never does, he knows that he's done the best he can for his family. The man there who is glaring at them -- he abandoned two different wives and five children. He blames his bad luck on everyone but himself."

Those weren't just words Darion had said. He knew the truth of what he saw, and so did I. We experienced the emotions both of the men and even picked up secrets which must have been a fae thing I had never considered. I had always known the truth-sayers from the liars. The problem was that sometimes the liars were not bad guys. Sometimes they were just trying to protect their own, fragile egos.

Blue looked at the man with the children as we passed them and then moved his hands, sending a wave of warm, powerful magic towards the stranger.

"Blue?" I asked.

"A person like that deserves luck. Someone will call his father tonight while they're visiting, looking for a good worker for a new job. By spring they'll be living in a better house and the kids will go to better schools."

I blinked and smiled. That luck had cost Blue power, which might have been unwise considering the battle ahead of us. I was glad he had done it, though. I wondered if Karma was a fae sort of thing. Maybe some of that luck would come back on us when we needed it in this battle.

We drove to a better part of town and parked in a lot beside a theater. That saved Darion from having to use magic to make the truck invisible. Blue held tight to the map as we climbed out into a brisk wind and the latest fall of snow. I glared up at the clouds. We were in for a long, cold walk.

Darion spread a little warmth over us before we had gone more than a block. Blue and I both looked at him, startled.

"We'll wear ourselves out before we get anywhere if we have to fight this cold and ice," Darion said. "We need more than magic right now. In fact, magic might be the lesser of our needs."

"We will fight them hand-to-hand for the stone?" Blue asked. He sounded worried and incredulous. We had walked faster now that we weren't cold or afraid of falling on the ice. "You do remember what these creatures have been doing, right?"

"I know. We need to use our brains and not rely on magic too much. We have the advantage there. Or maybe I'm just tired of being cold. At least we will get there faster this way."

"Is faster better?" I asked, looking ahead into the falling dark and the swirl of white snow. "It sounds as though we're running straight into a hell of a lot of trouble."

"Better to get there and get done with this problem," Blue said. He did not mention the other problem we still had to face and still had not found a single clue. Yes, get the gargoyle out of this mess. Both cases were time sensitive, but this one was the only one where we knew what to do.

Every time I thought about how this was taking me away from finding the two girls, I grew angrier. I said little as we headed back into the bad part of town. Soon I feared we would run into relatively mundane gang problems long before we found the trouble we wanted. People looked at us, scowling, which was inevitable. We were not only strangers, but we were *noticeable* strangers in a place where skin tones went from brown to black.

"Should we use a glamor so we fit in?" Blue suggested. He pulled back his jacket so that the long-bladed knife he carried showed. I didn't have a weapon, and I felt stupid for not even having brought one. I knew these streets better than my two fae companions, and yet they were the ones who had come prepared for trouble.

"Too late," Darion said.   He stopped and turned around.

A group of young men stepped out ramshackle bar's doorway behind us. They stank of beer, but none of them appeared to be particularly drunk. They had the glares of men who wanted excitement, and three blond idiots wandering into their territory looked like a lot of fun. I saw hope in the smile of the one who stepped forward, his hand in his pocket holding a switchblade. This could have been worse. No one had already gone for guns.

"You in the wrong place," he said, looking from Blue to me, to Darion -- and then back to me. He blinked. "I know you. Skye."

"Mateo," I said with a nod of my head, grateful that I could recall the name. I hadn't recognized him. He'd aged a decade in the last couple years since I'd seen him.

"What the hell do you think you're doing here with *them?*" he said, waving a hand -- without a weapon -- towards my two companions.

"Two of my half-sisters are missing, Mateo.   I'm desperate to find them."

"*Familia,*" Mateo said and silenced his companions who were still looking for trouble. That told me about the power he held these days. He'd come up in the world since I last saw him. "I didn't think you were tight with your family."

"I'm not. But they're only young girls, and if I can find them, then I will," I said. I reached into my pocket and drew out the picture of Kelly. "This is one. The other isn't oriental. They're both about sixteen, Mateo."

He took the picture and stared at it for a moment. Then he passed it to the others, asking something in Spanish. They passed it around, but none of them had seen her.

"Sorry, Skye. Wish we could help, *amigo*, but we'll keep an eye open. How can we contact you?"

I pulled out my card and handed it over to him. He smiled at it and whistled. "You come up in the world, friend. Your own business, eh?"

"It keeps me off the street."

That made him laugh. I remembered that sound very well. The last time I'd heard it was when the two of us went at each other, *mano-y-mano*, when I had come into his territory. I never took up with the gang, but they'd respected me.

Karma. It came back just then.

"Anything at all going on that is odd?" I asked.

That got a different reaction.

"Bad shit you don't want nothing to do with," Mateo said with an almost frantic shake of his head. "There's gang stuff that is way over the top. You want to know how serious? We're glad to see the cops step in."

"Well damn," I said.

Mateo nodded. "Nothing about missing girls, Skye. Nothing for you there. Don't head down toward the warehouses on Augustus. Bad shit happens there."

"Thank you," I said and nodded. "*Gracias*."

"You still going to be wandering around out here?"

"Yes."

He turned and gave orders to this people. They

nodded and took off in various directions. "There. That will keep you safe from my people. I give you leave to come and go, you and your wisely quiet friends. Just don't make trouble. Good luck."

I offered my hand. He took it, and we parted without any blood spilled.

"Warehouses," I murmured, as Darion pulled out the map. I looked it over while we walked. "There," I said, pointing to one of the spots Sand had marked.

Darion nodded and lifted his hand. He looked worried. "Trouble there. Lots of wild magic suddenly. We've found what we're looking for, but I'm not sure it's what we want to walk into."

"Do we have a choice?" Blue asked.

"None," Darion and I said.

We had over five miles still to walk. I wished for the truck, just to go there and be done with this mess. I wanted to face the enemy, but we were just as far from the theater, so there was no use going back for it.

Darion was damned worried, which made me rethink what I wanted. There were only three of us, and I had limited magic.

"What are we going to face?" I asked because I couldn't stand the silence and my own thoughts any longer.

"Something like this is --" Darion slowed, as though considering the situation made him reconsider rushing there. "The stone is wild magic. Untamed and unfocused, so it latches onto whatever is nearby. Humans touched by this kind of magic have no limits, and they'll go until their bodies give out. The stone is also apt to change them in ways that reflect what they already are. If the gang was already tough and cruel, they're bound to get worse."

That made sense of what Barber had said and the impression from Mateo. Things have gone over the top.

"Physically, they'll be far stronger," Blue added. "But we know that from what Detective Barber said, right?"

I remembered what he had said about how the Stones mutilated people. "They need to be stopped."

We walked faster again. We were fools to head for a place where we probably never should have gone at all.

There was trouble ahead. Police cars swept past us despite the weather heading for the area where magic spiked.

"What do we do now?" I asked and brushed snow from my hair.

"They won't stand up to the gang," Darion said as we turned a corner. The snow fell harder here, fueled by the sudden magic. That helped to hide us. "Damn. We need to get the cops away from here."

"Any plans on how to do it?" I said.

"Let's try to see more of the situation," Blue suggested. "Maybe we can create a diversion."

"This is going to be a mess," Darion predicted as we followed the police cars.

CHAPTER ELEVEN

S tupid, really. Of course, the police were watching for someone to arrive at their rear. At least we looked like stupid bystanders rather than more of the gang coming at them, so they didn't shoot us. When one grabbed me and threw me against the wall, I couldn't even say they were too rough.

"Cuff them. Get them out of here!" someone shouted as he started away down a narrow path between two buildings. "Move! We got more trouble!"

Darion stumbled over to the wall beside me, but the person who had been cuffing him stopped in mid-move. So did the one working on me. Blue took the cuffs from them and gently pushed the police up against the wall and into the shadows behind the police cars where they wouldn't be noticed. They looked back at us, blank-faced and empty.

"That's too dangerous for them, sitting there without

even the wits to run or fight," I said. "We can't leave them here like this."

We heard shouts and then dozens of shots. Voices grew louder, but above it all came an odd howling, as though wild dogs had been let loose in the middle of the city. Everything drew closer to us in a cacophony of chaos. Hell. None of us would be safe soon. Darion did something quick with magic, and the cops blinked, looked at us, and nodded. They headed towards the battle. I would have rather they'd gone somewhere else.

Darion gasped from the magic he had used. He waved a hand towards Blue. "Call in others. Call them fast. Tell them to get the police out of here so we can do something!"

Blue bowed his head. I looked around, frantic at the sounds of trouble and the touch of strange, dark magic in the air that came with the scent of burning wood. I might not be up to the fight which put us in a damned lot of danger.

Blue gave me a frantic nod; I hoped that meant the others were on the way. However, another cop car came screeching or way, lights flashing. Damn. I had hoped the car would keep going, but it slid to a stop ---

Barber climbed out.

"Glad I found you. Cherry said you were already down this way. What the hell is going on?"

"Sent for help," Darion said, even his voice trembling. He had a hand against the wall, still expending a lot of magic. Pale and sweating; he had to make an effort to speak. "Keeping the police back from them. They can't fight these creatures, Barber. My people will lead yours away."

"We might need --" he started, but then he stopped. "No. Your call."

Darion nodded.

I heard the sound of scraping claws on the wall and looked up, expecting the damned gargoyle again --

Something jumped from the roof above us. No wings, and human-shaped until the thing faced me. The mouth had become huge and almost muzzle shaped; thin lips drew back in a vicious grin showing sharp, dangerous teeth already stained with someone's blood. The thing snarled like an angry dog and came at me, but at that moment when we faced each other, I brought up a wall of magic, and he bounced against it and fell back, startled.

Barber had drawn his gun. He shot it.

The creature fell, jerked once and then surged back to his feet and started towards Barber, howling in rage. Barber shot again. This time, it didn't even fall.

I hurried forward, caught the once-human thing by a massive arm, and dragged it away from Barber. Once I had grabbed hold, the creature forgot the disagreement with Barber, even though it bled from a few holes in the chest. Now the eyes glared at me. I seem to have that influence on people. And things.

A hand swept at me, the claws growing longer as I watched. Scales erupted across the body and blood-red eyes that glowed like something out of hell itself as he turned to focus on me.

Blue attacked with a dagger in hand and tried to shove the weapon into the back of the neck. The creature caught him and cut across his chest as he threw Blue aside. I gave a shout of anger and sent magic against it. I aimed fire into the eyes, which worked better than I had expected. The thing howled and backed away from me. When I prepared to attack again, it turned and fled back towards the battle.

"Hell, hell," Barber said, his voice close to hysterical. "Bullets won't stop them. The others --"

"My people on the way." Darion went to his knees, startling us all. "I'm holding the creatures back. Skye -- help Blue --"

Blue sat up, a hand to his chest where he bled far too much. I went straight to him and used what magic I could to heal him. Why were the others taking so long? They had to know we were in trouble! Darion couldn't hold on much longer --

Sand arrived first. I hadn't expected her at all. She caught hold of Darion, closed her eyes, and fed more magic into him.

The others arrived though scattered throughout the area. So much magic swept up around the buildings that for a moment the air itself glowed. Barber, startled by the change, looked worried --

"Our people," I said. I had stopped the bleeding, but Blue wasn't much better. "Peren. We need Peren Ruby Day --"

"Not yet. Not here," Blue said, gasping. He got to his feet though I didn't think that wise. Then I considered how bad it would be to by lying there if more of those creatures came for us. "Don't want to bring the best healer the fae has into a battle like this. Risk losing him."

That made sense, but I panicked. Darion's people were having trouble getting the police out of danger. I stared into the night, trying to see anything. Barber moved up by me. I hoped he didn't expect that made him safe.

"The others are going," Darion said. "Created phantoms for them to chase out away from the true danger."

The sound of shouts and shots retreated from the area. Barber nodded, relieved, but the real evil still lurked there, and I sensed the darkness and hunger reaching for us.

I spun.

The creature had come back out of the dark and raced straight at me again. I shoved Barber aside and wished to hell I had a weapon. I tried kicking it in the groin which didn't slow the creature any more than a bullet had. It drove me down on my back against the hard cement.

Claws struck, straight down and into my chest --

The world went away.

Everything changed.

I felt no pain. Instead, I saw a different place: dark with only a single flickering candle lighting a corner where rats moved, slinking along the wall. Two girls huddled together, chained to a wall side-by-side, both of them afraid. One looked towards me.

"Skye," Kelly said, tears on her face run down past what I hoped was dirt and not bruises. "Skye, I can see you. Help us! Help us!"

The other girl looked towards me. I had not seen her before, but she had green eyes like mine and looked a little like Aria. She wore a long blue dress that had torn along the side. Her hair was short.

"Skye," she whispered, and I heard the magic in her voice.

Something held them here in this black abyss that was not in the world -- any world, I thought. Though the walls and chains were real, the rest was not. Power held this bit of reality in place, but something else pulled at them, and I saw the essence of their lives draining away to feed an evil I didn't see.

I tried to reach them.   I reached out and almost touched Kelly --

"No!"

Darion's voice and Darion's magic swept me away from the girls and back to the alley where Barber had hold of me. Darion knelt with both hands on my chest, healing and healing so that from one breath to the next to the pain I hadn't noticed before receded to a dull ache. I gasped and coughed tasting blood in my mouth. I felt very ill.

"Darion," I whispered.

He blinked and looked into my face.   "Praise the gods," he whispered.   "Praise every god that ever lived.   I thought we lost you that time.   Gods all, Skye.   It wasn't just the claws.   Something tried to drag your soul away."

"I saw -- saw the girls," I whispered.   "I saw them.   A dark place. One candle. Rats. Something drawing their life away."

"Skye --" he said, shaking his head.

"I saw them.   I recognized Kelly.   Lily -- I never saw her before.   Looks like Aria, but eyes are greener.   Wore a long blue dress.   Short blond hair."

He blinked.   Then he looked at Sand, who hovered close by, looking anxious.   "Find out, Sand.   Go and find out about Lily and if the description matches what Skye saw.   I want to know if this is more than Skye's mind trying to trick him into believing he's found the girls."

Sand nodded. She made a port -- an obvious one that she stepped into and disappeared. I saw Barber watch with eyes wide again. That had to be a shock.

"What -- where is that thing?" I whispered.

"It thought you were dead and left," Darion said.

"It was after me," I said. Not surprised. Not shocked. Things came after me all the time.

"Apparently so since it didn't try for any of the rest of us. I'm uncertain if we can put any real reasoning to what it did, though. It was too far gone, Skye."

I wished for a better answer, but I remembered how creature kept coming for me, and I had a bad feeling that wasn't chance. "What are we going to do?" I asked, looking around the area.

"We still have a gang to deal with," Darion replied with a snarl of his own. "We can't leave them here. Skye, I want you out of this area. If that creature was aimed at you --"

"Then going somewhere else won't help," I said. "I could go off alone and be attacked. I'm safer fighting it and all the others with you. If it is aimed at me, then I want to know now, not when I'm alone. Let's see what we can do. Let's get this cleaned up before we head into more trouble."

"I saw what that thing did to you," Barber said and stared at me, his face pale still. He stepped closer. Sirens and shouts were distant now, leaving just the fae to deal with the monsters. "And I heard what Darion said before you were conscious," he said.

I looked at Darion.

"I said that what the gargoyle did is killing you," Darion said. "You already know it, so we don't have to pretend. I stopped the worst of the damage, but that other problem is still spreading some kind of poison. I can't stop it, Skye."

No, I wasn't surprised. "Let's see what we can do about the gargoyle. I can't go on with the other problem before we settle this one and getting him his damned stone might take care of the poison."

That wasn't a certainty, though. The poison was in me, magical or not, and if the gargoyle had to draw the poison back . . . well, I didn't hold out much hope.

Darion turned to Barber, who appeared ready to argue. "It's Skye's life. He understands the danger, Detective. Let's just do what we can here."

I stood, moving slowly at first because the weakness was worse than I had expected. We left the area and headed towards the building that was still stood gilded in magic. I had never seen so many fae in one place. Their magic joined to keep the creatures inside the building. The magic within the structure pulsed as I watched, almost as powerful as the fae's magic. This would be a difficult battle and one I couldn't help since I was already so weak.

"Are they all Sapphire?" I asked, waving a hand towards the fae.

"Yes. There are people from some of the other clans who will come if we need them, but for something like this, it's harder to meld magic from outside groups. Rose?"

Rose pulled out of the group, stood with her hands on her knees while she gasped before jogging a dozen steps to us.

"They're powerful, Darion," she said and glanced back at the building. "About a dozen of them is what we can find inside. I have people following the other one. It seems lost as if he has no purpose."

"Doesn't realize I'm still alive," I said.

She gave a little nod and appeared unhappy at the answer. If it learned I was alive again, then just being here was putting my companions in danger. Being anywhere else would also put someone else in danger unless I found a location alone --

That idea came from insanity, and I was glad Darion couldn't read my mind.

"What are we going to do?" Blue asked. He had a hand to his chest appeared to be almost as spent as I felt.

"Something drastic," Darion said. He stared at the building. His hand lifted as he tested out the magic. "We can't fight them, hand-to-hand. I don't want to lose any of my people any more than I wanted to lose the police."

Barber agreed with a grunt. "Can you bring down the building on them?"

"That would be acceptable?" Darion asked.

The question startled Barber as he turned to Darion. "Look, I know that you're doing the best to save lives by destroying this group -- and I know they have to be destroyed. I saw what they can do, and I'm willing to sacrifice a building that's already deserted to get them. We can't let those creatures out in the city."

"It is not -- noble to do something like this. I don't want you to think the fae kill without mercy. It is not our way. However --"

"When one came at me, I shot it and didn't stop it. I saw Skye attacked. We can't let these things loose in the city, Darion. You people are the only ones who stand a chance of stopping them, and I want you to do it in any way you can. Pull the building down if that is what it will take. There would be no nobility in risking the chance of them getting lose among people who have no protection at all."

Darion appeared relieved by the answer. I looked at the building, already trying to figure out the weak points. The old warehouse was huge and solid despite its age.

"You stay back," Darion said, tapping me on the shoulder. "We can do this one. Keep watch. Make certain nothing gets out and we don't see it."

"I can't see the back, and my magic can't go around all the rest of this power."

"We have that area covered, but I suspect if they try to get out, they'll come this way," Darion said. He looked at me.

"Because I'm here," I said and gave an odd, wild smile.
"Yes."

"Do you have any idea why?" Barber asked.

"Probably because of the magic the damned gargoyle used to mark Skye," Darion explained. "They know he is associated with the gargoyle and wants the stone back. They aren't willing to give it up."

"I can't sort the stone out from all that magic," I added.

"Neither can the rest of us," Darion admitted. "We can't get to it until we've dealt with these poor people. They're too far gone. They'll never go back to what they were. Anything else in there -- bugs, rats, bats -- we can't let them loose either. Nothing that lived this long close to the stone would be safe."

I understood how horrible that admission was for Darion. We pretended magic could fix anything, but here was magic itself gone bad and beyond repair.

The storm had grown intense, but the fae had already made a shield around the area to keep others out. No one but those of us this close would see the magic around the building. I glanced back to see the storm raging through the city and hoped the weather kept everyone in somewhere safe. Then I turned back. I had my work here, and it wasn't something Darion had given me to keep me busy. We had to make certain no one got free.

The air had filled with a hundred scents overpowering the burnt-wood magic of those we faced. The scents combined into something pungent but not unpleasant. I watched the building as the others worked. The magic in the air changed, growing oppressive like a gathering storm-within-a-storm. I shivered at so much power and the magic it represented and ignored the little tingle of pain it set off in me. Lightning played at the walls and the broken windows. The air grew heavier all around us. Barber stood beside me, his face pale and his eyes large.

The building cracked along one edge and then in several other places. I heard howls from the inside and saw something try to beat against a broken window. The magical barrier kept the creature inside and what I saw had not been human. I looked away and watched along the upper floors and the roof.

The building creaked.

A moment later the wall gave way though it didn't fall naturally as magic held out against gravity. The weight should have pushed the bricks outward, but they stood while floors within crashed downward. I saw Darion give a wave of his hand and the walls shuddered and gave way as they caved inward and down so fast and hard that the ground shook all around us, and other buildings protested with loud creaks.

The magic died, including the shield, as the fae swarmed forward and into the debris. Nothing would survive, no matter how powerful it might be.

The winter wind swept in around us, snow falling harder again. This was a long, cold winter.

Darion crossed to where Barber and I stood. He sat on the ground, right there in the snow and ice and looked no better than I did.

"We'll have . . . have this done soon," he mumbled. "I don't want to leave until we're certain everything we've handled everything, and the debris is safe. Rest, Skye."

I settled at the edge of a building that still dropped dust around us but seemed steady enough. I was a little more out of the snow than him. Barber leaned against the building beside me. He stared at the ruins of the building, shaking his head.

"That was a damned lot of power," he said looking at Darion.

"Yes," Darion agreed. "A lot more magic than we ordinarily use in any circumstances, Detective. It's difficult for us to kill."

I don't know if the detective believed or not and I didn't care. I was cold and tired, and I wanted this done. But --

"The stone?" I asked.

"They're searching for it," Darion said and looked

bothered. "If it's there, we'll find the damned thing."

I looked at the ruins, feeling a new chill. "I don't think it's there."

Darion sighed with more worry than disbelief. "I know. Once the other things had died, we should have sensed the stone. They reeked of the stone's magic, but they're gone, and I still can't find it. I hope it's only because I'm weak."

"We don't have much time," Blue said as he came to rest with us. "The humans are coming to see the building."

"Damn," Darion whispered. He stood again and waved his hand, his eyes closed, and the power he sent out filling the air with light. The magic swept in over the building and into the crumbled walls while Darion held his breath, his face going pale and his arm trembling. I was ready to step in and make him stop when he lowered his arm and took several deep breaths again.

"Blue, tell the others to remove the bodies. We have to go. The stone isn't here," Darion said with a snarl that came close to rage. "It's not here, and it wasn't on the other one who attacked Skye. Where the hell is it?"

Darion angry was not something I had ever wanted to see. He was powerful, even for a fae -- but he usually had good control of his emotions. I wanted him to calm, but I said nothing since I couldn't be any less angry than he was.

"Something is playing games with me." I looked up at the surrounding roofs. "Where the hell is the gargoyle?"

"Not here," Blue replied with a glare of his own. "And I would have thought this was where he would want to be if we were close to the stone."

"Unless he knew we weren't. Why can't he find his

own stone of power?" I asked again and won a curt nod from Blue. There was more to this than what the gargoyle had pretended, and I didn't like being part of his game.

"We need answers. We need rest. We need --" Darion stood and took a couple faltering steps and then accepted Sand's help when it looked as though he might fall. "We need to go back to Cherry's apartment and rethink this mess."

Barber offered to give Darion, Blue and me a ride back to the truck which was a kindness since we couldn't have walked that far. We said little through the ride though Darion had magical messages passing to him every couple minutes. The storm was dropping a lot more snow, and I was the one who helped get Barber's car through the mess. We should all be worried when I was the one with any power to spare. Darion kept contact with the others, but he shook his head and I knew there was nothing new that came from it.

We had spent a long, dangerous night and as far as I could tell, we were no closer to finding any sign of the stone and as far from finding my two sisters.

The Gargoyle was waiting for us by the truck. I cursed and got out of the car to deal with him, but Blue caught me by the arm and wouldn't let me go closer.

"You did not find the stone," the creature growled and leaned towards me.

"It's your stone.   Why can't you find it?" Darion demanded.

"I do not speak with you --"

Darion was angry already and tired of this attitude. He had just put his own people in danger for this creature.

We'd done well to wipe out the mutated gang, but since we hadn't found the stone there, we might have to relive this battle.

I didn't think Darion had any magic left, but he proved me wrong. He reached out and grabbed the gargoyle with a rope of magic and threw it against the truck so hard that it dented the fender. The creature even grunted in shock and pain.

"Do I have your attention now?" Darion demanded and didn't let go of the magic. "I just had to kill a dozen humans tainted with your stone. I'm involved. All of the fae are involved. You *will* tell me why you can't find your own stone."

"Why do you aid it?" the gargoyle demanded, golden eyes flashing towards me. Did I see a little surprise and consternation there? "It is not one of you."

"That's none of your concern." Darion shoved the gargoyle back again when it started to straighten. "Why can't you find your stone?"

The gargoyle growled and tore free before taking a swing at Darion. Blue was ready and knocked the creature aside with enough force that it hit the building and cracked bricks. With a snarl of frustration and anger, the gargoyle leapt and took back to the sky.

"He will not be any happier next time we meet," I said, watching him disappear past the flurry of white flakes and up into the dark sky.

"No, but he will tell me why he can't find the stone," Darion said. He leaned against the truck, gasping and exhausted. "I have had enough of whatever game he's playing."

I didn't doubt him and hoped the gargoyle gave us an answer that would help.

CHAPTER TWELVE

Barber followed us back to Cherry's apartment. I wondered what he thought and if one of us should have ridden with him. Maybe not. Maybe it was best to let him have personal time, alone without a fae to bother him.

I drove the truck. I wasn't in the best of shape, but the other two were worse. Blue kept growing paler with every bump and Darion had slipped to the side with his head against the back of the seat and was asleep or unconscious. I said nothing at all on the long, treacherous drive.

I had plenty to think about, like stones that were not where they should have been, monsters coming after me for no good reasons, and two young girls missing and I feared sitting in a dark dungeon while a creature dragged power from them that appeared to be directed at one source.

Me.

I liked no part of this mess. I wanted to destroy my enemy -- and that wasn't possible because I had no idea what I faced. I needed the help of people like Darion and Blue and all the rest of Sapphire clan because I couldn't even find the enemy.

Or I could let whatever was behind this take me and be done with the entire mess, but that wasn't a reasonable answer. I'd learned that much from the trouble with Earis Ruby Day. She had wanted me, too. I am unique and a source of power no one else has, and though that power has never helped me much, I couldn't simply give it over to others.

Could I kill myself? Would that make it stop? If I did, I would never know if my actions saved the girls or not. I wanted real answers, not desperate hopes.

I pulled into Cherry's parking lot and looked around, wondering where the gargoyle was this time. If he showed up, Darion was in no shape to take the creature on, and neither was Blue. Detective Barber and his gun might be a better hope. Barber had pulled up beside us and was already getting out of the car despite the cold, miserable weather. Maybe his heater didn't work, and he was anxious to get up to the apartment. Maybe he wanted cookies.

I turned the car off and eased the door open. Blue slid out of the other side and kept on sliding down, too. Barber had reached him before I did as Cherry hurried down the steps. I worried about what her neighbors might see, but it was snowing, it was late, and I really couldn't care very much.

Darion woke up when the cold wind slapped him in the face. Good. Cherry would have panicked if he hadn't come out on his own. He seemed glad enough for her help as they went up the stairs, though. Barber had Blue in hand, and I followed behind, ready to do whatever I had to do if the gargoyle, or anything else, showed up before we got inside the apartment.

We reached the door without a problem and stepped past the wards and into the warmth and safety of Cherry's home. I closed the door and made certain the ward was in place. It wouldn't keep the gargoyle out, but it might keep some of the other things at bay for a while. There was still something after me if it realized I was alive.

"The others?" Cherry asked as though she was afraid to say the words.

"All right. They're cleaning things up," Darion said. He dropped onto the sofa and pulled her down with him. "We had to pull a building down on the people to destroy them. There was no other way. They were too far gone."

She looked startled by the words. Then she pulled Darion close to her. She understood how being forced to kill bothered him. Barber got Blue to the chair. I went to the kitchen and made tea. I couldn't be still. My mind swarmed with everything that had happened, and I felt the damned uselessness of it all. I needed to do something, so I concentrated on the tea.

"It's settled then," Cherry said.

"The stone wasn't there," I answered, coming back to the doorway.

"Sit down!" She got to her feet, worried. "You're bleeding!"

I looked down and saw she was right. The wound didn't particularly hurt, though --

Then I wondered if that wasn't still the magic Darion
had used earlier to help me gain a little more strength. I
headed to the bathroom to clean up, but Cherry caught
hold of me and took me back to the kitchen. Barber came
with us. He still looked lost and worried. I felt sorry for
him.

"Sit down," Cherry ordered again. "Both of you sit
down. Hell, Skye. What are you going to do now?"

"I don't know. I really don't," I said and dropped into
the chair and let Cherry fuss with me because her actions
were distracting and I needed that right now. She didn't
tell me to take the shirt off, at least. I couldn't have done
that in front of Barber, even having explained what I was . .
. and wasn't. "I want to tell the gargoyle to go to hell, but it
would still leave the damned stone out there, somewhere. I
want to find the girls, but I'm not any closer to them."

"We'll hear from Sand soon," Darion said. He limped
to the edge of the kitchen, paused there to catch his breath,
and then settled on the chair by Barber. "If those
nightmares are real, then we have a link at least. I don't like
the way it keeps grabbing at you, but even that makes sense
if taking the two is aimed at you."

"This couldn't be aimed at anyone else?" I winced as
Cherry brushed a cloth over my neck. I took it from her
and took care of the rest myself. "No, it's all right, Cherry."

I felt self-conscious with Barber there. I also wanted
to believe that all the bad things happening were not my
fault.

"Something is not right," Darion said. "Emerald
House should have been able to find Lily without a
problem, even if someone had killed her, no matter what

realm she'd gone to. Blood calls to blood."

The words struck me like a knife. I cried out -- and in the next moment, I was back with the girls. Oh hell, I knew beyond a doubt this was a true scene this time, and something pulled me here for a reason - and it wasn't to help them. The two girls sat huddled as close together as they could manage with the chains that held them. Magic played over their bodies, and I saw they were both weaker than they had been the last time I saw them, only a few hours ago.

"Skye," Kelly whimpered. "Skye -- stop her!"

I tried to reach out, but something held me back. I resisted being pulled away from the scene this time, even when I saw a tendril of the magic coming for me. I knew if it got me I would not leave again. Even so, I wouldn't abandon them.

"Skye! Help us!"

Cherry's voice! The panic I heard in her words yanked me back to the apartment. I would never turn my back on the one person who had always helped me.

I was on the floor.

A gunshot had fired before I realized there was trouble. In the short time I had slipped away, not only had the gargoyle come through the door but so had three creatures that had once been human.

They came *with* him.

And he had the stone of power in the staff he carried.

Used us. I don't understand what he had hoped to get out of his game and what purpose we had served. Did he come to kill us now because he no longer needed us? The reminder of the time he had wasted while my two half-sisters suffered gave me strength, but the rage stopped any coherent thoughts except to attack. I kicked the legs out from under one creature and threw fire into its eyes, blinding him. I didn't have a weapon except for what magic I could create.

Darion was trying to call for help, but as weak he was, the message couldn't reach the Clan House. I panicked, and I did something drastic. I caught hold of his magic and almost ripped the spell from Darion as I fed my power into it, and sent the message off so strong and loud that I thought everyone in the city would hear the cry for help.

That much magic work put me back down, but others arrived before I got back to my feet. Sand appeared first, but she was barely ahead of a couple dozen others, who swarmed in and grabbed the things that had once been human. The gargoyle howled and retreated but I saw someone following him and hoped that meant we would be done with that trouble. I can't say what happened to the once-humans. When I looked up again, the fae had taken them away.

I went back to my knees and then down on the floor with my head against the cool tiles. I didn't want to move. I didn't want to think.

"Careful with him," Peren said. His was a welcome voice though not the movement that came with it. "To the sofa. He's not too bad, just worn out. Sit down, Darion, before you fall down as well."

Someone lifted me, but I couldn't get my eyes to open. Once on the sofa, I wanted to slip away again, but I was suddenly afraid. Something had pulled me to the girls, and then the gargoyle had attacked the others. I didn't want to be helpless again, or to put the others in danger, either.

I opened my eyes just as Peren brushed a hand over my chest. The pain of the wounds eased again. The next breath came easier.

"There you are," he said with a nod. He looked grave. Cherry sat on the edge of the chair across from me. Darion stood beside her. They both looked pale and upset.

"What happened?" I looked into their bleak faces. "What's wrong?"

"Rose is dead," Darion said after a moment of silence. "One of the things broke her neck. We couldn't save her. Blue -- they took Blue back to our lands and hope to help him."

"No." I felt the loss of Rose, who had always been kind to me. The pain of loss doubled as I feared to lose Blue. "Why? What is going on?"

"We're trying to find out, Skye," Peren said. He helped me sit up and then settled on the sofa beside me. "The other clans have realized the importance of this battle. Although much of what is happening is aimed at you, without a doubt, it isn't only about you. We are all involved, and would have been anyway, with a fae child taken from her home. The gargoyle's involvement must be part of this as well since it appears he fabricated everything he told us about the stone."

"I am sorry," I said with a shake of my head. "I don't understand what is going on --"

"You have no guilt in what has happened. I sensed that emotion in you, Skye. This is not your fault."

I tried to believe what he said, but there had been too much death tonight with me the focus of what was happening. I still had no idea what to do. Darion, who probably felt as guilty as I did, lifted his head.

"We will find those responsible," he said.

I never doubted him.

CHAPTER THIRTEEN

We were not long in waiting for answers. Peren had been right about one important fact: all the fae world had taken up this battle as their own. Peren said they sided with us because this was about both the disappearance of a fae child and about the behavior of the gargoyle. The combination was enough to worry them all, and even Topaz was out checking into things along the edge of the gargoyle lands. I saw a rainbow array of rings on the hands of people who passed through the apartment over the next two hours though I did my best to stay out of the way and go unseen. The enormity of the problem became apparent when I realized they were ignoring me.

The news about Blue sounded hopeful which at least eased some of the fears I had been feeling. Aria arrived later and sat on the sofa where I had been resting -- Peren's orders still -- and nodded.

"I heard you were looking for a description of Lily and

that you thought you had seen her in some vision?"

"Yes. She and Kelly both, together. But we can't tell if what I saw was real for if this was something my mind created out of frustration at not finding answers. I think it's real, though, Aria."

She nodded and lifted a hand: a little image appeared there for me to see. She was wearing a different dress, but it was her.

"Yes, that's the girl I saw, except she wore a blue dress and her hair is shorter now."

"You're right. I was testing," Aria said. She looked hopeful. "Good. We have a link."

"We just have to keep Skye from getting killed to follow it," Darion replied. He looked much better. Cherry was baking a cake. She had to be very worried by now. Her place of refuge still wasn't safe as long as I was here because the gargoyle and his followers could use me to get past the ward. I knew there was no use saying I needed to go somewhere else, though. At least Cherry had a house full of people to help keep her from harm.

"We have to get them out," I said. "Whatever had hold of them is using magic to drain them and that apparently creates a spell that draws me. What is happening to them is slow and frightening, and I *will not* leave those two girls to suffer like that just because something wants to get hold of me."

The last thing I had expected was for Aria to reach over and take me into an embrace. In fact, I thought she was about to kill me herself, and I had almost jerked away before I realized what was happening. She left me more confused when she pulled back and looked into my eyes. I hadn't realized until then, but we both had the same green eyes, a sign of family ties that had only been words before this.

"It's not fae magic that's doing this," Darion said. He was talking to Donal, but he looked at me and nodded. "If it was fae magic, we could have done something by now. I can't get a trace on what has hold of Skye which means I can't come up with a spell to counter the magic. I can ease the power, and I can protect you somewhat, but I can't trace the path the power is taking to and from you."

"You people really don't know what's going on much more than I do, do you?" Barber asked, standing in the doorway to the kitchen. He had a bruise on the side of his face and had injured his arm. He didn't make those words an accusation. I heard surprise instead. "Skye, I sometimes get the suspect you don't even know what they're talking about."

"That's true too often," I confessed. "I was born on this side, and I never trained by the fae, so most of what I have learned has come in the last few months, and from Darion."

"But you knew about the fae."

"Oh yes," I said. I looked at Aria. "I had even met a few."

She made a sound somewhere between amusement and annoyance. Our first meeting had not been good. She'd kicked and broken a rib. The second time she stabbed me. I didn't bring those incidents up, though I thought I should avoid relatives with knives at hand in the future.

"What do we do now?" Barber asked. How odd that

he had joined with us so easily, though I suppose after what he'd seen, it was far easier to accept than to deny.

"We wait a little longer. Not too long," Darion said before I protested. "We are running out of time."

Cherry brought us chicken salad sandwiches. I had never been good at waiting, and that's part of why I became a detective so I could do things and keep working until I found answers. I didn't have to wait for others to find them for me.

Sand arrived just a little later. She looked around the group -- which was only about eight of us now -- and nodded.

"I was delayed by the Queen of the Fae," she said as she sat on the edge of the sofa by me. "She wanted to know what I could tell her, and it paid off. She asked the old ones to help, and they were glad to give aid to Skye. The word is that the magic that took the children is not human-made though it came from this realm. The Queen is hoping for more of an answer, but for now, that's a start."

We had expected human magic, but now Darion frowned and leaned forward, a hand lifted towards me as he tested the magic again. The hint of power brushed up over me, soft and a little intrusive, but I tried to not fight it aside, which was instinctive for me.

"If this isn't human made, then there should be a touch of something outside in it, something that doesn't belong here. The magic is subtle," Darion admitted. He shook his head and leaned back. "I like this less and less, but at least we can believe it is not a human with magic, which would have been worse."

"What's wrong with humans and magic?" Barber dared

to ask, one of the two humans in the room. Fae turned toward him, frowning. Most of them looked at Darion as though none of them knew what to say.

Or was it only because he was the ranking fae in the room? Barber, who was an ally, had asked an important question, and something Darion would be expected to answer as Sapphire House Ambassador. This was part of his job.

"Humans have to seek magic, detective," Darion explained. "They can sometimes stumble across the power, but even then they have to work to learn it, and they rarely do so for good reasons."

"Oh hell." I looked back at Darion and as a new wave of fear come over me. Darion noticed and looked worried. "Ian said that my mother had been reading books on voodoo and stuff."

Darion looked startled. Then he brushed magic over me once more. The tendrils of his magic carefully tested strands of the magic if found in me.

He sat back and nodded, his face grim. "I think that might be right, the Gods help us all. This might be, in part, the work of your mother. You are of her blood, and the magic she used is too close to your own signature to sort out. Hell, Skye. I don't know what to do now. We can't go to her and ask what she's involved in."

"And how did she get Lily? She can't be working by herself," Aria added. She sounded angry and looked my way, frowning. "You have been unlucky in your parents, Skye. I do not know how the two got together since they are both so blind to anything but their own wants and needs."

I agreed. "How can we be certain it's her? And if it is, what can we do?"

"We need to make certain of the first answer," Darion said. "That will be difficult enough. We must be careful. She might do anything if she learns there are fae watching her."

"And the tie to Skye makes this more dangerous," Sand added. "If she is working with magic, she might be able to sense when Skye is near, especially since this spell is aimed at him."

"And that would put the girls in more danger," I said, realizing what they were saying. "If she feared she was about to be found out she might do something drastic."

"She would kill them?" Sand asked softly.

"She is already killing them," I reminded her. They couldn't feel it as I did, so maybe they didn't understand. "The spell is drawing the life out of them to feed the spell that draws me to them. If this is her work, she might have allies including the gargoyle."

"Gargoyles would not work with humans," Peren said. "I suspect that part might be something else entirely. I can't believe that one as hostile as we faced would willingly work with a human on some wild scheme."

"I hate the idea that she would do this to her own daughter," Darion said.

"She has done horrible things to Skye," Cherry pointed out.

"But I am a unique case," I reminded her. Sometimes Cherry forgets.

"That makes no difference," she said and then shook her head before I could speak. "No, it really doesn't. You are her child. If she can treat you this way, I fear it's not much of a leap to do the same with Kelly if she told herself she had a reason."

"I watched them in the mirror," I said and regretted bringing up that moment because even I heard the hint of longing in my voice.

"Skye?" Darion said, looking troubled this time.

"I watched them in the mirror," I repeated and tried to control my own emotions this time. "Kelly was getting ready for school and my mother came in. For a moment, they looked like a typical mother and daughter. I saw everything I had never been. But —" I stopped and focused my thoughts elsewhere on that scene. The others remained silent. "But the moment Kelly walked away, she changed as though she dropped a mask she had been wearing, and there was nothing but cold, calculation in her stare. We can't judge her from that single look, but it was the morning Kelly disappeared."

"How are we going to get anyone close enough to find out the truth?" Sand asked. She looked more bothered than when she had first arrived. We might have a viable target to check, this wouldn't be easy. "How can we find out what she's doing and who she has contact with? We can't even get close to her —"

"I can," Barber said, stepping forward from the kitchen. "I can get her to trust me, too, if I hint I believe Skye is involved Kelly's disappearance. I've seen people like this before, you know. Not the magic part, but the rest fits the profile. I learned how to manipulate them."

"Can this help?" Cherry asked. "You don't have magic to test what she might be doing."

"He can help," Darion said. He looked hopeful again, and I held back my own protests, which came mostly from my fear of her. "I can create something small and subtle so we can keep track of her and hear what she's doing."

Other fae agreed. I wasn't certain what I felt, but I nodded agreement anyway.   The others got to work, which gave me hope. I watched Darion pull at a string on his shirt. At first, I thought it was nervousness, which worried me, but then I realized, from the care he took, that he did this for a reason. He looked at me and nodded.

"Cloth woven in the fae lands," he said and held up the long string. "It already has a little magic embedded in the structure, so that will make the rest of the work easier."

The string was only as long as his hand, dark blue and thin. He held it in his right hand and ran the left over it. A tiny trail of bright lights followed his touch, and I heard Barber make a little sound of surprise; magic was still very new to him.

"I need something from you, Skye," he said and looked bothered. "A little blood – just a drop, so I can key this to her. Since you are of her blood, that will reinforce the link."

I nodded. "Easy enough." I reached inside my shirt and tapped a finger at bandages. Aria looked troubled by my move. Darion ran the magical thread over my finger and nodded. He broke the thread in half and put part of it in his pocket. He held the other half out to Detective Barber.

"Place this on her and we'll be able to hear her and follow where she goes for the next few hours. We may have to do this again tomorrow if she does nothing tonight because the magic will burn the thread out. However, as long as she trusts you, this shouldn't be a problem."

"She'll trust me." Barber gingerly took the piece of thread and put it into his own pocket. "Let's do this now."

"We won't be far behind you," Darion said. "Let's go. We need to do this now, because if Skye's mother isn't involved, then we need to turn our attention somewhere else, wherever that may be."

We all felt time running out.

"Sand, I want your help. And you come with us, Cherry," Darion said, surprising us both. "I can't say the apartment is safe. The rest of you go back to fae and find out all you can. We need answers. I fear that even if Skye's mother is involved, finding the girls will not be simple."

Others nodded. Someone formed a portal, and a few were preparing to go back to the fae lands. I saw Aria grab cookies on her way which made me smile despite the situation. Cherry headed for the door and grabbed her coat and then handed me mine.

I didn't have to tell Darion that the draw to the girls was stronger now and that I didn't dare rest at all for fear I would not come back.

CHAPTER FOURTEEN

I had gotten used to having Blue with us and looking at Sand made me worry all the more about him. I hoped he was doing all right. The four of us rode in the truck, not particularly crowded – fae magic again, no matter what the car looked like on the outside. Detective Barber drove his own car and cruised along almost half a mile down the road in front of us. We had no trouble keeping him in sight since there was no other traffic on the streets tonight. Darion had made certain the man's car wouldn't bog down in the newly fallen snow. I suspected he would like that new feature, and Darion wouldn't take it away again.

We stopped a couple blocks back from the house and watched as Detective Barber pulled into the driveway. Darion made certain no one detected us, and he put the entire truck under a shield.

"Nothing obvious here," he said after checking the

area for magic. "I don't know what to expect. I half want it to be her, Skye."

"So do I. I want this done, and she is at least an answer. Without her, we have nothing to go on. Time is running out; I can feel it."

"What will happen?" Cherry asked with a bare whisper of sound.

Darion looked at me. I knew the answer. I had sensed the magic eating at me through the last couple days, first when Kelly disappeared and then, even stronger after Lily disappeared.

"The girls will die," I said. "And then I will. I'll be linked too closely to them, and I'll be pulled in with them."

Cherry grabbed hold of my arm, looking frightened for the first time. It would have been crueler not to tell her, but I hated upsetting her.

"Can't you protect Skye?" she asked, looking at Darion. "Can't you put her somewhere safe?"

"Yes," Darion said. He glanced at me and then back at Cherry, and he didn't even need to hear what I would say. "I could take Skye over to the fae lands with a shield around her that no human magic could break through."

"Then why not --"

"I would be trapped there for a long, long time. Spells linger when they can't find a proper end. *And the girls would die.*"

"The others might get to them first and could do something --" She caught her breath, and I put my hand over hers where the fingers had gripped my arm.

"The girls *will die* if I don't help, Cherry. I know they will. It's a fae sort of thing, to feel along a line of reality and understand what your choices will do. I've known this from the start, probably before Darion even realized the full extent of what was happening. The girls will die if I step away. There's no doubt at all. I couldn't live with that, Cherry, knowing I had backed away and let them be killed when I might have saved them."

"Might have. You don't know?"

"Not clearly. I have a chance, and I have to take it."

"I'll do everything I can to help Skye," Darion added, his voice soft as he stared out into the night. Sand nodded as well though she looked as worried and frightened as Cherry. I wondered why she cared so much. "This is the first step. If Tay isn't involved, we'll find another answer."

"He's going inside," Sand said.

I squinted through the dark towards the house where a porch light brightened the dreary night. The detective stepped inside, and I hated the thought of him in *that house*. My feeling towards the place had dramatically changed in the last couple days. This was not *home* in any form I recognized anymore. I was better for having let go.

We waited. I tried not to get anxious --

"There," Darion said, lifting the thread which moved and pointed towards the house. "He's placed the thread. We should hear --"

"I'm not sure what you think I can tell you," my mother said, her voice sharp and far too clear, as though she stood right before us. "I have answered everything for the police, and where has it gotten me so far? Where is my daughter, Detective Barber?"

"I'm not sure, but I have a hunch someone knows." A pause, the sound of paper as he prepared to write notes.

"Tell me about Skye."

I heard the hiss like the sound of a movie snake. She was putting on quite a show. "Skye is evil. Skye is involved in things that are dangerous to the rest of us, and I know it is part of the disappearance of my daughter."

"I fear you might be right," Barber agreed. "I mistrust Skye. He's hiding something --"

"*She.*"

"She? Well, there's another point against her, then. I thought she was male. And I don't much care for some of her companions, either. They all are hiding something."

"Sit down, Detective. I'll tell you everything I can. It's not a pleasant picture, I fear. Would you like coffee?"

"No, thank you."

I heard chairs moving. They were in the kitchen. The rest of the house was silent, and I suspected Ian and the children still weren't home. Good. I didn't want the children to hear any more tales about me.

"Skye -- Skye was cruel as a child. We didn't dare let her go to school with others because she liked to hurt things. She killed any pet we got. It's why her father and I broke up. I wanted to protect her and hope she got better, but he wanted her locked away. I fear he was right, and I was a fool to believe that a mother's love could make a difference."

She sniffed.

"Lying bitch," Cherry growled. She glared at the house snarling as though ready to leap out and attack something. I was glad she didn't have any power of her own. Darion was no better than Cherry, and he did have the magic to do something about it.

"Calm," I said. "Let's all be calm."

"How can you sit here and listen to her say those things!" Cherry demanded with her hands in fists.

"Because I know they're not true and with everything she says, she's getting closer to Barber. I don't care what she says, Cherry."

"You have other children. Didn't you fear for them?" Barber asked.

"I thought she had outgrown her problems and having other children would help. Or maybe I just wanted a *real* child that I could love without fear."

That much was probably the truth.

"Did it work?"

"For a while. But it -- she was jealous. I didn't dare leave the children alone with her. She would destroy their toys, and she would hit them, but I always caught her in time. I dared not leave her alone for more than a couple minutes at a time, day or night -- for years, Detective. For years, I devoted every moment to her and making certain she hurt nothing. It was only when she got involved with Satanists that I finally had to be rid of her. I asked her to leave. I gave her money to do so rather than turn her out. She left for a long time, off with those evil creatures she calls friends. But now she's back, and no sooner returned than my poor Kelly disappears! It is not a coincidence!"

"I suspected it isn't," Barber said.

"I fear -- I fear for Kelly," she said, and though her voice trembled, the tone was not one of fear. I caught the hint of barely controlled excitement as Barber listened to the tale she wanted to present to others. No one had listened until now, I suspected. She could never have told this to Ian. "I fear that Skye has already killed her, or else she and her friends are planning to kill her in one of their wicked, evil sacrifices."

"Do you know anything more about these people? Any links to them at all?"

"Ask my niece, Cherry. She's in with them. She was always a willful girl, too. Oh, her parents and sisters try to cover it up, but I fear she and Skye had far too much in common. There is bad blood somewhere in the family's past."

"I've met Cherry. She was not forthcoming on a few things."

"See!"

They continued to talk for another half an hour, my mother's voice becoming more strident with every mention of me, and her stories of my past becoming increasingly more elaborate. I listened with a shake of my head, and even Cherry had traded her anger for amazement at the lies. Darion still looked angry.

In a few more minutes Detective Barber said goodbye to my mother with a promise to keep her informed on anything about me.

He got into his car and drove away. We followed and pulled into the parking lot of a small, nearly empty strip mall. Barber hurried out of his car, slamming the door closed. He came over to the truck, and Sand let him in as Darion did a little wave of his hand and created a full backseat that hadn't been there until now. He looked a little drained by it -- not that easy! -- but the extra room helped. Otherwise, we would have all been standing out in the cold.

"I should have suspected her long before now," Barber said, startling me with his first words.

"You don't believe her --" I started.

"Hell no, of course not. Even if I hadn't met you, Skye, I still wouldn't have believed her after that last hour. She needs to work on her lying skills. First, she tells me how she never dared let you out of her sight, not for years. Day and night she devoted herself to making certain you hurt nothing and no one. And in the next sentence, she tells me how you got involved with Satanists. What? Did she introduce you to them?"

"Oh. Well." I took a deeper breath. "Never mind. That's old baggage of mine. But you suspect she's involved?"

"Yes. Skye, if I had been paying attention to her, I would have seen something was wrong from the start. Your mother has always been more concerned with turning people against you than she is with finding Kelly. Even tonight, what was the last thing she wanted from me?"

"To know anything you learn about Skye," Cherry said. She nodded. "She's not worried about Kelly at all."

"That doesn't mean she's the one, though," I said. "It just means she's not a very good mother."

"Well, that's true enough," Barber conceded. He sat back and frowned. "But Skye -- my gut instinct, which comes with being so many years on the force and a detective, says she's the one. What do we do now?"

"It would explain why every time she said I was involved it felt like the truth," I admitted. "It would be -- if she had drawn me into it herself, she knew I was involved, even if I didn't."

"She's on the move," Darion said. He held up the string. A car started and the string waver a little and point in another direction. "I hope we've nudged her enough that we'll learn something."

"Where were Ian and the kids?" I asked.

"She said they went to stay with his parents for a while, so the kids would be safe. I wonder if he did just that to keep them safe from her."

"Oh," Cherry said. "He knows now what she did to Skye, and he fears she did something with Kelly. God, this has to be a nightmare for all her children -- including you, Skye."

"I, at least, can help," I said.

She nodded.

A sudden pain in my side nearly doubled me over. Cherry caught hold of me and pulled me back, and Sand did something with magic which helped a little, but I caught her arm and stopped her from doing more.

"Save your magic," I warned. "Don't waste it. We'll need all the magic we can get soon."

"Skye?" Cherry whispered.

"I'll be okay."

I lied, of course. She pulled me into her arms, and I rested there, trying to conserve my strength now. Darion had pulled out of the parking lot, the string held in one hand as he drove. I didn't even care where we were going. For a while, I had trouble breathing, and I didn't want the others to realize.

We drove to the library. She parked, and I feared she would go in and --

"Library is closed," Sand said. "What is she doing

here?"

That drew my attention. I lifted my head and watched. Darion had never taken the shield off, so I didn't need to worry about her noticing us. Darion turned around at the next corner and came back. By then she had gotten out of the car, pulled her coat tight, and walked away with brisk, purposeful steps down the sidewalk.

"I wonder where she's heading," Barber said, leaning forward.

"If she's going towards something magical, we dare not follow too closely in the truck," Darion said. He pulled over and stopped. We might soon go out into the cold, and I was already dreading it. I tried not to shiver. "I hope that the string won't be enough to draw attention, wherever she goes."

We sat in silence, listening to her steps on the sidewalk. Darion moved the car forward a block while Sand tested out the area for magic. She found nothing which made no sense, especially since my mother was heading into an area known more for its porn shops and bar fights rather than the 'upper class' world she frequented. There were catcalls as she passed, and she cursed a little under her breath.

"They will pay when I'm done," she whispered once. "They'll all pay."

That was such an odd statement. I didn't trust this woman at all, and the more I listened to her, the more I became convinced of her involvement in something horrible that might go beyond the disappearance of her daughter. I heard the emotions in her voice and the pure hatred like she was driving knives into me with each step --

"Skye -- we need to get you someplace you can rest,"

Sand said.

"No. No." I put more power into those words and sat up straighter. Darion was moving the truck closer to her again. We passed by a bar where men huddled, looking for trouble. Why hadn't gone after her? Did they sense she wasn't someone to mess with--?

And suddenly the string dropped.

"What the hell?" Darion said.

He pulled over at the corner of a lot where the outline of a building, burnt down long ago, stood among the weeds. There had been destroyed buildings on almost every block, along with boarded up businesses that would never be resurrected. This wasn't a location for urban renewal.

Darion held up the string and frowned.

"Did it fall off her?" Sand asked.

"It shouldn't have," he said. "I made a strong magnet." He lifted fingers and brushed magic out ahead of us. "No, it didn't fall; it isn't out there. Gone. And I find no trace of Tay Fairbanks, either."

"No magic near here that I can find," Sand added. "Except a hint of something human that's not far away, but not enough to have any real influence."

"Safe to drive on?" Darion asked.

"Safe?" Sand said. "I don't know. The woman and the magic string just disappeared. Who knows what might happen to us? But we'll never know by sitting here."

"True." Darion pulled out and started forward again, inching the invisible truck through the snow covered road. Even the new snow hadn't kept the people from coming here. Addicted to this way of life. Addicted to the liquor and the sleaze, and nothing better to do with their lives. I couldn't make myself care about what they did. I wanted to find the girls. We had so little time.

I tasted blood in my mouth.

We found nothing in the next block. Even Sand lost the hint of human magic which might have been something normal. Little things happen around humans sometimes. She got out of the truck and went off on foot while we patrolled. Nothing. No sign of my mother, no sign of magic: we found nothing but cold and winter, and chills that came from fears and pains that were not all my own.

"She has to be here," Darion whispered as he turned around again.

We drove past boarded-up shops and a brothel where a woman stood outside dressed as though she never felt the cold at all. Barber made a slight sound, and at another time -- but not tonight. We had other worries.

We picked Sand up at the next corner, and she hurried into the still invisible truck. I saw a drunk coming out of a bar, stare as though he thought he had seen something, and then shuffle away again. It would have been amusing at another time.

"Not a damned thing at all," Sand said.

I lifted my hand. "I have the link to the girls. If I let myself go --"

"No, Skye," Darion said. He caught my arm and reinforced those words with an unexpected surge of magic that blocked part of the draw that had already tried to take me. I snarled in frustration, but he shook me, getting my attention. "*No.* Don't try to do that. It won't help. They want you there for a reason, Skye. Probably not to directly kill you, because that would have been easy compared to this. I don't know what your mother is involved in, but this goes far beyond her hatred of your father and you."

I blinked. "Oh. I suppose so. Gods, my head is pounding. It's hard to think."

"I know. But the only way you could go to the girls is by letting them into your mind and drawing you away. We couldn't follow. It takes your soul, your essence, and I can't latch onto it and hitch a ride with you. So we need to do this the hard way, my friend. And I'm sorry."

"Where is she?" I asked. "She has to be here somewhere."

And the string suddenly lifted.

"At midnight," a voice growled. "Return at midnight."

A door closed.

By the time we found her, she was almost back to her car. We didn't know where she had been, though we had a little better idea of the area. As she drove away, she turned on the music in the car and whistled along with classical stuff and in a good mood. Darion dulled the sound to a whisper.

"She is working with someone," I said. We had confirmation this time. "That makes the situation worse."

"We have to do more than just stop her," Darion agreed. "There is more going on, but we suspected as much. And now we have a timeframe -- and an area."

"Except she disappeared once already," Sand said. "We can't guarantee we'll do any better at midnight since we don't dare stay too close to her. There has to be magic, even if we can't find it."

"She's happy," Cherry added. "I don't like that she's so

happy."

"Maybe she scored some drugs," Barber suggested. "That could explain -- well, everything but her disappearing, I suppose."

"Right," Darion said. He had followed her but stopped the truck and pulled over, leaning back as he stared into the night. "She's heading for home. We need to stay here. We need to find something --"

"I couldn't find anything, Darion," Sand said. She sounded apologetic. "Perhaps someone else who is better with magic --"

"No. You would have located anything out of place. Even in this car, we should have found something." He stared at the string and then pushed it into his pocket. "I sensed nothing either, you know. At least we have an area, but we need more."

"We found Anna Cheshire not far from here," Barber said.

I looked at him frowning a little. The name meant nothing to me.

"She was the girl we found, the one you had learned about when you were out looking for Kelly. Locals found her about four blocks from here, down near the lake. We could tell from her wounds that someone had chained her up somewhere, but she was so far gone that we can't get --"

"Where is she?" Darion asked as he started the truck moving again. "Maybe she can help. Or maybe we can just help her. It's worth a try."

Barber directed us to a hospital that wasn't too far away. I didn't want to go. I wanted to get out and find Kelly and Lily.

"Midnight is only four hours away," I whispered.

Darion nodded and said nothing at all.

Chapter Fifteen

I balked at going into the hospital with the others. I have an absolute phobia of them and of doctors, and it's not an irrational fear, either. A few years ago people got hold of me. They knew what they were doing as they studied me. I survived, barely. They wanted to know what I was and how pain affected me -- and it makes me sick just thinking about what happened.

"I'll keep you safe," Darion promised and urged me towards the sliding door. The words surprised Barber, who looked at me with another frown but this wasn't the time to talk about my fears. "We can't leave you out here, Skye. We need you close by at all times because I'm the only one with enough power to keep you from being yanked to where we least want you to go."

I shook my head, trembling with the new layer of fear. "I can't go in there --"

"We're doing this for Kelly and Lily. We'll be as quick

as we can."

I took another breath, protests dying before I said more. The others followed us. Everyone was worn from too many days of chasing after this problem and not finding any answers. I bowed my head and walked with the four of them up into the building that smelled of death and pain and fear. Cherry caught tight hold of my arm. Sand kept a less obtrusive hand against the small of my back so I didn't slow or turn and run. I would have. I don't know how I kept walking, except that I hoped we would help Kelly and Lily.

Barber did the talking and flashed his badge, getting us through places we would have used magic instead, which might not have been safe with so much equipment in the area. We went up an elevator and down a hall. When we met with one person who balked at us visiting the girl, Darion used magic, and we were on our way.

"I don't like to do that," Darion admitted with a shake of his head. "And it's not wise to do it often. Some people are resistant to magic, and the problem gets worse rather than better. But mostly it's just not a good idea to magic people into doing things for you. It comes back on you at the worst time."

"Let's hope we get through this without trouble," Barber said with a glance back at the woman as she wandered off to do other work now.

Darion nodded.

We went into Anna's room. A thin girl with mousy brown hair rested in the bed, cradled by a pale blue blanket. She stared at the ceiling and blinking sometimes, but there was little else in her stare. She didn't see us. The equipment by her bed gave a drone of sound, and nothing changed at all.

I didn't think this would help until I looked into her hazel eyes, and there I saw the ghosts of fear, pain, and terror of the evil that someone had done to her. The power of the emotional turmoil behind her placid face took me by surprise, and I pulled back, nearly falling as Cherry caught me.

"Careful," Darion said. "You don't have the power or training for this work. You can see, though, can't you?"

"I don't know what I saw," I said, still gasping. "But it wasn't good."

He nodded and leaned over the girl, his fingers touching her arm. I saw a little whisper of magic and saw her give a little twitch.

It seemed a long time before her mouth opened, closed again. She frowned, and shook her head, as though fighting against the intrusion, knowing she didn't want to come back. Her eyes blinked and focused, this time, looking at Darion.

"Who are you?" she whispered.

"A friend."

Barber was already looking surprised and pleased.

"I don't want to be here," she whispered. The equipment protested, but Sand set it back to the same steady beat. I feared a nurse might come otherwise. Sand moved up by the door just to be safe.

"Here is good. Here is safe," Darion said, and a hint of lilacs overlaid the scent of the hospital room. "No one will hurt you here."

"Everything has always been bad. I want to go away

now." She turned her head and stared back at the ceiling.

"Please, Anna. Please help me."

She looked at Darion and frowned. "Who are you? I don't have any friends."

"Certainly you do, and friends help each other. I have helped you get past something horrible and dark, but now you have to help me save two other girls who may be even suffering something worse. I only need to know where you were."

"I don't think I can help you. That place. . . ."

Darion reached out and caught hold of my arm without even looking, and I shared the next few minutes with the two of them though Anna didn't realize what we did. Darion asked her questions, and she answered, recalling what had happened and the place where the man had held her. A tall man, with a strange voice. She never saw him clearly there in the dark with the rats. The only candle never seemed to go out, but the flame never lit him, either.

I recognized this place I saw in her eyes through the connection I had with Kelly and Lily. What I didn't understand is why she was there. She had no fae blood, nor did she -- obviously -- have a fae relative, since I was the only half -fae alive. Why they had taken her made no sense at all.

But there in her mind was the answer. Practice. She shivered at the memory of a blade cutting across her arm, but Darion took the memory away and the scar as well.

This was the link I had been looking for, and she told us a great deal -- except for the most important part. She had no idea where she'd been held.

I wanted to howl with frustration, but Darion's fingers tightened, and I held back my emotions for her sake. He had helped her through the worst of her problems, and he had cleared the drugs from her body and repaired broken pieces in her head. She would come out better for this, so we had done well. But still, but still --

"There was a woman who came once, right towards the end," she said.

My heart missed several beats. I saw Cherry and Barber both take steps closer, but Sand stayed by the equipment and watched the door. Darion leaned over her, and his hand touched her face, drawing her to look back at him. She was prettier than when we first saw her, and it wasn't that Darion had done anything physical to her looks. Anna had just lost a lifetime of troubles along with the more recent nightmare.

"She came not long before he got rid of me," she said. Her voice no longer trembled. "I couldn't really see well by then, but I heard her --"

Darion pulled me right down into the memory with him. I saw the shape of a head bend low over Anna's face.

"This will work?" she said. "You can kill it like this?"

There was no doubt at all. This was my mother's voice.

"You'll have proof tomorrow at the hospital," another voice said -- distant and distorted. I wanted to see that one.

"The woman is already ill. How do I know the death will be your work?"

"I will set a time. 11:23 pm tomorrow night --"

"Can you make it earlier? I don't want to stay up that late."

So typical, I thought. About to have someone killed, and she didn't want to be bothered staying up late. I had never considered how she treated others who were a bother to her. No one in the world mattered except for Tay Fairbanks. If she'd really had power, she might have been as bad as Earis had been.

We didn't need more people like her.

"Fine. I will kill her at 7:23 pm tomorrow night. Does that suit you?"

"Yes." The head pulled away. "You'll kill them both."

"I'll kill the mother. There's no reason to taint this place with the death of the girl which might draw others here. She'll die on the street soon enough. I need to maintain the purity of this place for what we want."

They went away, the two of them. Anna turned her head slightly, watching as they walked away and for the briefest moment she thought she saw a window and the ruins of a building across a street --

A place! I tried to grab a mental snapshot of the scene, concentrating on the fleeting image. We wouldn't have much time.

Darion let go of me. I staggered back to Cherry, who pushed me into a chair. Barber brought me water and Sand sent away a nurse. I gasped so badly that I couldn't speak.

"You need to sleep now, Anna, and later you'll wake up, and you will be better. You will not remember that we were here --"

"Please," she whispered and caught hold of Darion's arm. "Please let me have at least that memory. I *want* friends."

Darion smiled. "Yes. Sleep and be better and when

we meet again, you'll know we are friends. Your life will be better. I *promise* this will be so. Sleep now."

She had no idea the power in that promise.

Anna closed her eyes, smiling a little as she drifted back to sleep. Darion took one step back -- and then he was on his knees.

"Damn, that was a lot of work," he said, gasping. Sand had started towards him, but he waved her back. "I'm all right. We have something, my friends."

"It was your mother?" Cherry asked, looking at me.

"Oh yes," I nodded. "And we have a location."

Darion agreed, pulling himself back to his feet. He stood there for a moment, and then glanced at the clock. "Time to go."

I looked back at Anna as we left the room and wondered what her life would be like in the future. Darion had made her a promise, but all of us -- fae and human -- who had been in that room would do our best to make it come true.

CHAPTER SIXTEEN

We got into the truck. Snow fell, some of it because of the magic in the air from the battle with the gang. We headed to the library and parked the truck, all of us climbing out into the cold and dark night. Nearly eleven already, and the wind had kicked up as the temperatures dropped. No one walked the street, and even the bars had shut in the face of this storm.

We didn't care about the weather tonight.

I didn't feel the cold. Instead, I counted seconds in each step, pushing us faster along the paths. We'd seen more than one ruin on these streets, so I paused to stare at each one, crossing back and forth across the street to get the closest to the view that Anna had seen. Darion seemed content to let me take the lead, and I didn't take long to find the place and looked from the ruin to the boarded up shop at my back. I could barely make out the sign, the paint faded and covered over in snow and ice. The place hadn't been closed more than a few months. The windows were dusty but not broken.

"Looks like it was a bookstore of some sort. New Age? Wiccan?" Sand asked as she stared inside at the ruined shelves. "Sometimes they happen on magic manuscripts in places like this, but I still don't feel any magic here."

"Let's go find out," Darion said.

He went to the door. I caught hold of Cherry's arm and wished she wasn't here. I wanted her safe. We were all the way to the boarded door before the pain hit me so hard that I thought I was about to die. I was face down in the snow. Darion said something I didn't understand them, and I choked on blood --

Magic came between me and the pain, or at least most of it. Sand's work. Darion looked worried.

"Quickly," I whispered. "We have little time."

He got me to my feet, but then Barber took hold of Cherry. I stayed close. I looked at the building and felt dread and fear and --

Darion waved his hand and blew the door off the hinges, letting it fly inside before we stepped through the opening.

The place smelled of old wood and dank, rotting paper. I feared I was slipping away again when everything blurred and blended. I grabbed at Barber, but he caught tighter hold of me first, and from the look on his face, I knew the reaction wasn't just me.

Once we had crossed past the door, we found that we were no longer in the shop. I looked back and saw a thin facade behind us. Through the window, I saw the ruins across the street, dull gray and covered in snow. I tried to place where Anna had been to see that view --

There were others here. I hadn't noticed until a shadow moved, stepping forward into the light.

The gargoyle.

Why wasn't I surprised? And even less so to see his companion, my mother.

"You are a hypocritical lying bitch," I said.

She took offense. I suspected I had only amused the gargoyle. The girls sat huddled in the corner across the room, the magic still playing across them. Although only a few steps separated us, I would never reach them without help. My legs felt leaden, and my head bowed with weakness. I wiped the blood from my lips as I stared at the woman who had given me birth and wondered how she lived with her own lies.

"We're no longer back in the city," Darion said. Barber glanced behind us, frowning. "Never mind what you see there. We came through a portal. A clever one made straight in the lands of the gargoyles. You fueled this with human magic."

The gargoyle bowed his head in an almost regal move as he preened, the staff in his hand and the stone I had been searching for -- and which he had never lost -- glowing yellow on the top. "Earis Ruby Day came looking for allies. She told me about Skye, but I wanted nothing to do with the fae. Instead, I found this place. I planted a magical book and the humans running this shop opened the portal, so only human magic was used. I kept the portal open, destroyed them and the store, and hid here, waiting while I drew in the threads that would link Skye to me. Skye is unique. I want it."

"I am far too popular," I mumbled and moved to get between Cherry and this creature though I could barely stand now. "Why did you send the black monster after us?"

"It was to kill your Sapphire Guard and to make you easy to take," he said. "I was anxious, but even when that didn't work, I knew you would come here," the gargoyle said. The eyes still glittered. "I had only to play the game well. And now you are mine, little thing."

The gargoyle waved his hand and stepped towards the girls. I went that way as well because the draw was so strong I couldn't hold back. Besides, I didn't want him to hurt the girls who were staring at the rest of us, a whisper of hope in their faces, and the emotion so strong in their hearts that the power of their combined hope tore at me, but also gave me strength. I would not fail them.

Darion grabbed me as I started past him. That wasn't a good idea. The pull towards the girls and his pull to hold me back felt like a knife trying to cut me in half. I cried out, but Darion would not let go. The gargoyle made a sound of annoyance and stepped closer to the girls. He reached out and with both hands, ran his claws down both their right arms.

The girls had cried, but the pain and the wounds disappeared in the next moment. My arms bled instead, in a tricky reverse mirror.

"How strange," the gargoyle said. He reached out again, this time to cut across Lily's chest. She looked into the gargoyle's face with such hatred that he must have felt the emotion from the fae girl. He cut deep, but she never felt the wound and Darion did all he could to stop the new bleeding on my chest.

"Help coming," he whispered. "Help coming. Hold on."

I didn't think I could.

"Kill them and kill it," my mother demanded, coming forward at last. "Kill them so this abomination will be dead at last!"

"In my time, human. In my way."

"Now. I demand --"

"*Be silent.*"

That had the sound of someone who had already spent too much time with my mother. She snarled but said nothing more for the moment.

We were running out of time. Midnight was almost upon us, and the power of the gargoyle's web of magic grew, draining life away at me. I'd be dead soon. But maybe. . . .

"Let the girls go. I'll stay. The others will take the girls and leave."

"Skye!" Cherry cried out, frightened by the words. She looked frantic as though she didn't understand that I wouldn't survive anyway. I wanted the last of my life to count for something.

I pulled free of Darion and stayed on my feet. "Do this and you will not have a fight with me. If you do not, I will have Darion kill me now, and you won't have the power at all."

The gargoyle blinked. I had surprised him. "You could not --"

Darion brought out his knife. "If the choice is to see them all die and you gain power, I will do it, gargoyle. I will do it, and then I will come and kill you."

I had never heard such hatred and conviction in his voice. That promise became a living thing, a swirling color dancing like fire through the air, swarming around us. I hadn't known fae were capable of such power, and I wished he hadn't done this for me, though the Gargoyle, at least, looked worried. He believed Darion. So did all the others.

"Let the girls go. And let Skye go as well if you are at all wise because if you don't, there will be a feud between the fae and the gargoyles and you cannot win against us."

"Feud for this half-breed," he said, contemptuous of the idea.

"Skye is befriended by the Queen of the Fae herself. Do you think she'll look away? Are you willing to take that chance?"

"Give your word you will not kill the half-breed if I let the girls go."

That was as good a compromise as we would get. Darion turned my way, his eyes angry. I nodded.

"You have my word," Darion said and put the power of truth in that statement. At least we appeared to have won something here.

The gargoyle gave a bow of his head, but now we faced another problem.

My mother had panicked at the agreement.

"You can't! You can't let them go! They'll tell the others about me!"

"Shut up, you stupid human." The gargoyle leaned so close into her face that I thought he would bite her -- and even still, even after all of this, I would have moved to protect her. I don't know why. "Do you think I did any of this for *you*? I put books in your path, just as I did for the shop owners. I manipulated you to do my bidding, so I had your daughter and you as a link to this half fae. Should I care what problems you created for yourself? You were my tool, nothing more. You brought me what I needed to draw the half-breed here, and now I will have the power it holds. I don't care about you."

The gargoyle lifted that damned staff with the stone of power, and the magic flashed brightly in the dismal little room. I saw the chains gone from the girls. Part of me suspected he did this simply to get back at my mother. I couldn't imagine she'd ever been a pleasant partner.

My mother screamed with mindless rage, a sound I'd heard too often. She dashed towards the girls, grabbing something out of her pocket: a gun. I gave a shout of my own. My legs wouldn't work, and I sprawled short of catching hold of her. Cherry moved faster and drove her into the rock wall with such force that my mother gave a muffled cry of pain as something clattered against the floor, lost in the darkness around us. She turned as though to grab Cherry, but slid down, reaching a hand towards her face. I think Cherry broke her nose.

Cherry grabbed both girls by the arms and helped them away along the edge of the wall and back to where Darion stood over me. The gargoyle watched in silence, but I sensed power forming around him. The stone glittered with gold and blue light. He would strike soon. I didn't know what to do, except that I made it back up to my knees which was only nominally better than lying down and giving up.

Cherry looked at me, her eyes filled with tears, as she

and the two girls went past me. The girls had trouble moving, but the magic had left them, and they would be fine given a little time. I hoped so. I wanted all of this to have ended well for someone.

"Take them to the truck and go back home," Darion said, handing her the keys. Their fingers touched for a moment. "The others will protect you."

"Darion --" she whispered.

He put a hand to the side of her face and she bowed her head. She turned and held out a hand; I touched her fingers, but she gave a nod, her eyes filling with tears again. I wanted to tell her that everything would be fine though it would not.

"Go," I whispered. "Get them to safety."

She left with the girls, holding to each of their hands. Kelly looked back and tried to pull away, but they were going out through the portal and back to our world. The magic swirled where they passed, and I hoped they didn't get too cold. It wasn't far back to the truck. They would be safe.

I heard an almost inhuman cry of fear and worry as my mother surged out after them. I feared what would happen, but Darion trapped her for a moment in the portal. Cherry turned one way, and when my mother got free, she seemed confused. She went in the other direction. Darion gave a nod, so I suspected Cherry and the girls were as safe as he could make them.

"There. My end is done," the gargoyle said, taking a step towards me. His magic crawled over me, and the lust for my power became a blanket smothering the world, like the black things he had sent after us.

Darion moved forward, the knife in hand.

"You gave your word, my fine fae ambassador," the gargoyle mocked. He knew Darion wouldn't kill me.

And he was right.

"Sand," Darion said. "If I fail, kill Skye."

She nodded.

And then Darion leapt forward and attacked the gargoyle.

CHAPTER SEVENTEEN

Blinding flashes of power filled the area as the two drove at each other. The gargoyle's touch on my soul disappeared. I struggled to my feet, trying to call up some magic of my own to help Darion survive even if I didn't. The fear he would get himself killed while trying to protect me nearly drove me mad.

Sand had raised her hands and prepared to help, but we both knew that it would be dangerous to throw all our power in together. The chaos might ruin any hope Darion had of winning.

Barber stepped forward and held me to my feet. He tried to back away towards the door opening intending to go out, but I wouldn't leave.

"Go," I said. "You should go. This is dangerous -- dangerous enough for those with magic."

"No," he replied. He'd seen magic before, but not used like this as Darion tossed power from his hands into the gargoyle's face and the creature sent bolts of yellowish-red light at Darion. So far, both had scattered the power of the other's attacks. "What do you need?"

"Rest," I gasped. The magic that had been holding the girls had spread over me. Little bits of lighting flashed up over my body, and draining more power and giving it to the gargoyle -- feeding him power while Darion lost more --

"Sand! Kill me now! The gargoyle feeds on me!" I shouted.

She looked my way and shook her head. "He hasn't lost yet."

But Darion would lose: I knew the truth, like seeing the future with the girls dead. I could see what would happen if we didn't change this battle. Darion would be dead, and I thought Sand and Barber would die, too. I saw chaos, trapped --

The flashes grew less intense. Darion staggered away from the gargoyle while he gasped and put hands to his chest where wounds bled too much already. I saw the way his head came up and his shoulders straightened. He wasn't dead yet. He hadn't lost.

Outside in the snow, I saw fae arriving, but the gargoyle saw as well and with a growl and a wave of that staff, he locked the way for them. If they could break through -- but I didn't think they would make it in time. I considered grabbing the dagger from Sand, but right then she sent a wave of magic against the gargoyle that swept it backward hard enough that the creature went to his knees when he hit the wall, giving Darion a little longer to recover and giving the fae a chance to break through to this place. Giving me a few more moments to breathe -- but my vision for the future had not changed.

The gargoyle growled and rose back to its feet, lifting the staff and that damned stone. It glowed with a bright sickly yellow --

Barber leaned close to my head. "What if I shoot the stone?" he asked.

Gods and gods. "It could be disaster and death for all of us," I whispered.

"And if I don't?"

"Pretty much the same, I fear," I said.

"Then let's take a chance. Better than doing nothing."

Darion or Sand wouldn't care much for the idea, but I nodded agreement. Barber and Sand wouldn't get away if Darion fell. This at least gave them a chance. My vision of the future wavered at that moment. It might change.

Barber shifted slightly, drawing the gun from beneath his jacket. Darion was about to leap back into the attack, and the yellow light the gargoyle caught in his hands flickered as though about to explode into a tremendous fire. I didn't want to see what would happen if the magic swept down on Darion.

Barber brought up the gun, aimed carefully and quickly, and fired.

Chaos engulfed us.

Sound shifted as the light went dark and bright and everything turned strange. A sharp pain shot through my chest, but even as I glanced down, I saw the spell the gargoyle had put on me torn free and scattered like drops of blood through the air. I could almost breathe again, but I was no stronger for it. Darion and grabbed hold of me, not daring to use any magic. We somehow found Sand.

Barber still had hold of me. We held on, the four of us, while everything around us changed and reshaped. Colors melted into sounds and sounds swept into infinity -- no end, no beginning -- no --

And then I saw a shot of green through the chaos. I grabbed hold and with the last of the strength I had, I dragged all of us towards a path I understood.

My path guardian welcomed us. She took hold of me and pulled us from the chaos and into the green that was a part of her, and I think, a part of me. I had never experienced the power and peace of this place so completely until this time. I could breathe again as I knelt, safe. Barber still looked frantic, but I patted his arm.

"Safe," I said, then amended what I said. "Safer."

He nodded and said nothing at all.

"He's trying to follow," Sand said, waving her shaking hand back behind me.

I looked to see the gargoyle trying to push his way towards us. The path guardian stood in the way, and he would not get past her and was even crazy to try. Path Guardians are not like other magical creatures.

"We're safe. We're here." Darion lifted his head and looked at Barber. "You are crazy and dangerous."

"Yes?"

"You fit in fine with the rest of us," Darion said and patted him on the arm.

Barber gave a little laugh though the fear remained in his face. This was nothing he understood, and the three of us were still too weak to even stand, let alone find the way out. I might locate a mirror, but I wouldn't be able to hold on to such a portal just yet. Rest seemed the better idea.

Darion's wounds still bled. Sand took care of him, a gentle wash of magic as she brushed her fingers across his chest, and then lingered a little longer on the bad cut across his right cheek. "No scars," Sand said sounding a little breathless now. "We wouldn't want to mar that perfect fae beauty."

Darion snorted but bowed his head in thanks.

"What do we do now?" Barber asked.

"Rest, just for a while," I said. I looked back at where my friend guarded for us. "But not long. She shouldn't have to fight for us. If we go on, the gargoyle will leave."

Darion looked back and nodded. "Can you find your way out, Skye?"

"I hope so. Just let me rest a moment."

Darion nodded, and then brushed a hand over my shoulder, magic healing some of my wounds. "The gargoyle still has a link to you, though not as strong as it was before. I don't have the power to sever it, either."

"Let it be, then. Don't try."

He nodded.

I knew the danger of sitting there and losing track of things. Before too long I got to my feet and glanced around, trying to find my bearings in a place where that was impossible.

"No mirror," I said with a shake of my head. "And I can't concentrate enough to find one."

"Mirror?" Barber asked.

We had started walking in an arbitrary direction. I didn't think it mattered which way we went, anyway. Space, direction and even time didn't mean the same things here.

"Skye can travel from one mirror to another, following

this path," Darion explained. He barely stayed on his feet, even with Sand holding him there. "This is the path he takes."

"And we're lost here?" Barber asked, sounding worried again.

"I have faith we'll find our way out," Sand said. "Or that the others will track us down. Darion is too important to just forget."

"Not to mention too pretty," Darion added, which made Sand laugh. The sound was good; everything brightened around us. When I looked back, the gargoyle was no longer in sight, and the Path Guardian trailed behind us.

"Darion is important," Barber said and sounded surprised. "You know, with the way everything has been going, I would have thought Skye was the important one in this group."

"I'm more trouble than important," I admitted. We hadn't walked very far, but it seemed as though miles of green had fallen in behind us, a bastion of protection against the gargoyle. I lifted my hand, but I couldn't form the image of a mirror to get out. I looked back at Darion, gasping and shaking my head.

"It's that damned gargoyle magic," he said. "It still has you tied to the girls --"

My head came up with an odd surge of hope. "I can still get to the girls using the magic the gargoyle used to tie us together. It is still trying to pull me to them."

Darion looked startled and then reached out with magic and nodded. "Yes, it should work."

"Grab hold and don't let go." I took several deep

breaths. Darion had hold of one arm and Sand the other, and Darion took hold of Barber with his other hand -- Darion would not let go of either of us. "I've never tried this with other people to pull along. A mirror would have been easier but --"

"But time is passing," Darion said. He looked at Barber. "Time passes differently here on the paths. There's no telling how long we've already been here. It might have been days."

"Hell," Barber said. "I will never be able to explain this."

"We'll fix it," I said. Darion nodded agreement, but Barber still looked worried. "We will. Ready?"

The others nodded.

"Blood calls to blood," I said aloud, and let the words take hold of me rather than fighting it this time. The magic pulled me towards them so that everything around us swirled again. I sensed Lily, Kelly and even Cherry, all close together, praise whatever gods were looking over me. If they had not been together, I don't know what would have happened, but I had hoped (without telling the others what the problem might be), that I could focus on one. The three together was far better. The power dragged me straight to them, so powerful that it hurt, but I didn't let go. I had never pulled people along, though, and they were anchors, trying to hold me back.

"Let go," Darion said. "Send back for us --"

"No. Might not find you. Hold on!"

We kept going. Closer, but I feared I would pass out, that we would not make it -- that --

We fell into Cherry's apartment, the four of us

tumbling over each other, loud thumps --

I was staring up at the ceiling. Yo-Yo came over and looked me in the face. I laughed while I still gasped for breath. Laughing felt good. We had done the impossible.

"Careful," Blue said. He caught hold of my arm, and I was damned glad to see him here, alive. I caught hold of his arm and held on tight because I still had the feeling of movement, of being pulled away and apart, and I couldn't even speak just then.

I turned my head and make certain my companions had made it here. Someone had gotten Barber to the chair where he leaned back, pale and shaken but all right. Cherry had wrapped her arms around Darion, and someone else had taken hold of Sand.

Safe. Safe -- but why didn't it feel safe? I looked up with a start as Kelly, Lilly -- and Anna of all people! -- came towards me. Blue had hold of me and used gentle magic so I could breathe again. My thoughts still swirled as much as the world had when we moved.

"Is Skye all right?" Kelly asked. She knelt before me while the other two stood behind her. I hadn't seen her in years. She was lovely.

"He'll be fine," Blue said. "Don't worry."

She didn't believe Blue. I looked into her face and saw pain and fear in her eyes and I wanted to take those dark emotions away and give her back a normal life of a teenager. I even lifted my hand, but Blue caught my fingers before I could do anything.

"Careful, Skye. Careful. Just rest a moment. Lean back. Can you get a pillow from the sofa?"

Anna hurried to do the work. I wondered what she

was doing here. I wondered if this was real. Had I created this scene out of my own need? Maybe I failed them all --

"Skye, look at me."

I turned back to Blue and blinked -- but was he here? Wasn't he injured, and they feared for his life? Was this all my dream, of things working out well and everything right --

"Skye!"

I couldn't focus. I was drifting, going away --

"Skye!"

But I hardly heard his voice this time, and I thought that would be best. I was a problem for them and drew trouble like a magnet --

"Don't give him the power, Skye. Don't do it after all we went through!"

Damn. Darion's words hit me with a new fire. I don't know if they gave me strength or if they made me remember how damned stubborn I was. It didn't matter. He called me back either way.

I was on the floor, a pillow under my head, gasping for breath and still not quite connected to the world yet. I watched the others who were alive, fearful: all of them gathered around me and wishing me well, even while Blue used more magic to make certain I didn't slip away again.

"You are real?" I whispered, looking at him.

"Very much so," he said. He sounded relieved, perhaps only because I had spoken. "Peren. Good."

Peren Ruby Day sat down by Blue. He gave me a wry little smile. "I'm not used to sitting on the floor. Does this often happen in the human world?"

"Happens often with me," I replied because talking

seemed to bring me closer to *here*. "What happened?"

"You were too weak to fight off the last of the gargoyle's spell," Blue said. He sat back, looking shaky. "I could only try to give you strength, but Darion knew what to say to you. I feared we had lost you, Skye."

"Maybe better if you did," I said and meant those words. "So much trouble --"

"No," Peren said. He caught my hand and fed so much healing magic through me that the power hurt as it healed. "There. Sorry, but that work needed to be done quickly. That damned gargoyle purposely poisoned you. He wanted you weak. There was never a missing stone and even the blackness that chased you and Darion turned out to be his work to keep you weak in power and off guard."

"Ah." I saw the pattern of everything falling together. "Cherry got the girls here, though."

"Yes," Blue said. "We brought Anna since she would leave the hospital and we wanted her safe, too."

I happened to glance at Anna, who looked surprised and shocked by those words. I suspected no one had ever cared if she had been safe before now. Odd how I felt such a kinship with her just then, something that went far beyond anything of blood.

But that brought another thought.

"My mother?"

"We don't quite know where she is," Peren said. "Hiding."

I nodded and tried to sit up, but every bone and muscle ached now. I gasped and decided to just stay still and breathe for a while.

"Rest, Skye. Just rest. Sleep if you can."

I closed my eyes, too tired to care that I was on the floor. This was comfortable enough, and Cherry brought me a blanket. I opened my eyes and whispered a thank you, and closed them again. The hum of people was reassuring and comforting. Peren stayed by my side. Yo-Yo curled up on the blanket and slept with me.

"We could take Skye to the bedroom," Blue suggested.

"No. Let him sleep right here for a while. He's doing well. He needs to be with us."

Peren understood.

I slept. . . .

DAY FOUR (MORE OR LESS):

CHAPTER EIGHTEEN

I slept until the gargoyle crashed through the apartment door. I should have expected him as soon as I tried to sleep in Cherry's apartment. At the moment between sleep and sanity, I realized the creature was coming for me. Sand tried to stop him, but he swept out one huge arm and knocked her aside; he had strength and anger on his side and I feared for the lives of everyone that got in the way.

Time we settled this problem.

I got to my feet which surprised everyone, including the gargoyle who backed up a step and stopped as he glared. He did not have his stone of power. The bullet must have destroyed the thing. Good.

"Mine," the gargoyle said and reached out with a long-clawed hand, his magic reaching for me.

"I do not belong to you." I pushed the magic aside which was not as easy as it sounds, but unless I won this battle, the gargoyle would come after me again. I wanted the gargoyle out of my life and my friends safe.

Darion moved up to help me. Dangerous to do, the two magics trying to intertwine, but he controlled his part -- I had never been trained -- and the power shoved the gargoyle back again as it drew the gargoyle's spell and magic out of me and flung it back at the maker. He howled so loudly the walls shook, and I saw a crack appear. Magic surged up around the creature like a whirlwind, and the others were trying to throw wards into place to protect everyone --

Something hit me in the back. I almost went down, but caught myself and lifted my hand again. Anger gave me more power. I try not to use magic that way because it harder to stop, but I had suffered through enough pain already. I pushed and shoved and tried desperately to find his weakness.

The gargoyle howled and rushed at me using one great shove of power to get through our magic; claws caught at my shoulder and ripped. Blood flowed, a warmth down my arm, but I still didn't feel more pain. What I felt, instead, was the fear from Lily and Kelly, afraid that the creature would take them back, afraid that the safety they had found was an illusion. I glanced their way, seeing the two of them and Anna, huddled close to Cherry and Barber, who had that gun in hand again. He wasn't too quick to use it, at least. I didn't want that chaos again, especially with so large a group. We would lose some of them. I wouldn't be able to find them again.

Darion had beat the gargoyle back, but now I shoved magic straight into his face, blinding him for a moment. Darion followed me and tried to stab the gargoyle with a glowing, magical blade he had created with a flick of his hand. The gargoyle snarled and hit his arm. I heard a bone break, and Darion fell. I created more magic, and I would have to quit soon, for the sake of those around me. More fae had arrived. If they could --

And then I saw that we had no hope at all.

More gargoyles arrived at the door.

I screamed and shoved the first gargoyle back into them, trying to bring up more magic, but I was already going to my knees. The other fae moved up to help me, even Darion, with his broken arm pressed to his chest, and his face pale and damp. Four gargoyles came through the doorway. Others were close behind them --

They grabbed the first gargoyle. He fought, but one bit him in the neck, and he went limp, though not dead. They dragged him away.

One stopped at the doorway.

"This battle is done. He will not be back to this reality again." The golden eyes, so like the one I had fought, looked at me. "It wanted power. You are unique."

Then he turned and took to the air. The others had already taken away their companion.

Outside the wind blew in a sudden gust and snow fell harder again. I looked outside with amused shock, realizing I would have to worry about the cold again. Peren had taken hold of Darion and led him over to the chair. The others moved around me, and I heard them say they were safe now. I did not trust so easily.

CHAPTER NINETEEN

I stared into the night sky, listening to what seemed like the faint sound of large wings, heading away from here. I didn't trust what had happened. This had to be a trick.

"Skye?" Sand asked, coming close enough to take hold of my arm. "Come on. It's cold out here. You should be inside."

"Is it over?"

"For now," she said.

Those were words I understood. Nothing was ever *finished*. I let Sand close the door and herd me back to the sofa. Cherry sat beside me, but she looked around with worry. The three girls stood behind us; living and warm and no longer as frightened as they had been. Good. We had won.

"What the hell just happened?" Blue asked. He stood by the chair where Darion sat, and he stared at the door.

"Someone overstepped the line," Darion said. He still looked white-faced and in pain, but Peren had worked on his arm, and it no longer looked broken. "The gargoyles have a hierarchical society. Everyone knows his place. I suspect the one that came after Skye was already stepping out of line just by being here. He found out about Skye and worked at trapping him so he could gain the power to move up in the ranks."

"My mother helped that creature," Kelly said, and the anger and betrayal in her echoed a long ago pain of my own. I shivered.

"She opened herself to it by trying to study magic," Darion said, looking at her. "He went looking for a key to Skye. She was easy to manipulate."

"She gave me to it," Kelly said. Her voice sounded small and hurt.

Cherry reached back and caught hold of her arm.

"I'm sorry," I said and looked at her. "I'm sorry this happened --"

"This is not your fault," Kelly said, and her sense of loss disappeared in a new a surge of righteous anger that took me by surprise. "I know you didn't do this, Skye. I know what she did to you, too. Cherry told us. I missed you after you left and that made her mad. She never trusted me because of how I felt."

"I never thought she would do anything to the rest of you," I admitted. "I thought by staying away, I kept your safe. I'm sorry."

She leaned over the back of the sofa and hugged me. I remembered that embrace -- how Kelly would hug me like that when she came home from school and found me waiting on the sofa, anxious to hear what she had done, the people she'd talked to, and what she had learned. The memory came back like a new wound, something cut open that I had worked so hard to seal closed. I hoped I hid the pain.

"The gargoyle likely manipulated her to get her to give you over, Kelly," Darion said. "This wasn't all her, though I won't make any excuses for how she treated Skye."

That was a little balm for my half-sister, at least. Darion might even have been right. My mother would have been easy to lead to what the gargoyle wanted, but giving her real daughter over might have needed extra magic.

"What are we going to do?" Kelly asked.

"I don't know," I admitted and looked back at Darion.

"I'll find an answer. We just need a little time --"

He stopped. Every fae in the room turned, hands lifting -- and dropped again with sighs of relief. More people arrived through a portal by the door, and it wasn't until I blinked that I realized who I saw: Donal Emerald McFaelyn and the Queen of the Fae.

Many of us bowed. Even Darion and I managed to get to our feet and do so. Those who didn't realize who stood there followed our examples.

"Oh dear," the Queen said. She wore a simple blue gown, sparkling with a touch of magic that must follow her everywhere with a scent that mingled orange blossoms and vanilla. "I will never get used to this. Skye, Darion -- sit down before you fall down. Wouldn't that be embarrassing?"

She made me laugh. She was still Lacey Weaver in my

eyes though the Queen of the Fae gave up her name when she took the position. To the fae, she was The Queen, but to those of us who lived in the human world, she still had a human name. She was the tie that would help in a time when there was too much magic drifting over into the human realm.

I had me her under the worst of circumstances when we were both prisoners of Earis Ruby Day. But even then I had sensed the goodness in her and knew she would make a great queen. So far no one, even Topaz House, had a complaint about her. She brought joy to the fae lands.

I turned and sat on the sofa -- well, more like dropped back to the pillows. It was not graceful, and she was right; I would have fallen if I had tried to stay on my feet any longer. She and Donal crossed the room. Darion gave up his chair to her. She settled there and smiled. Donal stood at her shoulder, and I suspected that the former king of the fae had become an advisor to the new Queen. Excellent choice. Donal was a good man.

The Queen settled back, sniffed delicately, and looked at Cherry. "Tell me I smell some of those fantastic chocolate chip cookies you make."

Cherry laughed and went to the kitchen. She had known Lacey long before Lacey learned she was fae, let alone before she became queen. Before long we were all having milk and cookies with the Queen of the Fae.

Yes, it was surreal, but wonderful, too. She brought peace, hope, and joy into the apartment. I felt the sort of healing balms you cannot get through magic and pains eased again, especially those of a heart that had been stabbed a few too many times of late.

"This has been a troubling time," she said, looking at Darion and me where we sat side-by-side on the sofa. Even talking about the problem didn't seem so bad now. "Donal has been helping me to sort things out. With everything that's gone wrong of late, I'm in way over my head in a new job. I'm grateful for his help."

"Have you learned anything?" Darion asked.

She looked to Donal and gave a little nod. He sat aside his cookie with obvious regret, which made me almost laugh again, despite how serious he appeared.

"Something is out of balance in the fae lands," he said. Darion shifted at that news and frowned with a new worry. "We've seen it happening too much of late: a little trouble here, a little trouble there. Then the larger things, like the Unnatural and the problem with Earis. This latest dispute with the gargoyles only adds to it."

"One gargoyle," I said. "The others didn't seem to like what he had done."

"True," Donal agreed. "Still, this is an imbalance. The gargoyle was a lowly worker, Skye. It should never have had the power to do anything like what it did."

"We fear more such problems," Lacey said. "I can sense them, like little ripples across the land. Some, like the gargoyle problem, will drift into this reality. We'll do our best to control them, Detective Barber. I wish I could promise you more."

"We can't control our people," he said. "I suspect the work is no easier for you."

"I'm part of the problem," I said as I realized the implications. She focused on me again. "I'm part of the strange things that have been happening."

"Yes," she said.   "You are unusual and are obviously part of the pattern, Skye, and that gives me hope."

"Hope?"

"Because you are not like the gargoyle or Earis Ruby Day. You are a good person and have helped others. That makes me hope that not everything I sense will be trouble, but even if it is, I still have you."

"What is it about my powers that are unique?" I asked. "What do the others hope to gain from me?"

"You have some of the usual fae powers," Donal said. "And you have others I've not seen before. Your ability to mirror, and to use mirrors -- that is the stuff of legends, Skye. That is a magic we have not seen in our own very long lifetimes. This is the real reason people like Lord Iron Topaz Fair fears and loathes you; not because you are a half-breed, or because of your gender, but because you have powers that make you more akin to the Old Ones than to us."

I felt very odd.

The queen smiled. "We will watch over you, Skye -- oh, not in the way others watched before. Don't worry. We will not interfere in your life, but you will not be without help if you need it."

I wanted to argue, but a wiser part of me remembered all the others who had suffered in this, so I bowed my head in acceptance.   Darion watched over me already, and I suspected all of his friends from Sapphire House did the same. I wondered what their leader thought of them taking me in, but I had never dared ask about clan politics.

Donal Emerald McFaelyn headed Emerald House now. He and I got along well. I hoped I did nothing to change that situation, or that nothing happened to him. How many of my clan might be more like my father rather than like Donal? It was possible that none of them liked me and might wish me dead and out of the way, an embarrassment they could soon forget.

Associating with the fae was dangerous, but I had no choice given how fae and other magical creatures showed such an interest in me. I wouldn't have walked away. I was more like the fae than I had ever expected and sometimes I even forgot that I wasn't one of them although I was always aware that I was not human. Darion and his people treated me as though I was fae, and I only now realized how much of a gift they gave me with their casual acceptance.

"Are the girls safe now?" I asked, waving my hand back towards Kelly, Lily, and Anna

"We cannot be certain so we will keep them in safety for a while longer," the Queen said. She smiled. "I know a place I think the three of you will enjoy. I've already talked to my mother and father -- my adopted parents, here on this side."

"Oh!" Kelly suddenly squealed. "You're Lacey Weaver! I've seen pictures of you!"

"Yes, I am." She smiled with delight. "My parents are human -- the people who raised me. My mother would love to have the three of you come and stay with them. The house is huge and has always had magical protection while I grew up. I'll stop by now and then. You'll like it there."

"But my father -- he's already upset about me being gone --" Kelly began.

"We will make certain your father knows, Kelly. It

might be good to bring him and the rest of your siblings to the house, at least until your mother is found. From all I've seen, I suspect he might need a rest, too."

Kelly nodded agreement. "They haven't gotten along for years."

"I have already talked to your mother, Lilly, and I know she's been here to see you, so this will not be a problem."

"But I -- I don't belong with the rest of you," a quiet voice said, and I turned to see Anna standing a little apart from the other two girls. "You are family, and you don't need me --"

Lily caught hold of Anna's arm and held tight. "I want you with us," she said. She seemed quieter than the other two though perhaps that came from being in the presence of the Queen of the Fae. "I like you. And we share something, the three of us. It was horrible, but it is a link."

"She's right Anna," Lacey said. The girl looked at her, shocked to be called by name. "Oh yes, I know who you are too, and what that horrible creature did to you. You lost your mother because of it --"

"I never knew her. I was only a few days old when she left me with her sister and my aunt threw me out when I was fifteen --"

"But the gargoyle used you to do his evil, and you have a new scar over old ones. It's time for you to heal, Anna. Darion started you on the way, and you were wise enough to grab hold of what he offered. So now you're stuck with us, my friend."

She blinked and looked startled. "I've never lived anywhere around rich people."

"You'll be surprised how much like real people they are," she said with a laugh. Then she looked around again. "There is something else we have learned, and this will affect all of you. Magic is coming back to this reality. It's being drawn as though into a vacuum, and I can't say if that's good or bad. We can't stop it, but we can try to temper what happens. Sapphire and Emerald Clans will have the lead in this work because we have both always been closer to the human world than most of the others. We will have trouble. Lord Iron Topaz Fair will try to carve out a kingdom for himself on this side and to remake the world to his liking. We must be on the watch for him and his companions."

I tried not to snarl. I had no liking for the head of the Topaz Clan, who had already tried to kill me once. Stopping him was a battle I wouldn't mind taking on -- in the future.

"Rest for a while," the Queen said. She stood, and the rest of us did as well, despite the exasperated shake of her head. I think she wanted to be Lacey sometimes, but that would not happen here and now. "Rest, Skye. We'll talk again soon."

"Thank you," I said, bowing to her again, though Darion had to catch hold of me before I fell.

I watched as she gathered the three girls with her and left in a flash of light and the scent of oranges. They were safe in her care, and her parent's house would be a good place for them. It had both magical and human guards, and they would have all the care and attention needed. I wanted to see all three of them healed.

I was still staring at the door when Cherry came and

took hold of me.

"You need sleep, Skye."

"Nearly ready," I said. I turned back to Barber, despite Cherry's little grunt of frustration. "We disappeared for a while, Detective Barber."

"I know. I checked the date. We disappeared for three days. I don't know how the hell I will explain that one," he admitted. He looked flustered.

"We have it covered," Blue said, surprising him. "We've made it look as though one of the gang members held you captive. The police department to kept it quiet, so they didn't put you in more danger. Now you can turn up, none the worse for it and the gang member will have disappeared so no one will ever know differently."

"Hell," he said. He looked startled, worried, and then nodded. "Thank you. And you did that with the Lacey Weaver case, too."

"Yes," Darion said. "I'll tell you about that one after we all rest for a while.

Blue smiled. "We don't like to mess so much in human affairs, but we owed you the help for what you have done to help us."

"Barber -- I can still make you forget everything," Darion offered.

Barber looked at him and frowned again. "No, I still would rather know the truth and know where to turn to, rather than forget. If what your Queen said is true, then it looks like there might be more trouble coming, right?"

"Right."

"Then you might find having another human who can help out is good."

Darion gave a bow of his head in agreement. Good. I was glad to see that settled.

"I'm tired," I said.

Cherry took my arm and led me to the bedroom. No one else got in the way. I looked at the front door, half expecting it to come off the hinges and another monster to come stomping into the apartment. The door remained blessedly quiet and still. I reached the bedroom and sat down on the bed though I wanted to go home to my place.

"You're going to sleep here," Darion said when I suggested I go home instead. "It's safe here right now. Let's make certain everything is cleared up before we all go off in our own directions again."

I didn't argue as I kicked off my shoes and rolled over on to the nice, soft bed. Cherry pulled the comforter up over me and headed out of the room. Darion said something to her, whispered words that almost pulled me back up from the near sleep. I ignored them.

Darion came over and sat on the edge of the bed beside me. I looked at him, frowning. "What *now?*" I sounded petulant.

"You still have the link to the girls," he said.

Ah. That. "I know."

"I could get rid of the link now that I understand the source and they are free from the gargoyle."

"No."

He looked at me, head tilted a little.

I sat back up and pushed my hands through my hair. "We don't know that they're really safe, do we? If we did, the Queen wouldn't be so worried about getting them somewhere they can be watched, and you would have severed that magic without even bothering to ask me."

"It's still drawing from you, Skye."

"Not much. I can handle that part for now." Neither of us said that it also hurt like all magic does for me. It was only a little sting, though. "I want to know where they are and that they're safe, Darion."

"I thought as much."

"Now let me get some sleep!" I threw myself down, pulling the blanket up over my head as though it would block out anything bad that might happen.

Darion chuckled and stood. He moved to the door, but he hadn't gone out. I pulled the blanket back down and looked at him, half annoyed --

"You did a good job, Skye."

"We all did. We got the girls back, and we survived. Go spend time with Cherry."

He smiled and gave a nod of his head -- or did he bow? -- as he left the room.

The last look I had seen in his face as his left gave me a chill. I tried to banish it from my thoughts as I closed my eyes.

More akin to the Old Ones than to us.

I shivered again.

But I drifted off into sleep, doing the only thing I could for now: I hoped for the best.

The End

###

PREVIEW: KAT AMONG THE PIGEONS

Tap, tap, tap.

The incessant drumming of small bird beaks against the bedroom window brought me out of a deep, blissful sleep. I tried not to curse.

Tap, tap, tap.

"Go 'way." I pushed my head under the pillow. Cato, a big lazy lump of an orange tabby cat, made a sound of protest and burrowed his head into the blankets. I started to fall back asleep. . . .

Then I heard the little bird voices.

"Big wings! Big Wings!"

Tap, tap, tap.

"Don't care," I mumbled.

Tap, tap, tap-tap-tap-tap. "Big-big-big wings!"

I rolled over and stared at the ceiling as I contemplated

what kind of ecological disaster the earth would suffer if I wiped out the nuthatches.

"Big-big-big-wings-wings-wings!"

Tap tap tap tap tap tap tap tap.

The combination of their tiny high-pitched voices and the pounding of their sharp little beaks sounded like a badly sung round robin and with a drummer out of beat as well. This was not a sound someone can sleep through. I sat up and focused on the window. I squinted and found a dozen or more panicked nuthatches holding to the wooden frame. A few hung upside down and all of them tapped ceaselessly at the glass. Their voices rose in shrill cries of frantic worry.

Tap-tap-tap-tap.

"Yes, yes, I got the idea. I'm getting up!"

I climbed out of the warm bed and yanked on my robe. Soft light drifted through the window which meant it dawn had barely touched the sky. I muttered things again.

Cato pulled his furry head from under the blankets, blinking sleepily. "What's wrong with the nuts?" he asked and yawned.

"Not nuts," I answered batting at his head as I went past him. I missed as he stretched. "Nuthatches."

"All the same to me." Cato settled into a plump circle, his tail curled around his nose. "Do you think you might quiet them down?"

"Sure. I'll throw you out the window. They'd find that interesting enough to shut up about the eagle or hawk or plane that upset them this morning."

Cato snorted and mumbled something I didn't quite hear. Probably just as well.

Understanding animals is common among the fae.

This is part of what makes us good at our work, even on this side of the Edge. I have a problem though since I'm not blessed with the ability to understand all animals the way most of the fae can. No, I got lucky enough to catch only two: birds and cats.

It's not a good combination.

I still work as a border guard like all of my clan. We watch over parts of the human world where the Edge is unstable, which is usually wilderness areas. Magic abhors technology, so wild magic like the Edge stays clear of large settlements. I've been here on the outskirts of Estes Park for the last four years, living in a pretty A-frame house on land which has belonged to my family for generations. Down at the base of the hill is the main road to Rocky Mountain National Park. My location is lovely and peaceful.

Except sometimes things upset little birds, especially with the seasons changing from winter to spring and the migrating birds passing through the area. It's not their fault a big bird came sweeping over the trees and terrified the little guys.

I buried my anger as I cranked the window open. Nuthatches held on to the frame, some of them upside down as they stared in at me.

"Big wings, very very very very big big big wings."

"Everything is okay guys," I said. They stopped tapping on the window, at least. "The big wings aren't here."

Dozens of feathered heads turned, craning around to watch the sky between towering pines where the mountains come down in graceful cliffs behind my house. They scanned left, right and back again.

"What are the guys saying?" Cato asked. He pulled his nose out of the blankets and it twitched a couple times.

"Something big frightened them -- but it's not here." I looked out into the gray light of the yard and found quite a few more nuthatches on the trees. "Something set them off."

"Ah," Cato said and his nose twitched again. "Do invite the little ones in for breakfast, Kat."

"Why? You're so lazy you couldn't catch one if it landed on your head."

"I resent that," he replied with the prissy sound only an annoyed cat can get. "And I'd like to see you catch one."

"Would you?" I held out my hand. Four swept down to grab hold of my fingers.

"Show off." He curled up and put his tail back over his face.

I spent the next few minutes doing my best to calm the birds. A couple dozen came to my fingers while I stood there. The day brightened into a gorgeous dawn of dark blues, fleeting clouds, and fog. No big wings came around the house and many of the little birds settled onto the trees nearby.

Nuthatches, like most of the tiny birds, panic at *everything.* If I weren't close by they'd fly off in all directions. I'm a beacon to birds. And cats. I spotted three of the local strays lolling near the pine at the edge of the yard and eyeing breakfast on the wing if the birds weren't careful.

"Don't do it, guys," I said to the cats. They'd been hanging around for over a year but I watched them turn my way with a moment of 'dare I pretend I don't understand?' in their eyes. "I'll bring food out for you in a few minutes."

"Some of the canned stuff," a big grey tom called Pawford said with a flick of his tail. "If you expect us to leave the birds alone, I don't want the dry crap."

I leaned out the window and stared at him. Most of the nuthatches headed upwards onto the tree branches, except for two who burrowed into my hair. I plucked them out while I kept my eyes on the cats. Ears flickered and tails twitched. Pawford finally gave a great sigh as he dropped onto the dirt, his head on his paws -- the perfect picture of apparent kitty dejection.

"Food would be nice," he mumbled. "Anything you can spare. Thank you."

I smiled and drew my head back into the room. Cato had sat up once he heard the other cat and seemed far less interested in the birds. He and Pawford had faced off in a few clashes during the last year and he had two nicks out of his left ear. Cato surprised Pawford when he proved he could hold his own. He may live in the house, but he's not soft.

I'm not even certain how he got to be a house cat. He wandered in one day and I found the company . . . well, nice enough for a cat.

Not lonely here. Nope.

A couple more nuthatches swept down at the window when I pulled myself inside, almost starting another panic.

"Everything is all right." I brushed my finger the tiny heads and used a whisper of magic to settle them. "Everything is fine now. The big wings are gone."

They scanned the sky again, this time including the trees and even the cats, as though they would sprout wings to come after them.

I sent them flying to the trees, watched for a moment to make certain the poor guys remained settled, and then cranked the window shut. I pulled several feathers from my hair and dropped two in front of Cato's nose.

"Tease." He didn't move his tail or open his eyes.

I laughed as I headed for the bathroom and then on to the kitchen where I grabbed the cat food, including a couple cans for the outside guys. They were good for strays, and they behaved around the house. I can't stop them from doing what's natural elsewhere, but here -- where I can understand the screams -- well, they know better than to go after the birds.

The Big Wings didn't worry me, but something seemed odd this morning. I couldn't put my finger on anything out of place and suspected the changing seasons might be affecting me too.

Then, as I leaned down to open the cabinet, a surge of magic spread so quickly and strong through the air that the sensation almost made me ill. I stood and spun, my hands coming up to protect myself, and startling Cato who had followed me into the kitchen.

"What!" His ears went back and his fur fluffed out, making him appear twice his normal size.

"Magic," I whispered, as though afraid a loud noise would bring the power back. The surge had unsettled me. Free magic running through the ether makes me twitchy.

"Is it all right?" he asked, eyes narrowed and ears slanted back still.

"I can't sense anything solid out there. The magic came from far back in the park -- a lot of magic from out of nowhere. I hate it when the Edge acts up!"

Cato made sounds of agreement. He'd noticed the open cabinet and at the sight of cat food he would pretty much agree he was a bird and could fly if that would get me to open one of the coveted cans for him.

I closed my eyes while I reached out with magic, but still found nothing out of place.

I love my job most of the time and I adore living here, meeting tourists and talking with humans. Yes, I miss home. We all have to work this side of the Edge for a few years and there are far worse places to be. This is a relatively stable area. They gave me this location because I'm not the strongest person in my clan. The rest of my cousins were out in the tough areas: The Sahara, the Gobi and a few places that make Antarctica seem like an easily accessible vacation destination.

Free magic can play havoc with the weather, though, and we were already having a stormy April. If the Edge continued having problems, I feared things would get worse for a while.

"Meow?" Cato said, drawing my attention back to the kitchen.

"Very funny." I tried not to smile.

"Hey, you're standing in the magic place." He purred as he rubbed against my legs. "I needed to get your attention before I fell faint from lack of food."

"Oh yeah, you look as though you're going to starve, pudge."

"Huh."

I got the food out and gave him a can of his own because I wanted him to be in a good mood. A happy cat makes me happy. Cato may be a sarcastic furry pain in the ass, but he's a good guy.

"Thanks," he said as I put the plate down on the floor.

Polite, too, which is more than I can say for many humans -- or fae -- these days.

I pulled down more paper plates, spread two cans of food out on them and grabbed a huge dipper full of dry cat food to add to the mix. A quick inventory of the refrigerator found a few things I would not eat before they went bad. I dropped them into the mix, adding a piece of ham to Cato's food.

"Ah, food of the gods!" he said with delight.

I laughed and gathered the plates, using magic to balance them on my left hand. I may not be the strongest with magic, but I am not powerless. There are nice easy things you can do with a bit of reality nudging and that makes life easier on this side of the Edge where there's so little magic in the air to work against you.

I have to be careful going past any electronics. The brush of technology can upset magic and magic can play havoc with technology. If I use any piece of technology, I have to lock my powers down and bury the magic.

Fae to learn these things on this side of the Edge. I wouldn't even have such items in the house except I needed to seem as normal as possible for my neighbors and friends. Besides, avoiding destroying things in my house was good practice for me whenever I went near them in other places.

As I came out of the kitchen I glanced over at Shakespeare, a lovely African Grey parrot I'd acquired a few months ago. There's just one problem with him --

"I have not always been us now, the fever'd diadem on my brow."

That's the problem. Shakespeare doesn't speak parrot. He only speaks human words and those in odd bits of verse. I can talk to any bird in the world . . . except for this one. If he would speak in parrot, I would learn what's bothering him. Well, other than his former owners turning him loose in the Rocky Mountains and Shakespeare not exactly being the type of bird that would do well in the local climate. Rangers found him before he froze to death. They brought him to me.

Shakespeare nodded and preened. He'd been horribly shy the first few weeks and given to shouting things at odd times of the day or night. Lately I thought I'd seen resignation in his eyes.

"Not hell shall make me fear again!" he shouted, startling me.

"Right. Good."

I glanced outside the big plate-glass window where mist wreathed the trees in front of my home. From here I saw no more than a few roofs in Estes Park though I heard the sounds of cars headed towards Rocky Mountain National Park despite the early hour. I didn't blame them: First light was the best time to watch the valleys come awake. The big horns would rush down to Sheep Lakes this morning; I loved to watch them go bounding down the mountain side. Beautiful animals.

I saw no one nearby, so I scurried out in my robe and bare feet, using magic to brush away the pine needles before I stabbed myself. Pawford stood sniffing as I came closer, and his tail went straight up in the air with delight. He even rubbed against my legs, his matted fur rough. I brushed the burrs out with a quick sweep of magic.

"Thank you!" he said with real enthusiasm as I dropped the several plates on to the ground. Abbie, a small black and white cat and Trouble, a young pure black tom, mumbled *thank you*. They were a little warier than Pawford as they turned their attention to the food. Anywhere else they would have been at each other, but I enforce calm between the cats in my yard.

Quite a few nuthatches had taken to the trees, mingling with house sparrows and dark-eyed juncos. They all acted agitated, which often happens with the smaller birds. It's as though they're psychic or something -- or maybe psychotic. If one gets upset, the panic spreads through every tiny bird brain in the area.

And they come to me. It's just part of the job.

A little magic still lingered in the air. I turned and headed back to the house. The Edge got unsettled now and then. Nothing serious.

ABOUT THE AUTHOR:

Hello!

I am an eclectic and prolific author whose has published in a number of genres, including Young Adult Mystery, Urban Fantasy, Epic Fantasy, Science Fiction and numerous works on writing. While I started on the outer edges of traditional publication with sales to small press and magazines publishers, I have since moved most of my work to the Indie world and I am madly in love with the new world of publishing and the direct contact with readers.

I live in Nebraska with my husband, my cats and a small but entirely useless dog.

I also own Forward Motion for Writers and the ezine, Vision: A Resource for Writers.

Connect with Zette:

Web Site: http://lazette.net

Twitter: http://twitter.com/lazetteg

Facebook: http://www.facebook.com/lazette.gifford

Joyously Prolific Blog: http://zette.blogspot.com/

Smashwords:

http://www.smashwords.com/profile/view/LazetteG

FIND WORKS BY

LAZETTE GIFFORD

ON

CREATESPACE

SMASHWORDS

A CONSPIRACY OF AUTHORS

NOOK

LAZETTE.NET

www.ingramcontent.com/pod-product-compliance
Lightning Source LLC
Chambersburg PA
CBHW070838250626
47159CB00003B/835